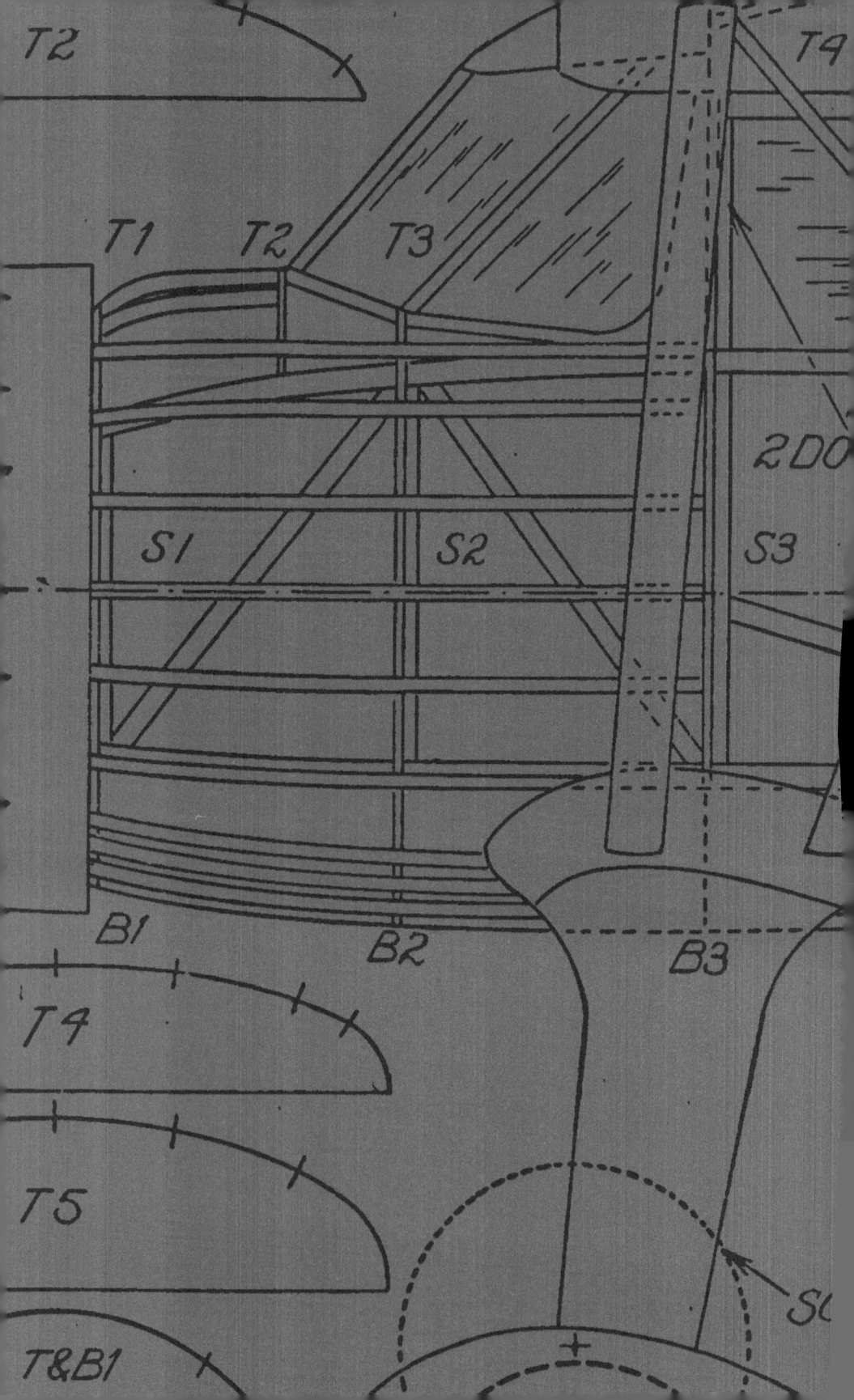

THE COMPLETE ADVENTURES OF
THE GRIFFON
VOLUME 4

BY
Arch Whitehouse

ILLUSTRATIONS BY
Al McWilliams

COVER BY
August Schomburg

ALTUS PRESS

2023

© 2023 Altus Press, an imprint of Steeger Properties, LLC • First Edition—2023

PUBLISHING HISTORY

"Griffon's Nemesis" originally appeared in the January 1938 issue of *Flying Aces* magazine (Vol. 28, No. 2).

"Coffin in the Fog" originally appeared in the March 1938 issue of *Flying Aces* magazine (Vol. 28, No. 4).

"Death Haunts the Clipper" originally appeared in the May 1938 issue of *Flying Aces* magazine (Vol. 29, No. 2).

"Clipped-Wing Clue" originally appeared in the July 1938 issue of *Flying Aces* magazine (Vol. 29, No. 4).

"Black-Out Vultures" originally appeared in the September 1938 issue of *Flying Aces* magazine (Vol. 30, No. 2).

"Fog-Flyer's Fate" originally appeared in the November 1938 issue of *Flying Aces* magazine (Vol. 30, No. 4).

Visit *altuspress.com* for more books like this.

TABLE OF

Contents

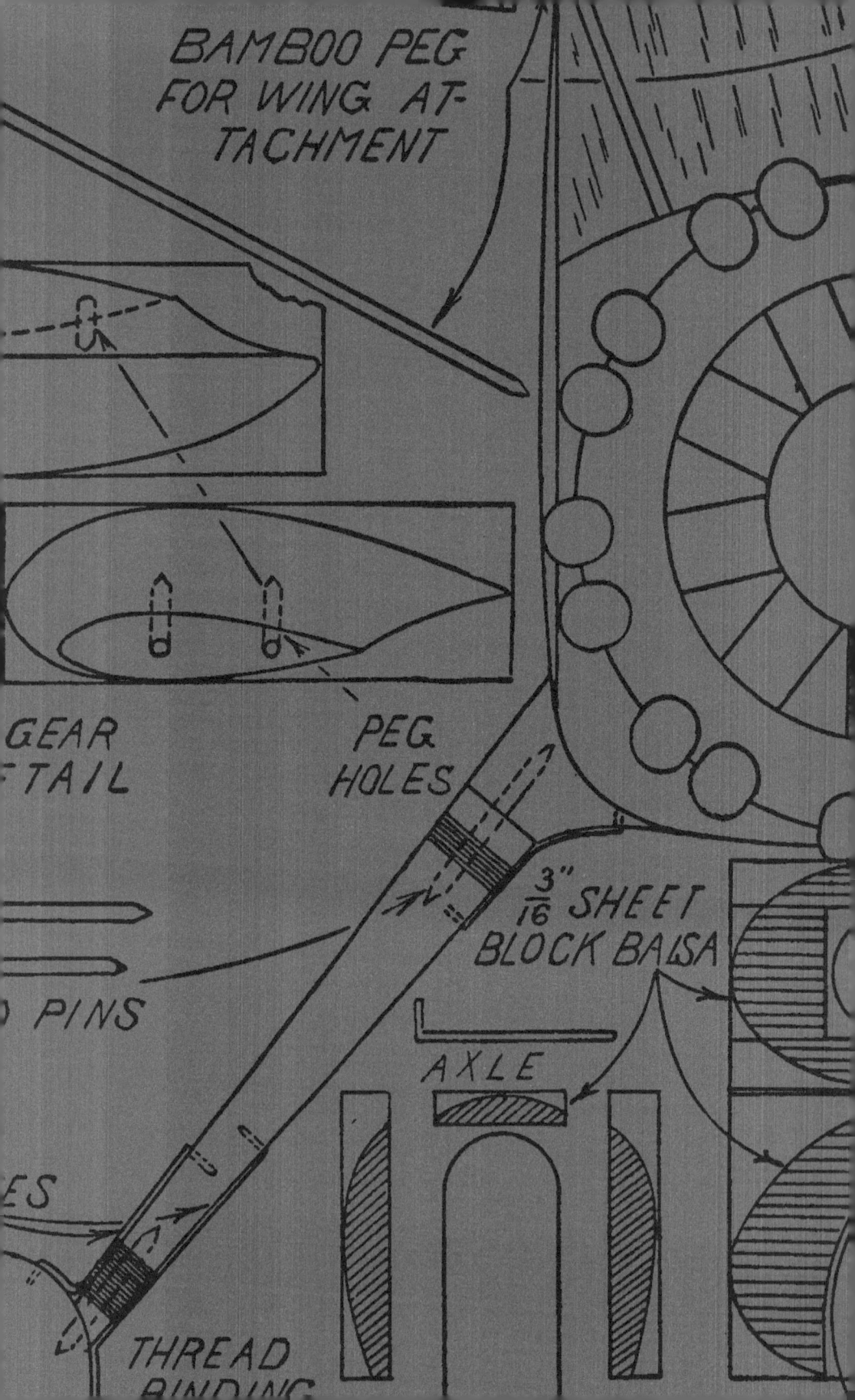

BAMBOO PEG
FOR WING AT-
TACHMENT

GEAR
TAIL

PEG.
HOLES

PINS

$\frac{3"}{16}$ SHEET
BLOCK BALSA

AXLE

ES

THREAD
BINDING

Griffon's Nemesis

THAT YELLOW monoplane kept pace with the black amphibian no matter what the Griffon did to get more power out of his Avia motor. This had been going on for more than thirty minutes now—ever since they had passed over the south-western tip of Cape Cod.

The Griffon turned, glanced at the man behind him who sat peering up through the Plexiglass top of the Black Bullet. His gnarled hands gripped the black handles of the twin-Browning guns that snuggled under the fuselage hump.

"Take it easy," the Griffon warned. "He'll get tired of following us."

The man in the rear pit grunted, then said: "But what's he tailing us for? I'm not taking any chances on him. But hey! There's that strange light again. What's that?"

The Griffon looked up, saw two sharp pencil lines of light flash out from the forward portion of the yellow monoplane. He instinctively flinched, drew back half expecting to feel the thud of a bullet.

"That's the second time he did that," the man behind growled. "What's he doing?"

The Griffon stared up again, waited. He had an idea about that strange light. The realization made him go cold, and his mind raced like wildfire turning over the details of a new science of which he had recently read.

But when he quickly pushed the throttle of the Avia, she

Quickly the man behind the Griffon unlimbered his twin guns, poured a hail of lead across the sable sky. But from that eerie yellow monoplane there came only a weird beam of white light—a merciless luminous finger that the Griffon could not evade!

responded perfectly. No, that was not it. The engine purred beautifully. Then what the devil was that man doing up there?

Again the weird light flashed, and again the Griffon winced. Then there was a sudden scuffle as the man behind the Griffon quickly unlimbered his twin guns. The Brownings danced on their mountings, poured a hail of lead across the sable sky. That withering fire bit into the fuselage of the eerie yellow monoplane.

"No! No!" the Griffon yelled. "You shouldn't have done that," he barked, expecting to see the yellow intruder disintegrate in mid-air. But then he was startled to see the weird ship continue on its way as though nothing had happened. Now it was curling up in a beautiful arc, slipping over sharply—and coming down upon them hurling four streams of battering fire!

The Griffon acted fast. He had to, to get clear. The yellow monoplane slammed at them with all the fury of hell, gave the Black Bullet a terrible beating around the tail surfaces.

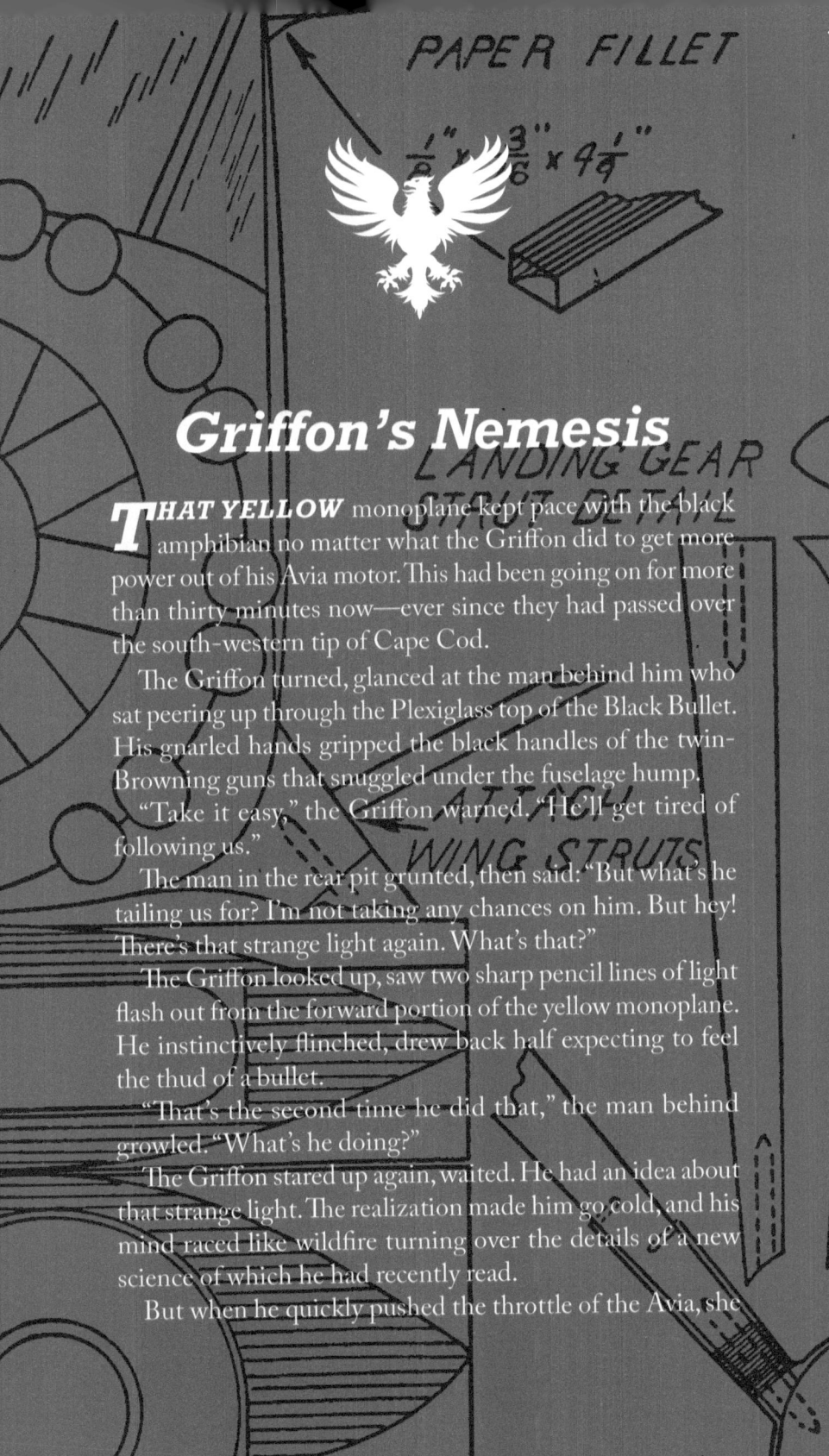

Griffon's Nemesis

THAT YELLOW monoplane kept pace with the black amphibian no matter what the Griffon did to get more power out of his Avia motor. This had been going on for more than thirty minutes now—ever since they had passed over the south-western tip of Cape Cod.

The Griffon turned, glanced at the man behind him who sat peering up through the Plexiglass top of the Black Bullet. His gnarled hands gripped the black handles of the twin-Browning guns that snuggled under the fuselage hump.

"Take it easy," the Griffon warned. "He'll get tired of following us."

The man in the rear pit grunted, then said: "But what's he tailing us for? I'm not taking any chances on him. But hey! There's that strange light again. What's that?"

The Griffon looked up, saw two sharp pencil lines of light flash out from the forward portion of the yellow monoplane. He instinctively flinched, drew back half expecting to feel the thud of a bullet.

"That's the second time he did that," the man behind growled. "What's he doing?"

The Griffon stared up again, waited. He had an idea about that strange light. The realization made him go cold, and his mind raced like wildfire turning over the details of a new science of which he had recently read.

But when he quickly pushed the throttle of the Avia, she

Quickly the man behind the Griffon unlimbered his twin guns, poured a hail of lead across the sable sky. But from that eerie yellow monoplane there came only a weird beam of white light—a merciless luminous finger that the Griffon could not evade!

responded perfectly. No, that was not it. The engine purred beautifully. Then what the devil was that man doing up there?

Again the weird light flashed, and again the Griffon winced. Then there was a sudden scuffle as the man behind the Griffon quickly unlimbered his twin guns. The Brownings danced on their mountings, poured a hail of lead across the sable sky. That withering fire bit into the fuselage of the eerie yellow monoplane.

"No! No!" the Griffon yelled. "You shouldn't have done that," he barked, expecting to see the yellow intruder disintegrate in mid-air. But then he was startled to see the weird ship continue on its way as though nothing had happened. Now it was curling up in a beautiful arc, slipping over sharply—and coming down upon them hurling four streams of battering fire!

The Griffon acted fast. He had to, to get clear. The yellow monoplane slammed at them with all the fury of hell, gave the Black Bullet a terrible beating around the tail surfaces.

The man in the back seat now went into action again, and as
the yellow monoplane swished up over them he directed a
deliberate stream of spinning lead full into the mud-flecked
belly of the ship. But again, nothing happened!

"Holy Mither o' Moses!" the gunner guy gasped. "What
is that damnable thing?"

The yellow monoplane cleared, curled over in that skilled
turn, came back at them once more. This time, the Griffon turned sharply, drew his stick smoothly, and pressed his
nose gun triggers. The two ships came at each other head-
on, spurting streaked fire. For a few seconds it appeared
that they would meet in a terrible crash. True, the Griffon
held his course, ducked low behind the big 1,000 h.p. Avia,
and hammered through. But the yellow plane swished up,
clearing the Black Bullet by inches. Then it hoiked hard and
climbed high.

The Griffon was perspiring. He had seen with his own eyes
something that even he could not believe. He had encoun-

tered a bullet-proof plane—there was no question of that now. But what was its strange secret?

He renversed, watched as the yellow craft held its same position just above them. The man in the back seat continued to flame off short bursts at it, but the weird monoplane never wavered.

"Get the divil oot o'here," the man behind almost whined. "We can't do anything against that bird. But look! There's that light again!"

Two more fine jets of light flashed out—and the Griffon knew he was trapped—knew that this was the outcome of their secret trip north.

They'd taken a few weeks of rest, camping in the Hudson Bay section, thus regaining strength and enthusiasm for what might come in the future. It had been a happy month only interrupted when they made a couple of secret trips down to Montreal to arrange for shipment to Graylands of some necessary equipment.

But that was all over now. They were back, facing grim facts of intrigue. Already they had tasted gunfire—and with it came the realization that something had slipped up. Who was this swine in the yellow monoplane who had so easily intercepted them at 10,000 feet over Cape Cod? What did it all mean? What was this man in the bullet-proof plane after?

The Griffon and his gunner knew they were in a tough spot. They had to land soon. And even though the night was perfect for a secret landing at Graylands, there could be no secrecy unless they could get rid of their yellow nemesis.

THE GRIFFON sat back. They were over Block Island now and already had spotted the telltale beams of Montauk Light. Their secret hide-out was only a few miles south-west of that light.

With a quick move, the Griffon made an adjustment on his variable pitch prop. Then he set his wing-flaps and gave the man behind a signal.

"Chuck everything that we don't need overboard. We're

going upstairs. You may need your oxygen, so play safe. If he is armored, he'll have a devil of a time getting up there."

Then began a mad duel. The Black Bullet climbed like a fiend. The Griffon kept pushing her higher and higher, watched the needle of the altimeter pass the 15,000 foot mark. The yellow monoplane tried to keep up with them. But by the time they had reached 18,000, the Black Bullet was several hundred feet above her.

The man behind kept one eye on the yellow monoplane as he jettisoned box after box of sporting-rifle cartridges, hunting clothing, hatchets, and knives. A complete camp kit went next, then the parts of a folding gasoline stove. Finally there was nothing left but three expensive sporting rifles and a brace of revolvers.

Twenty thousand feet! They were well above the yellow monoplane now. The Griffon sucked on his oxygen tube, adjusted his throttle and supercharger level, and sat back. The Black Bullet was still climbing. They had checkmated their pursuer!

"What is that bus?" the Griffon turned and asked.

"Looks like a Seversky P-35 to me. Has all the lines of one, anyway," the man behind him replied. "But I don't get that bullet-proof business or that funny light business."

"I do!" the Griffon growled. He was obviously very perturbed.

They finally eased off at 26,000 feet and peered about. The yellow monoplane was nowhere in sight now. Relieved, the Griffon headed away for Montauk Light. Their journey ended, they spent several minutes circling cautiously, then the Griffon shut off the motor, put the Black Bullet's nose dead on the ringlet of lights that represented East Hampton, and let her drop like a plummet. For what seemed hours they dived, while the slipstream screamed its banshee wail.

As the short-line of Long Island became more distinct, the Griffon turned back toward Montauk. Then with a quick curl, he eased out of the dive, cut in the Skoda mufflers to deaden the Avia's roar, and S-turned down to a smooth landing.

Gently the sleek ship taxied across the inky smooth waters to a dim boathouse. Then the amphibian's wheels came in contact with the hard-packed sands and she quietly crept up the beach, rolled over the well-groomed turf, and found the shadows of a great arbor.

Within another minute, the Black Bullet rumbled through the great rock garden doors and into the secret hangar.

TOGETHER, THEY studied the plane after the great doors had folded back, and they found that in spite of the heavy armament of the yellow monoplane, comparatively little damage had been done to the structure of the Black Bullet. A few metal patches here and there and she would be ready for action again.

They went upstairs, tired and hungry. The gunner chap threw off his flying kit and hid it away with that off the Griffon's. Then he broke out a bottle of O'Doul's Dew, a bottle of champagne, and a large dish of crackers and cheese. And together they sat swigging and munching while they pondered on the events of the night.

The Griffon finally went across to a bookshelf, selected a volume and fingered through its pages until he came to a treatise on black light. Then he sat down to read.

"Here we are, Barney," he suddenly cracked. "It was just as I thought. That bird was using a black light camera on us. He probably got a few neat shots of the Black Bullet tonight—and of me."

"Wow!" gasped the Irishman. "That does cop the prize, huh?"

"Well, that means we've got to get a new bus. If we can't run away from ships like that, we'll have to quit this game and go to work—and nothing annoys me more than work."

"When did you ever work to find out?" Barney asked, grabbing another hunk of cheese and pouring himself another drink.

"We'll skip that," the Griffon said. "But we've got to do something about this yellow monoplane bloke. He's bad news."

At that instant the telephone bell rang. Both the Irishman and the Griffon exchanged a glance.

Barney started to pick up the receiver, but the Griffon signalled him off, took up the receiver himself, and listened a moment before he spoke. All he heard was a low annoying chuckle.

"Hello!" the Griffon said in a well-modulated voice.

"Hello!" came the answer from the other end, followed by another low chuckle. *"That you, Mr. Keen?"*

"Keen speaking. Who is this?"

Again came a chuckle, then a name was given which was not quite distinct. Keen queried again, but the man on the other end only laughed aloud this time. Keen then gave Barney a signal, whereupon the Mick darted into another room.

"Nice ship you have out there, Keen," the voice said.

"What are you talking about?" the ballistics expert asked, stalling for time to give Barney a chance to check where the call was coming from.

"Stop it! Stop it!" the voice said. *"I just want to say that I got some nice pictures of you—and you won't be able to talk yourself out of that evidence."*

At the word "evidence" Keen went cold.

"Is this you, Lang?" he asked suddenly; for there seemed to be a certain timbre to the man's voice which reminded him of Drury Lang.

"Never mind who it is. I'm wise to you, Keen. How about getting in on your racket?"

"I don't know what you are talking about?" Keen parried.

"So you didn't fly down from Canada tonight. And you didn't exchange a few shots with a yellow monoplane, and you didn't climb up to about 25,000 feet to evade me, eh? Well, you'd better

have a good story ready when the authorities get the evidence I have."

"What's your game?" Keen asked.

"The same as yours, and I'd like to get in with you. You seem to have the inside on a lot of things. What about it?"

"I'd better have a little time to think it over," answered Keen, who knew when he was cornered.

"All right. I'll give you a few hours. I'll call you at your 55th Street place in New York City tomorrow."

"You mean you'll call on me tomorrow?" asked Keen.

"Oh no. I'll simply call you on the telephone—and then we'll plan a joint meeting somewhere else. I'm not dumb, you know."

"All right, and good night," Keen replied, hanging up the receiver. But he did not hang up quick enough to avoid hearing that taunting laugh again.

KERRY KEEN stood there for several moments, stared into space and tried to figure what the man was getting at. Why had he so carefully followed him? How did he know he was on his way down from Canada? And how did he know who he was and where he lived?

He pondered on the voice again. Certain words and phrases the man had used reminded him of Drury Lang. But it *couldn't* be Lang. Lang was not a pilot, and he was certain that the yellow monoplane was a single-seater.

Then Barney came in wearing a puzzled frown. "He was phoning from a booth in a cigar store in New London," the Irishman said.

"New London?" Keen replied, wrinkling his brow. "Then it really *could* have been the same bird that was in that yellow monoplane!"

"Faith, and I think we'd better be packing our bags," Barney cracked glumly.

"You can buzz off if you like, but I'm sticking around here," said Keen sternly. "He's not frightening me out. He's got to come out in the open and tell his story first. I have an idea he's trying to work me for something. But still I can't figure out how he traced me—and the Bullet."

"What are we going to do?" asked Barney, indicating his loyalty in spite of his reference to the business of packing bags. "You say he wants to get in with us? What for?"

"That's what we'll have to find out tomorrow. He's calling at 55th street."

Then the telephone bell rang again, and once more they exchanged glances.

Keen took up the receiver, and this time it was unmistakably Drury Lang.

"So you got back, eh? Where you bin?" the Secret Service man asked at once.

"Oh, just tootling about the country, keeping away from telephones," explained Keen blandly. "What gets you to a telephone at this time of night? Someone swipe an aircraft carrier?"

"It's worse!" Lang wailed over the wire. *"Do you know anything about codes? The Navy's lost theirs."*

"Probably some gob dropped it down a funnel while he was chipping paint," chortled Keen, wondering what Lang was getting at.

"No, this is real. The new Navy Yarnell code, supposed to be the only unbreakable code in the world, has disappeared. I thought you might have an idea about it. We're stuck."

"My line's ballistics. Pop-pop stuff, you know," Keen went on, winking at Barney. "I don't know much about codes."

"Will you be in town tomorrow?" asked Lang *"I'd like to see you about it."*

"I'll give you a ring sometime before noon."

"Well, here's the dope. It'll be something for you to think about. A young Navy Intelligence Service Captain named Walter Glendon, who has been conferring with a Professor Neville Letchworth of Yale—he's a cryptologist, or something—was on his way down from New Haven with a complete copy of the Yarnell code. He was found in his compartment when the train pulled

in, drugged and his brief case cleaned out. The Yarnell code book was missing, and the Navy is raising hell about it."

"He was carrying the code book? What for?" asked Keen.

"I tell you, he'd been up to New Haven conferring with this Professor Letchworth. From what I can make out this Letchworth is hot stuff on this sort of thing, and I suppose he's in with the Navy, and had been asked to clean up a few of the points about it."

"Then Letchworth knows all about the code, eh?" Keen queried.

"No—not all of it. Only the particular points in question. As far as I know, not even Glendon knows the full details of the thing. He was really little more than a trusted courier."

"When did all this happen?" cracked Kerry Keen.

"Three days ago—on Tuesday night."

"Three days! Then they've had ample time to photostat the book from cover to cover. There's nothing you can do about it."

"That's what I thought, but Glendon says no. It is useless unless they have what he calls a key book. The key book itself is useless without the code book. From what I can make of it all, the key book changes with each day in the year, and any messages sent on a certain date are keyed to that date. So actually, then, the code book is really 365 codes all in one."

Keen growled. "Well all they have to do is stop anyone from getting the key book."

"That's the way it stacks up with me. But the Navy wants that code book back, and we're tagged. You'd better run in here tomorrow. I'm getting sick of it."

"I'll give you a ring," Keen said, and he hung up.

Barney drained his glass, glanced up, his mug mournful. "We'll both probably end up with a hunk of chain dangling from our ankles," he said. "I'll niver be able to sleep a wink this night."

KEEN SANK into a large leather club chair, lit a cigarette. For the first time in his career as Raffles of the airways, he caught himself casting quick glances about the room and inspecting the windows. When a log in the open fireplace crackled, it made him jump.

He got up, paced the floor back and forth, and tried to fathom the meaning of it all. Who was the man whose voice at times sounded like Drury Lang's? He kicked himself mentally for not checking Lang's call.

Finally he went into his library, found Professor Neville Letchworth's biography in a scientific tome, then checked back through his elaborate file system and uncovered a full-page photograph of the man. The latter had appeared with an article on the Rosetta Stone published in a fairly recent edition of *Scientific Digest*.

Keen studied the photograph, re-read the man's biography. The son of an English savant, Letchworth had graduated from Harvard with high honors and had then spent considerable time in Egypt with the Harvard Archaeological Association. He'd been responsible for deciphering several important tablets that had been unearthed at El Qaitara in 1927. He was about five years older than Keen, but his photograph proved him to be a man in splendid physical condition. The rest of the biography related to his skill in the art of cryptology.

Keen returned to his studying of the portrait. Letchworth certainly did not look like the accepted criminal type. He had a broad forehead, an aristocratic nose, a firm jaw. Then suddenly something in the picture caught Keen's eye and he peered at the picture with a magnifying glass.

Finally, he smiled, took down a violet-colored book from a shelf, and flipped its pages. He came upon a reproduction of the tiny emblem he had discovered in the lapel of the man's coat.

"Now we are getting somewhere," he said aloud. "Just suppose that someone has a copy of the code key book and has already photographed it without anyone else knowing. Then all he'd have to do would be to get together with the thugs who stole the code book and split the profits."

He pondered on that angle for some time, jotted down several notes. "Glendon and Letchworth," he finally muttered, "could be in this together. Glendon could have faked that hold-up gag. He probably didn't have the book with him at all during the return journey. Very likely Letchworth had it all the time and is now trying to contact the man who has the key book. But if it's Glendon who has the key and knows that Letchworth has the code book, they already have all they want and can sell out quickly," he argued with himself. He looked at Letchworth's picture again. "No, Letchworth may have stolen that code book, but he doesn't look like a double-crosser. This business is a last effort toward something or other. Glendon may be the dark guy in the woodpile."

Keen suddenly got a new idea. He remembered that he was slated to meet the man who had flown the yellow monoplane—the man who threatened his whole existence… his freedom. The old fear came back. But with a sudden decision he folded his papers, put the books away, and went to bed.

AFTER A good breakfast and a glance over the morning paper, Keen hurriedly packed a bag with a strange selection of garments, small boxes, and bottles. He gave orders to Barney to get the Black Bullet into shape for a possible flight that night.

Then he stowed his bag in the Dusenberg, slipped behind the wheel, and drove toward Manhattan. It was refreshing to speed along the broad concrete ribbon, but he realized that he had a tough job ahead of him. This time it was something more than a matter of bullets and air speed. He had to outwit someone, and first he had to find out who was his real enemy.

His 55th Street penthouse apartment was neat and ready. He quickly changed into a drab, baggy Harris tweed suit, and a pair of thick soled shoes. Then he took out the photograph of Professor Neville Letchworth and placed it against the mirror of his dressing table.

His fingers worked fast. First he trimmed his eyebrows to

get that upward curl so noticeable over Letchworth's right eye. Then he drew up the skin of the bridge of his nose, and injected special wax with a medical syringe, thus producing the slightly hooked nose of the Yale professor. After shaping the abbreviated sideburns of hair in front of his ears, a small military mustache carefully applied and a pinked in chin cleft completed his disguise into the character of Letchworth. And the result was astonishing.

"Very satisfactory," he agreed, selecting a battered felt hat. "If Letchworth is the man, all well and good. If not, I may learn something intended only for Mr. Letchworth's ears."

He stood off, practiced a self-satisfied smile in which one corner of the mouth turned up higher than the other. He had nearly perfected the grimace when the phone bell rang.

"Hello?" he said, taking up the instrument.

"*That you, Keen?*" It was the voice of the man in the yellow monoplane.

"Right. What's your plan?"

"*Can you meet me in half an hour?*"

"I can—and will. What place would be convenient?"

"*Anywhere you say.*"

"What about the Armor Room at the Metropolitan Museum of Art? You're an armored plane expert!"

"*That's Okay—but be sure you get there.*"

"Don't worry," replied Keen. "I'll go directly to the 16th Century Armorer's Shop exhibit."

"*Very good. I know it well. I once did some... well, never mind. In half an hour, then.*"

"But do you know me?" Keen asked. "I mean will you recognize me?"

"*No. I've never seen you—that is, no closer than we were last night. But we should have no trouble at the Armorer's Shop, should we?*"

"No. There won't be any one there at this time of morning, except perhaps a few tourists—and I assure you I don't look like a tourist."

"Neither do I," the voice at the other end said.

"Half an hour, then," concluded Keen. And he smiled to himself—for the man had taken the bait.

SLIPPING ON a pair of dark glasses, Keen left his apartment fifteen minutes later, walked a few blocks, then signalled a cab. He arrived at the museum exactly on time and hurried upstairs to the Armor Room.

He first wandered quietly through the exhibits, taking his time about heading toward the Armorer's Shop set up on the west side of the museum room. He feigned interest in a French collection which included breastplate and headpiece for the charger. He was really listening, rather than seeing, however. Finally he took off the dark glasses and moved on slowly. A gray-haired caretaker in Museum uniform came up, glanced affectionately at a suit of a Crusader's armor, then went out a door at the other end of the room.

Kerry Keen halted and glanced about. He sensed that something unusual was about to take place. Footsteps could be heard hurrying up the stairs at the end of the room, so he darted behind a case of ancient weapons and listened. The footsteps crossed over to the north side, then slackened down on nearing the 16th Century Armorer's Shop.

Keen was about to step out from his shelter when he caught the sound of another set of footsteps, hurrying up the stairs. He pondered on that, hesitated a minute. Since the footsteps followed the others, he decided to investigate. Keeping well in the shelter of exhibition cases and mounted armor sets, he worked his way across the south side and peered around.

There was a man standing there—a fairly tall man, wearing a trim worsted suit, who stood erect in what might be described as a painful way and kept both hands in his pockets. He was listening to the approaching footsteps.

Keen knew at once that this was not Letchworth. He sensed too that something had slipped up—either that or he had been tricked into a meeting with more than one man.

The man suddenly looked up the aisle, saw Keen who had stepped out from behind a Flemish exhibit and was now in full view.

"Letchworth!" the man called. "Hey, Letchworth!"

The footsteps hurrying along the other side of the room seemed to hurry faster. Then as Keen started to step back, the man at the Armorer's Shop suddenly let out a low scream, staggered, and fell forward on his face!

There had been practically no sound, but Keen had sensed the quiet chug of a silenced pistol.

Keen waited a moment, heard retreating footsteps. Then he darted to the fallen man and turned him over.

"Letch... he got me... from behind," the man gulped, trying to struggle to his feet. "Got me in my... in my back. Can't make my legs work."

"Why did *you* come here?" Keen asked.

The man looked up at him, a glassy stare already creeping into his eyes. "I phoned you... this morning. Guess the wires got twisted... twisted somewhere. I heard your conversation... with that Keen guy. Figured you were... double-crossing me, Letch. So I came, too. Must have been... Keen that... got me, Letch."

"Why did you distrust me?" the ballistics expert asked realizing now that this might be Glendon, the Navy man.

"I figured you... would duck out on me... and contact Zorros," the man said, rolling back.

"But the book was no good without the key," probed Keen, his mind working fast now.

The dying man wagged his head: "No good... without the key... but I wanted to make sure. I didn't like... that business with Keen. Too many chances... chances I took, eh, Letch? Now you got it all... to yourself if you can contact Zorros."

"But the key?" Keen said quickly.

"Sorry, Letch. I must confess that I double-crossed *you*. Zorros has the key. I got it to him... to him, last night... and got my money. You'll get yours when you get... get...."

"When I deliver the book?" Keen whispered.

The man nodded his head, then his whole body was racked with spasmodic jerks. He stiffened out.

The man was dead.

Keen hurriedly ransacked his pockets, took his wallet, a time-table, an oiled-silk tobacco pouch, and, strangest of all, a motor distributor head. The wallet contained a roll of bills amounting to well over $1,500, also a celluloid calendar put out for advertising purposes by an insurance firm. For some strange reason, Keen took the calendar but returned the money. He also left a small white card.

Then he darted away, dashed down the aisle between the exhibition cases, and made his way around the room to the stairway door.

The old caretaker on the stairs gave him a puzzled look as he passed. "Back again?" he said. "Forget something?"

"Yes, I wanted a sketch of that Flemish breastplate scroll for a design. I just took a pencil rubbing. Very interesting, that scroll."

"Ah, yes. A beautiful piece of work that."

Keen went on down to the street, walked around the corner, and jumped in a cab.

He gave the driver his address, then added: "Take a jaunt through the park for about fifteen minutes, first. I'm in no particular hurry. So take it easy."

REACHING HIS apartment, Keen removed his Letchworth disguise and slipped into other clothes. Then with a glance at the clock, he went to work on the things he had taken from the man who had been murdered in the Armor room. The wallet, just as Keen had expected, indicated that the dead man was Walter Glendon, a Captain in the U.S. Navy. But there was really nothing of interest in the leather case outside of the general identification.

The time-table, however, was for the New Haven line and seemed to have been lightly penciled for trains running between New Haven and New York.

As for the Bosch distributor head, that unit seemed to have no particular significance at first. But Keen pondered on the fact that a man dressed so neatly should be carrying such an unusual item in his pockets. Obviously a used part, it was well cleaned; but it still bore certain scratches and marks indicating it had been used on a radial aircraft motor of some kind.

He inspected it carefully, saw that it was bored to take the central high tension lead and had nine openings around the side. It was made of black bakelite and the inside had been carefully cleaned of all oil and grease. He poked about with it for some time, still wondering why the Navy man had carried it about with him.

Then becoming interested in the inner plate of the device, Keen decided to investigate with a small screwdriver. But just then his telephone rang. He picked up the receiver, heard the voice of the man who had called before.

"*Well, where were you?*" the fellow asked at once.

Keen had to think quickly.

"I came up there a few minutes late. You see, I had a special call on a matter of ballistics; and when I got up to the Museum, it was closed off by the police. I was told that someone had been murdered in one of the exhibition rooms. Were you there?"

"*Of course. But when I found that you were not about, I left at once. You say a man was killed in the Museum?*"

"No. I didn't say a man had been killed. I just said that someone had been killed. I don't know whether it was a man or a woman," Keen continued, smiling to himself.

"*Looks like your friend the Griffon has been getting in some soft shooting, eh? Well, what about a meeting later in the day?*"

"You seem very anxious to see me now," Keen taunted. "But you were in quite a hurry this morning. I was only a few minutes late."

"*I didn't like the smell of the arrangements. We'll try it again tonight about 6:30—say at the Police information booth on Times Square. That is, outside the booth."*

"That suits me," Keen replied. "We're not likely to be murdered there," he added cryptically.

"You can't tell where you're going to get murdered, these days. Okay, then—6:30. And you'd better be there, or your friend Lang will get a very interesting letter."

KEEN HUNG up and went back to the motor distributor head, pondered on the man who kept phoning him as he worked over the unit. He was certain now that it was Professor Neville Letchworth. Letchworth had murdered Captain Walter Glendon in cold blood in the Armor Room of the Metropolitan Museum of Art! But why?

He kept recalling the conversation of the dying man, as he sat fumbling with the bakelite distributor piece. Glendon had told his story believing he was talking to Letchworth—but it must have been Letchworth who had killed him. Letchworth was the only other man who would have come to the 16th Century Armorer's Shop at the Museum.

Keen knew he had enough on Letchworth. Nevertheless, he also knew that Letchworth had *him*. Both could hold something over the other. But Keen knew that any man cold-blooded enough to shoot a man in the back would stop at nothing to gain his ends. As long as Neville Letchworth was still alive, Keen's own freedom wasn't worth a thin dime.

He sat staring at the bakelite block, suddenly realized that it was particularly heavy for such a device. He inadvertently poked inside one of the cable stems, pressed down on the small brass disc plate at the bottom. As he did so, he sensed that he had actuated some kind of geared mechanism.

For a moment his hackles stood up on the back of his neck. This was eerie. Fascinated, he tried it again in the same stem marked "1." Again, there was that whirling sensation inside.

"What the deuce?" he muttered, inspecting the block more closely. Then he looked into the larger high tension cable orifice. There, glinting against a white background, was the letter "J."

He pressed the base of the No. 1 plug cable a third time—and the disc behind the large orifice whirled, stopped, and showed the letter "S."

Something began to dawn on Kerry Keen. He laughed to himself and said: "Here I decided to have nothing to do with codes—but I've certainly got myself in for one now."

He counted the number of stems, saw that there were nine. Mentally he divided nine into twenty-six and found that each stem must provide three letters in some way. Three times nine was twenty-seven, that is, one more than the regular alphabet. Perhaps that last stem, if pressed three times, cleared the dial.

"I'll try that," he mused, jabbing a pencil into the No. 9 plug hole. The first push disclosed the letter "I" in the high tension hole. He pressed again and said, "This should bring out 'R,' the eighteenth letter of the alphabet."

He peered in. Yes, there was the letter "R." And when he pressed the third time, he drew a blank. He had been right—that cleared the dial.

Now he took out a sheet of paper and jotted down the letters of the alphabet, ending with the word "clear." Then opposite each of these characters he listed the corresponding numbers, 1 to 26 and with 27 after the word "clear."

"Now," he argued, "if I push No. 1 once, it should bring the letter 'A.'"

He did—and the first letter of the alphabet appeared. He cleared the face with three jabs in the No. 9 hole, then trying his theory further, he pressed No. 7 twice and got the letter "P," the sixteenth letter in the alphabet. Now if only the third sequence of the nine holes worked, all would be Okay. So he pressed No. 6 three times, and to his joy the letter "X" appeared.

He had solved the mystery of the distributor block!

"A very smart system," he grinned. "Now all we need is something to work with it."

But instead of pondering further, he put on his hat, grabbed a buckthorn cane, and sauntered out. A taxi quickly took him to the local Secret Service office.

BOTH DRURY LANG and John Scott were there, poring over several newspapers which they had spread out on a large table.

"Is this the way to look for missing Navy code books?" demanded Keen gayly. "Or are you catching up on your comic strips?"

"This ain't funny," Lang barked pointing to a headline. "How do you like this?"

Keen peered down, saw the first reports of the murder in the Armor Room.

"This sure is a pip!" Lang snarled. "A guy killed in the Metropolitan Museum. No one knows who he is. But twenty people see the guy we think did it leave in as many different ways. There was only two guys who went into that room this morning, outside of the caretaker; and the one who came out is the bird we want. But some say he was wearing a *brown tweed* suit, and others are equally certain he was wearing a *gray* suit. Then the caretaker thinks he went out and walked across to the park. But others swear he leaped into a cab right outside, and we've found a taxi-man who says he took him to Grand Central station. If this isn't one for your whiskers!"

"But have you got anything on the code book?" asked Keen, apparently disinterested in the murder case.

"Code book? Don't mention that to us," moaned John Scott. "That one has us dizzy—for that Captain guy, Glendon, is missing now."

"Say," broke in Lang. "Where were you about—about 10:30 this morning, Mister Keen?"

"In my apartment. Why?"

"Nothing much. But we found another Griffon card—on the body."

"How interesting," grinned Keen. "Well, I *have* got a brown suit and a gray suit—but I didn't go to Grand Central station. Too many funny people get into Grand Central station. But you say you've got nothing on the code book yet?"

"Nothing. And how those Navy guys are squawking about it! Got any ideas?"

"Well, if they're upset, it's quite obvious that they've not only lost the code book but the code key, too," Keen said, pacing up and down the room.

"What makes you say *that?*" Lang sputtered.

"Figure it out yourself. The key book might have been photographed right in the Navy Intelligence Department's office without ever leaving the building."

"I thought you didn't know anything about codes," Lang said with a strange gleam in his eye. "Frankly, none of us thought of that possibility."

"Perhaps it's because I know nothing about them that the most obvious point should strike my untrained mind first," Keen said flipping his cigarette into an ash tray.

"You got *all* the answers, ain't you?" Lang said. "In fact, you got too many good answers, Keen."

Scott looked from one to the other, and Keen knew trouble was brewing.

"But," continued Lang, "I'll bet you ain't got no answer to *this* one: There was a large crate shipped from the Aldis Motor & Engineering Company plant two weeks ago and addressed to a party over in Jersey. The crate arrived at Jersey City and was placed on board a truck to be drayed to a small air field outside Westfield. Know anything about it, Keen?"

"My line's ballistics. I've told you that over and over," Keen parried.

"Well this sure has a touch of ballistics about it. That crate carried a 1,500-h.p. aero motor specially designed to carry a 37 m.m. air cannon. Now do you know anything about it?"

"Two weeks ago? Why I was up in Canada then with Barney."

But Lang kept on: "Yeah, and that truck carrying that motor disappeared for several days, then was traced to a spot outside Montreal—was found in a ditch and no crate aboard!"

"The Griffon again?" asked Keen in all seriousness.

"Yeah—The Griffon again!"

"How odd!"

"Of course, *you* wouldn't have no use for a 1,500-h.p. aircraft engine, Keen. But I figured your pal—"

"My pal?" broke in Keen.

"Well, that Griffon guy might want to use one… in some way."

"So what?"

"I'll tell you what. We gotta get that code book back—and we thought, John and I, here—that if you could help us out, we might forget that Aldis motor thing. It was hijacked—a serious offense, you know—and Canada don't like it a bit. Still, we can overlook some things—if you need money bad enough to give us just a little help on this code book business."

"I still don't get what you are driving at," Keen cracked back.

"Okay! We'll trace that motor if it's the last thing we do! That way, we'll get the Griffon. And when we get him, his pals, such as you—"

"Wait a minute," smiled Keen. "What did you say about money?"

"Look here, Keen. We're not dumb. Either the Griffon swiped that crate to use himself or to sell it. It's worth about $80,000."

"Why don't you let me try to find the motor?" Keen asked blandly.

Lang was disgusted "We don't *want* the motor, we want the code book. And you'd better do something about it. You're not so dumb. As for that business of photographing the key inside the Intelligence Department office, where did you get that one?"

"I guess I read too many detective stories when I was young," Keen replied dumbly.

Lang was ready to explode again, but Scott checked him: "You have helped us in the past, Keen," he said quietly. "And we've always seen that you got a good break on the rewards. I think you can help us. You've got a good mind. And being on the outside, you are not hindered by the routine that often interferes with us. We're simply asking a favor of you—"

"Favor, hell!" Lang burst out. "I'm *ordering* him to go to work on it. He knows more about this thing than he'll admit, and I'll bet ten bucks he had something to do with that Aldis engine. Get going, Keen!"

Keen smiled and lit a fresh cigarette. He had won a valuable point, and he was satisfied.

"See you sometime tomorrow," he said with a jaunty air as he strode toward the door. "And by the way, you say that this Captain Glendon is missing. Well, I'm just dumb enough to have an idea that the man found murdered up at the Metropolitan Museum might be Glendon." And with that Keen opened the door and went out.

Drury Lang let out a gasp—and sat down hard.

FOR THE rest of the afternoon, Keen did a lot of telephoning. He called Barney, gave him orders for the evening, then turned his attention to a drawing board. For three hours he fussed and fumed over a sheet of white paper, fumbling the while with a slide rule, calculating instruments, and some rough sketches he had made.

Then at 6 o'clock he went out, stopped for a bite to eat at the Astor Hotel grill, then quietly sauntered across the street to the safety island in the center of Times Square. There he stood looking up at the newsflashes on the electrical sign board running around the Times Building. The New York Police information booth was only a few feet away.

One news flash caught his eye. It read:

Man Murdered In Metropolitan Museum Identified as Captain Walter Glendon, Navy Intelligence Man. Secret Service Men Throw Out Dragnet For Foreign Spy Syndicate.

"But have they ever caught anyone in one of those dragnets?" a voice whispered behind him.

"I wouldn't know," answered Keen. "I never read the papers."

"You're likely to know if your friend Lang ever sees one of those photographs I snapped last night. You were a little careless that time, Keen. You should have worn your mask. My black light camera brought out your features very clearly."

"Okay, what's the gag? You're trying to contact a man named Zorros, eh? Or do *I* have to contact him?"

"No, you did enough contacting with Glendon in the Museum this morning. And what was the idea of that Griffon card gag, anyway?"

"So now you're worried?"

"Well, it doesn't make any sense."

"Neither does your game of trying to sell a code book that is useless without the key."

"I suppose it does sound foolish. But we all work in our own way, you know. And now let's go where we can sit down."

They sauntered over to the Astor, went into the bar room, and sat down. Keen ordered the drinks, then they sat studying each other for several moments.

"You've got a fine background, Letchworth," Keen finally said. "What got you into this mess?"

"What got you into yours? You're smart, too, Keen."

"The drabness of ordinary life, maybe the Robin Hood in me."

"We're kindred souls, then. Only I'm Robin Hooding for myself. I need money."

"So you're selling the country out to a gang of international spies. That's not my idea of playing the game," Keen said.

"You've had money and still have plenty, I presume—but

I have been struggling along for years on the paltry salary of a professor, giving out my knowledge virtually for nothing. But it's my turn now—my turn to do something for myself."

Keen frowned. "But how did you find out about me?"

"That's a long story. Glendon had the idea first. He heard one of your lectures before the Ordnance Department and figured you would be a good man to contact for some of these jobs. Then he got wind of all this 'Griffon' business. We worked on that together, soon figured you out. As a matter of fact, I followed you all through that Aldis motor business. I was the man who drove the truck."

"You are a member of the University Flying Club," Keen said with a glance at the small badge in Letchworth's lapel. "I have been looking you up, too. You'd make a smart partner— if we could get that warped mind of yours straightened out."

Letchworth bristled. "But why did you look me up?" he almost hissed.

"Lang phoned me and explained about the Navy code book business, so naturally I checked both you and Glendon. I found a photograph of you, spotted that flying club button, and thus got you definitely identified with that yellow monoplane."

LETCHWORTH WAS silent for some time. "You're a strange man, Keen. You pinch everything you can lay your hands on, then salve the police off with a few interesting assists on some of their dumb plays. Yes, I've got to hand it to you. But what did you want that new motor for? I'll confess that you licked me when you grabbed it."

"I wanted it just in case," Keen replied enigmatically. "Just in case you don't come back tonight with my Black Bullet. Yes, I've guessed your little game. Loss of my Black Bullet would mean I'd need a new plane—to put that engine in."

"But you didn't know about me when you swiped that motor."

"That's right. But I knew I'd have to be getting something faster in a short time. Now what's the rest of your story?"

"Well, you've doped it right. I'm contacting someone tonight—at midnight. And I need your bus, since it's an amphibian. I have a plan to pick you up at a certain spot, say about 10:45. I'll take your ship and go about my business, while you wait on the island with mine. And when I get back, we just switch over again—you go your way, and I go mine. Simple, eh?"

"Simple for you. But what do I get out of it?"

"Just a package of pictures and—the negatives. You can do with them what you wish. It's all on the up-and-up, and no one else knows that Mr. Kerry Keen is the Griffon."

"Well, I grant you've got me cold," Keen said. "All I can do is to say Okay and hope for the best. Now where do we meet?"

"I'm flying a Navy Seversky X-BT. Glendon got that for me. I'll pick you up here," Letchworth said indicating a spot on a small map he now shoved forward. The point he'd chosen was on Nantucket Island's southern shore about two miles east of the road that ran south from the town of Nantucket.

"That's a strip of beach that will be above water after 10 o'clock. You can come in and land from the south, and I'll be high and dry on the sandstrip with my Seversky. You'll come alone—and there'll be no funny business, remember."

Keen studied the map for several seconds, then nodded. "We'd better get moving if you expect me there by 10:45."

They rose from their chairs still scrutinizing each other.

"Don't think too harshly of me," Letchworth said, with bitterness. "I never had the chances you've had."

"You mean, you've never taken the chances I have," corrected Keen.

"I've given my whole life to study. There aren't ten men in the whole world with my knowledge—but what has it brought me? Less than four thousand dollars a year! I've always been a seedy university professor wondering where my next pouch of tobacco is coming from."

"There should be a certain amount of satisfaction in your success, your standing in the university world, and the respect the Navy Intelligence Corps holds for you. Money isn't everything."

Letchworth sneered. "No, money isn't everything. But it begins to become mighty important at my age. It's pretty important in yours, too, Keen."

"Let's go," the young ballistics expert said. "This time I'll play the game as you have laid down the rules. But when it's marked 'Paid,' I'm going to get you—if that code book has gone out of this country. Is that understood?"

"Let's not go into heroics, Keen. We meet at 10:45 at Nantucket." And with that, Letchworth hurried across the sidewalk and leaped into a cab.

Keen frowned, then sought a phone booth. A few moments later he was giving Barney a long string of orders and stating with emphasis that they must be carried out at once. What Barney said in return would have curled the corners of an asbestos curtain.

"Don't be silly," bantered Keen, "you'll have a lovely night."

RUSHING BACK to his 55th street apartment, Keen gathered up whatever things he thought he would need. He also took all the items he had taken from the murdered Glendon, particularly making certain he had the distributor block device, the time-table, and the celluloid calendar.

Then he dashed downstairs again, climbed into his Dusenberg, and shot out for Long Island. It was well on toward 9 o'clock when he finally crunched up the driveway and put the car away at Graylands.

He dressed carefully, selecting clothing that bore no markings or identification of any kind. Finally he pulled on a new suit of coveralls, a kapok-lined life-jacket, and a brand new parachute. Lastly, he stuffed his scarlet "Griffon" mask into his thigh pocket.

"If I only knew where he was going to contact this guy Zorros," he muttered as he checked the Black Bullet five minutes later. "I might get away with something." But as he climbed in and started the big Avia engine, he realized that Letchworth held all the trump cards. The professor had planned well. Keen could only hope he had made some mistake.

The Avia caught, hummed into a low thunderous boom of power. Keen snapped in the Skoda mufflers, then toned the engine down to a low rhythmic beating that threw eerie vibrations from the black walls of the secret hangar.

Keen now grew morose. "I wonder if I shall ever get back to run a ship out of here again," he said to himself. "We've had some grand times here, Barney and I. It would be too bad to have a louse like Letchworth break it all up now."

With a last look back at Graylands, Keen let the Black Bullet roll down the padded turf, and into the water. Then the Black Bullet streaked away in comparative silence. Keen had plenty of time, so he let the Black Bullet climb steadily to about 4,000 feet before he opened up the mufflers. Then he continued on for about a quarter of an hour, pondering over the situation as he flew. None of it offered him an opening, because he did not know where the mysterious Zorros was to be contacted.

At 10:15 he turned the Black Bullet north-east and headed for Nantucket. "He'll take my bus," Keen went on to himself. "And maybe he'll come back and maybe he won't. But by that time, it will be too late to save the code, even if I do get those incriminating pictures. Yes, I was certainly a bonehead not to have been wearing my mask when he leveled that camera."

He sat back and reflected that this time the Griffon was in a real spot. He could knock Letchworth off the minute he landed at Nantucket—but that would be dangerous. He could not be certain that the cryptologist had the pictures with him. He might have left them somewhere to be mailed to Drury Lang in case he failed to turn up within a stated time. Letchworth was not the type of man who would take any chances now. There were too many points involved.

By 10:35 he was within sight of the island. Letchworth had indeed selected a God-forsaken point for their contact.

WITH A last careful investigation of the ground below, Keen snapped in his Skoda mufflers and let the Black Bullet glide down to within 500 feet. He inspected the strip of sand which was now high and dry above the water. It lay there like a long brown sea monster of some kind. Smooth and well packed, it provided a reasonable stretch for a landing.

The Black Bullet soon rumbled over the sand. And Keen shut off the engine. How long he sat there, anxious and on tenterhooks, he never knew. The time was spent staring out to sea, wondering where the man known as Zorros hid. He stared down at his small map, reading it by the light of the instrument board. Then suddenly he caught the sound of a powerful motor. Keen sensed that it was the Seversky.

And now Letchworth had landed, letting the plane run well clear of the Black Bullet by pulling her up on the wheel brakes about seventy-five yards away. Keen waited, and Letchworth also sat in his cockpit several minutes before he got out.

But finally he came forward with a sub-machine gun under his arm. He was dressed in field boots, riding breeches, and a heavy leather windbreaker.

"All right, Keen," he said in a domineering tone. "How is she?"

"She's ready. There's plenty of fuel for several hours. I'll show you how to set the landing gear, if you wish."

"You just tell me—and keep your distance, I'm taking no chances on you."

Keen then went into detail explaining the mechanism of the retracting gear. Letchworth listened carefully, nodded.

"And now what about the pictures?" Keen asked.

"I have the pictures here with me," Letchworth said, tapping his jacket pocket. "You'll get them when I get back: All you have to do is sit tight here for about an hour or so. No one will bother you, I'm sure of that."

"What about my taking your ship if I *have* to beat it?"

"You're here until I return, Keen. I've taken care of that. I just emptied the tanks."

"Swell! And how are you going to get off here after you get back?"

"We'll split up what fuel you have left in yours. That's simple enough, isn't it?"

"Okay! Here's hoping."

"Fine! Now you just walk off about twenty or thirty yards—and don't try anything funny, or I shall be tempted to spray a few slugs into you. Understand?"

Keen walked away and watched Letchworth climb up into the Black Bullet. He let his hands drop into his pockets and his fingers came in contact with the time-table, the calendar, and the bakelite distributor block. His fingers were twitching as he fumbled nervously with the paper and strip of celluloid.

He heard the Avia motor catch and saw Letchworth wave to him from under the covered hatch. Then without knowing why he snatched the calendar out of his pocket and ran his fingertips over the glossy surface. He had discovered a number of pinprick spots marked on the calendar!

The Black Bullet was now taking to the air, but Keen took no notice of her. He rubbed the surface of the calendar again, then hurried down the sand, climbed into the Seversky cockpit, and switched on the dash lights. There he studied the calendar for several seconds, then noticed that by marking down the various numbers underlined by the pin-pricks in month-by-month sequences, he had a set of figures that looked suspiciously like a code.

He smiled as he caught the idea of the pin-pricks. They'd been jabbed in the calendar sometimes singly, sometimes in twos, and sometimes in threes. That system, he decided, corresponded with the number of pushes called for in the distributor head holes.

Just then, he heard the chug-chug of a motor boat. He snapped on the landing lights of the Seversky, then went back to his list of figures. Taking out his pencil, he now went to work on the distributor block device and worked out the following:

BLAZERIPLIGHTMIDNIGHTFRIDAYZORROS

Those letters, correctly spaced out, gave him:

"Blaze Rip Light, Midnight Friday—Zorros."

That was it! The contact was to be made at Blaze Rip Light at midnight—tonight!

He leaped out of the cockpit, raced toward the shore line. A glinting hooded motor boat was nosing toward him.

"Barney! Barney!" Keen yelled. "Come on, we've got to move fast."

They lugged out large five gallon cans of fuel from the stern of the boat and hurried up the sands to the Seversky. While Barney unscrewed the tank caps in the wings and set in a funnel, Keen dived underneath and tightened up the dump valve. Then for five minutes they worked like beavers, Barney transporting the cans up the sand spit from the boat while Keen poured the fluid in.

"You're a marvel, Boss," said Barney. "How did you know he'd dump his fuel to hold you?"

"I don't know, really. I tried to figure all the angles and I guess it was a lucky hunch."

"There's the last ten gallons. You got plenty now. When do we leave?"

"We both leave, now—but you leave in the motor boat," said Keen, fumbling with some smooth projectiles he was fitting under the wings.

"You mean I don't go with you?" asked Barney incredulously.

"Exactly. You head straight back for Graylands. I may pick you up somewhere between here and home—and then again, I may not."

BARNEY DID not answer. He simply walked down the sand, sloshed through the water, and climbed into the boat.

Keen followed him, shoved the boat clear, and waved as the craft backed into the easy rollers.

"I'll be seein' you," he grinned. Then he hurried back to the Seversky X-BT and started the 775 Wright Cyclone engine. He drew a line on his map running due east from his position on Nantucket Island, then figured the position of Blaze Rip Light. The distance was approximately 110 miles, which gave Letchworth plenty of time to make his midnight contact.

Keen climbed the Seversky fast, turned inland for a short time, then headed out to sea. He wanted height, and he wanted to make certain that his take-off had not been detected.

He needed plenty of time, too; for he had to work out several plans. What did Letchworth expect to contact at Blaze Rip Light? Had his gang taken over the lightship— or was that position simply a general marker for something else?

Once he had reached 6,000 feet, he set his course for Blaze Rip Light. He knew he could soon overtake Letchworth in the Black Bullet if he headed the fast X-BT direct for Blaze Rip. That much would be easy—but the rest would be harder.

"Harder?" he almost yelled. "It'll be impossible!" he snapped to himself, suddenly realizing that he was flying a land plane. What a fool he had been! This scare that Letchworth had handed him had completely disrupted his ability to think clearly. He was licked. Zorros had the code key; Letchworth had the amphibian… and the Navy Code book. If he shot Letchworth down now, he could not get the code book. With a land plane, it was impossible to get down and take it; thus all his work, effort, and planning had been for naught.

The Griffon was helpless!

He squirmed in his seat, mentally scourging himself for being trapped like this. He had gloried in his trick of having Barney bring him fuel. He had triumphed in solving the riddle of the distributor block and decoding the pin-pricked message. But he had been just a buffoon in the matter of greatest importance. He had been tricked out of his amphibian and given a land plane which was about as much use to him now as a bank vault door.

He flew on, scanned the skies above, and the sea below as though expecting to find an answer written there. The sky was black, the water blacker, and the outlook blacker still.

Then he got an idea. He peered about the cockpit of the Seversky, found its radio set. He did not touch the wavelength lever but switched on the set and clamped the headphones down over his ears. He sat there waiting, listening intently.

As he pondered, he found himself gradually increasing the speed of the Seversky. And now he finally caught the gleam of Blaze Rip Light. But so far there was no trace of the Black Bullet.

"I've got to take a chance," he muttered grimly. "It's neck or nothing now." He flipped the radio switch over to "Transmitting," then spoke into the mike in a low voice:

"Calling Zorros… Letchworth Calling Zorros!"

At first there was no answer. But in a few minutes he called again. This time there was a reply—a cryptic reply.

"Two miles south-east." The phrase was repeated, then silence.

"I hope Letchworth didn't hear me," Keen mumbled. "My one chance is that he'll have so much trouble worrying about the gadgets aboard the Black Bullet that he won't have time to fiddle with the radio."

Keen now changed his course slightly and carried on for a few more minutes. Presently he saw a small vessel apparently at anchor a few miles ahead. It was at the position indicated in the message—two miles south-east of Blaze Rip light.

He worked fast now, for a plan had formulated in his mind. He slipped out of his parachute harness, made certain his automatic was safe, then calmly cut his motor.

From that altitude Keen would be able to approach the

ship with ease. He studied the craft as his glide brought him lower and lower. It was a trim steam power yacht with a white bridge, a red and black funnel, and an air of luxury about it. Finally, he shoved back his coupé top, released his belt, then spoke into the hand mike: "Letchworth coming in. Pick me up, Zorros."

ALMOST INSTANTLY a loud explosion echoed above his head. A gun had been unshipped from a position aft of the yacht's funnel. Another streak of light flashed out—and he knew his trick had been nipped in the bud.

BR-R-RONG! CR-RASH!

Through it all he could hear the raging voice of Letchworth coming through over the radio.

Nevertheless, Keen held the X-BT in her glide. And when two more shells burst over his head, he shoved the stick forward a trifle more.

SMA-A-ASH! The Seversky hit the water, then bounced!

Keen quickly rammed the stick forward and gave the rudder a last kick which sent the nose around and covered his next move from view of those on the yacht, which now lay not forty yards away.

The Seversky again hit hard. Then when her tail snapped up, Keen threw himself forward and hit the sea in a perfect dive. He went down deep into the icy water.

He swam under the water for what seemed minutes. Then he cautiously came to the surface sucked in his breath, he went down again, and swam toward the stern of the yacht. This time he stayed below until he thought his lungs would burst.

When he came up again, sailors on the vessel were playing a blinding light on the wreckage of the Seversky. Keen smiled. They had not seen him, and he was now under the cover of the yacht's overhanging stern. And when a couple of men clambered into a dinghy on the port side, Keen made his way around to starboard.

Aboard there was plenty of action. Two seamen were

running wildly along the decks, another was booming orders through a megaphone. Keen moved cautiously, made his way to the anchor chain in the bow.

Just when he had recovered his breath, he heard the roar of an aircraft engine. He recognized that roar—it was the Black Bullet bringing Letchworth! With a quick glance upward he clambered up the cold chain, worked his way over the bow rail. A sailor in the fo'castle was too interested in the Seversky wreckage and Black Bullet to know what was going on.

With a quick movement, Keen slipped up behind the sailor, brought his automatic down on the fellow's head. The man dropped like a pole-axed steer. Keen caught him, dragged him to a shelter forward of a winch. There he quickly slipped into the sailor's clothes, then calmly sauntered along the starboard deck.

The Black Bullet now screamed low over the yacht, and Keen slipped through a companionway door and disappeared.

SOON THE Black Bullet slithered in for a bumpy landing, but Letchworth steadied her in time and finally nosed her around near the wreckage of the Seversky. The man in the dinghy bellowed to him, and he eased over to them so that they could pass a line through a pontoon ring. Carefully they rowed back to the yacht and tied the Black Bullet up on the lee side.

Letchworth was non-plussed as he stared back at the wreckage of the Seversky which was now sinking lower and lower in the water. "What happened?" he asked as he climbed out.

"We put a couple of shots into him and he—well, he just nosed down into the water. We can't find the guy at all."

"That's funny. That whole cockpit is armored. The engine cowling is armored. I don't believe he was shot down. Did you see him get out?"

"No, the plane hit pretty hard and went straight over on

its back. We think he was thrown out unconscious and then drowned."

"I don't trust that guy," said Letchworth as he climbed up the side. "Go back and have another look. And two of you stand by here with this ship."

Once aboard, the professor made his way to a group of men standing near the bridge.

"How did that fool get away like that?" a big brawny man in evening clothes demanded of Letchworth. "I thought we ordered you to take no chances of any sort."

"I left him with my plane—but there was no gas in it. How the hell he got away is more than I can figure. The dump valve must have closed and left enough fuel in one of the center-section tanks for him to chance it. But what I really can't fathom is how he knew enough to come here."

"Well, he took one chance too many. They can't find the body, eh?"

"So they say," Letchworth said, looking over the rail to where the searchlight still played on the wreckage. "But I still don't—"

"Come on in and let's get it over," the big man in evening clothes broke in.

They went along the deck, passed down a dark companion-way, and entered a spotless cabin. A table had been cleared, and they drew up their chairs.

"You got it?" the man in evening clothes asked Letchworth.

In reply Letchworth drew out two packages from his windbreaker and slid one across the table. The other he kept in his right hand. The man in evening clothes nodded to a young narrow-faced man at the other end of the table, then he began to untie the cord that bound the package.

The narrow-faced man went to a safe, twisted the knob a few times, and opened the door. He brought out a long black book, fitted with loose-leaf binder clasps. This he carried to his superior who was still busy untying the string on the package Letchworth had brought.

"What happened to Glendon?" asked the latter, suddenly looking up at Letchworth.

"I had to finish him because I was afraid he was going to double-cross me," answered the professor. Then he told of the incident in the Metropolitan Museum of Art.

The man in the evening clothes nodded as he opened the package. "I didn't like the way he was working," he said. "I had to take the key book at his price, and I still think he would have double-crossed the lot of us."

"Well, what about *my* money, Zorros?" Letchworth demanded. "I've taken plenty of chances getting that book."

"Give him his money, Pierre," the man called Zorros said, nodding to the thin-faced man. Thereupon, a package was thrown across the table to Letchworth with a disdainful gesture.

"Yes, this looks all right," said Zorros, taking the Code book and checking it with one of the photographic pages of the key. "You've done a good job, Letchworth. A good—"

But before he could finish the sentence a door opened behind Letchworth. Zorros went white as he stared up and faced a man in a scarlet mask—a man who brandished a blue-black automatic.

"A pretty fair job, Zorros—but it's all over now," said the Griffon. "I'll take those two books—and also your wad of dough, Letchworth."

Letchworth turned, tried to stop the Griffon from taking the two packages. But the Griffon brought his gun down hard on the man's hand, and he drew back.

"Now the code and the key book, Zorros," the Griffon demanded.

"How the devil—?" Letchworth started to say.

Zorros was crouching over the table, his hand shoving the books forward slowly.

"Make it fast. I haven't all night," the Griffon barked.

"He fooled you, too, Zorros," Letchworth started to say.

"Yes, he fooled us, too," hissed Zorros, bending forward to shove the books nearer to Letchworth. "He certainly *did!*"

The Griffon, suspecting a counter attack, suddenly jumped to a position behind Letchworth. Zorros made a quick move, and a gun blazed out from somewhere near his hip.

But the man in the scarlet mask was ready. He pulled his trigger once, a sharp crack sounded, and Letchworth fell forward over the table, blood spurting out of a great gash in the top of his head. Then a second report rent the air, and Zorros jerked up, dropped his gun, and grabbed his massive stomach. And when the thin-faced Pierre made a quick move, the Griffon slammed him back against the wall with a bullet that drilled his shoulder.

Finally, the masked man snatched up the books and packages, stuffed the lot into his shirt, and backed away.

Zorros was still standing, hunched against the heavy teakwood table, an insane mask of hatred distorting his face. He choked on an oath as he clutched his stomach.

"That's all, Zorros," the Griffon snapped. "You had your run and you've played out your hand. It was great while you were winning, but this time you tackled the wrong outfit. The United States Navy puts up with just so much—and no mo—"

That was all Zorros heard. His legs twisted under him like a pair of corkscrews, and he went to the floor in a heap. Then the body of Professor Letchworth gave a last convulsive jerk and rolled off the table.

THERE WERE still two men alive in that room. The Griffon quickly backed them against the wall. One raised both hands high above his head, the other could raise only his left arm, since his right hung helpless and bloody at his side.

"I'm leaving here," the Griffon said. "And I'll give you birds twelve hours to get away somewhere and ditch this tub. That's my proposition, and you'll like it."

The two men gave grunts of assent, and the masked man

backed out of the door with a final admonition: "If you birds show your heads out of this door before ten minutes are up, I'll blow them off for you."

Now he slipped quietly up the companionway and went out into the shadows of the deck. Then skirting the wall fast, he quietly worked his way up to the section of rail where the two sailors stood at the boarding ladder.

"Zorros must have given that guy Letchworth the works," one was saying.

The Griffon caught them flat-footed. When he displayed his gun, the two men gasped, raised their hands. One tried to let out a yell, but a short hook to the jaw brought him to his knees, and he only gurgled.

"Fast!" snapped the Griffon. "Over the side, both of you!"

"What's the idea?" the second fellow started to say.

"Over, I said—and dive deep," the Griffon snarled through his mask.

They both climbed up on the rail, whereupon the masked man gave them both a shove. They dropped over with a stomach-slapping splash. The Griffon then grasped the line to the Black Bullet and dropped down onto the port pontoon. He quickly untied the rope in the pontoon ring, then shoving the Black Bullet clear of the yacht, he clambered up over the wing, dropped into the cockpit, kicked the starter, and rammed the rudder over.

The left wing-tip scraped against the hull of the yacht, but the Griffon finally got her clear and slammed the power to her.

Abruptly, a crackle of gunfire spat from the deck, and he ducked as a burst pounded into the fuselage somewhere behind him. But he got the Black Bullet off and was soon circling tightly over the yacht.

He went down once and gave the deck a terrible hosing of fire that scattered men in all directions. He could see the two seamen in the rowboat working madly to get back to the yacht. With a last salute that spattered sparks off the deck and the funnel, the Griffon zoomed up through a trickle of tracer and headed west.

IT WAS afternoon the next day when Barney wandered into Kerry Keen's bedroom with a comforting tray of piping hot breakfast. He had a doleful expression as Keen climbed slowly from the pillows and blankets.

"Have a nice ride home?" Keen asked, slipping into a bathrobe.

Barney did not answer. Plainly peeved, he simply went about pouring the coffee and dishing out the griddle cakes.

"I couldn't help it, Barney. I didn't know I'd get the old boiler back the way I did," Keen tried to explain. "I had to change my plans at the last minute when I suddenly realized that the Seversky was a land job."

"Ye needn't make any excuses to me," Barney growled. "A foine night that turned out to be. I do a long distance patrol in a motor boat—while you have all the fun. I'm just a galloping gas station attendant now."

"Oh, go and put your head in soak," laughed Keen.

"In what?" came back Barney.

"Well, here's a few bucks I lifted last night. Go buy yourself a couple of cases of O'Doul's Dew and soak your obstinate noggin in that!"

Barney took the package, flipped open the end, and ran his thumb across the crisp edges of a stack of one hundred dollar bills. Slowly his face lit up. He beamed and smacked his lips.

"Why didn't you say so before?" he said. "I'll see you later."

"And don't forget you have a crate to pick up somewhere before the week is out," reminded Keen sinking his aristocratic beak in a steaming cup of coffee.

Barney went off and Keen heard him spinning the knob of a safe in the other room. He smiled, then took another package from his pile of damp clothing on a chair. He opened it, studied the photographic prints inside, then fingered the fine grain negatives he found in another envelope. Without a second glance at the prints he walked across the room and dropped the lot in the crackling fire Barney had just lighted to warm the room.

THE TELEPHONE bell rang. "I'll take it in here," Keen called to Barney, and he picked up the receiver with a bland smile and said: "Hello!"

"Hello, my eye!" the voice of Drury Lang snapped from the other end. *"How did you do it this time?"*

"Whatever are you talking about?" Keen said in mock surprise.

"You know what I'm talking about. That code book and the photographed pages of the key book. You left them in that table drawer yesterday. You must have had them all the time!"

"I think you're mad, Lang. What are you trying to say?"

"Well, whatever your story is, the story at this end is that we have just found the code and key in the drawer of the table where you were standing when we were looking over those newspapers."

"You think I put them there? How the devil could I?"

"I don't know. I'm just asking. Oh, I know there was a Griffon card in the package. But this time, I don't think the Griffon did it. I think you did it by faking that card."

"I'm telling you Lang. I did not have the code or key yesterday, I did not put anything in your drawer yesterday, and frankly I have no idea what you are talking about!"

"Where were you last night?"

"We took my boat up toward Nantucket—just for a ride. You can check that with Barney. As a matter of fact, we were stuck on a sand bar for some time."

"You're a clever guy, Keen," Lang finally spluttered. *"And if your story is Okay, you certainly could not have planted the code last night."*

"I certainly didn't plant anything yesterday afternoon. I give you my word of honor. But are you sure you've got what you want?"

"Sure? Why, it's the biggest thing we have pulled off in this division. They had a photographed key, too. We didn't know that."

"All right, then. Everything is swell. What do you care how you got it, as—"

"... *As long as we forget about that Aldis engine business, eh, Keen?*"

"Oh, I wouldn't worry about that, Lang. As a matter of fact, it's all taken care of."

"*What the deuce are you talking about?*" stormed Lang.

"Well you see, Lang, I really wanted that engine to put in a motor-boat cruiser. But we were so dumb, we didn't know that the Aldis engine was an inverted Vee job. When we really went into it, we found out that it could not be put into a motor boat, so we had to give up the idea entirely."

"*Good Lord! You were dumb,*" said Lang, "*and there was me figuring that you really had some idea of using it for flying. Ha! Ha! What a fine pair of cookoos, you and that Mick guy are!*"

"Yeah, just a couple of cookoos," agreed Keen. "Still, I'm glad—"

But Lang had hung up with a derisive chuckle.

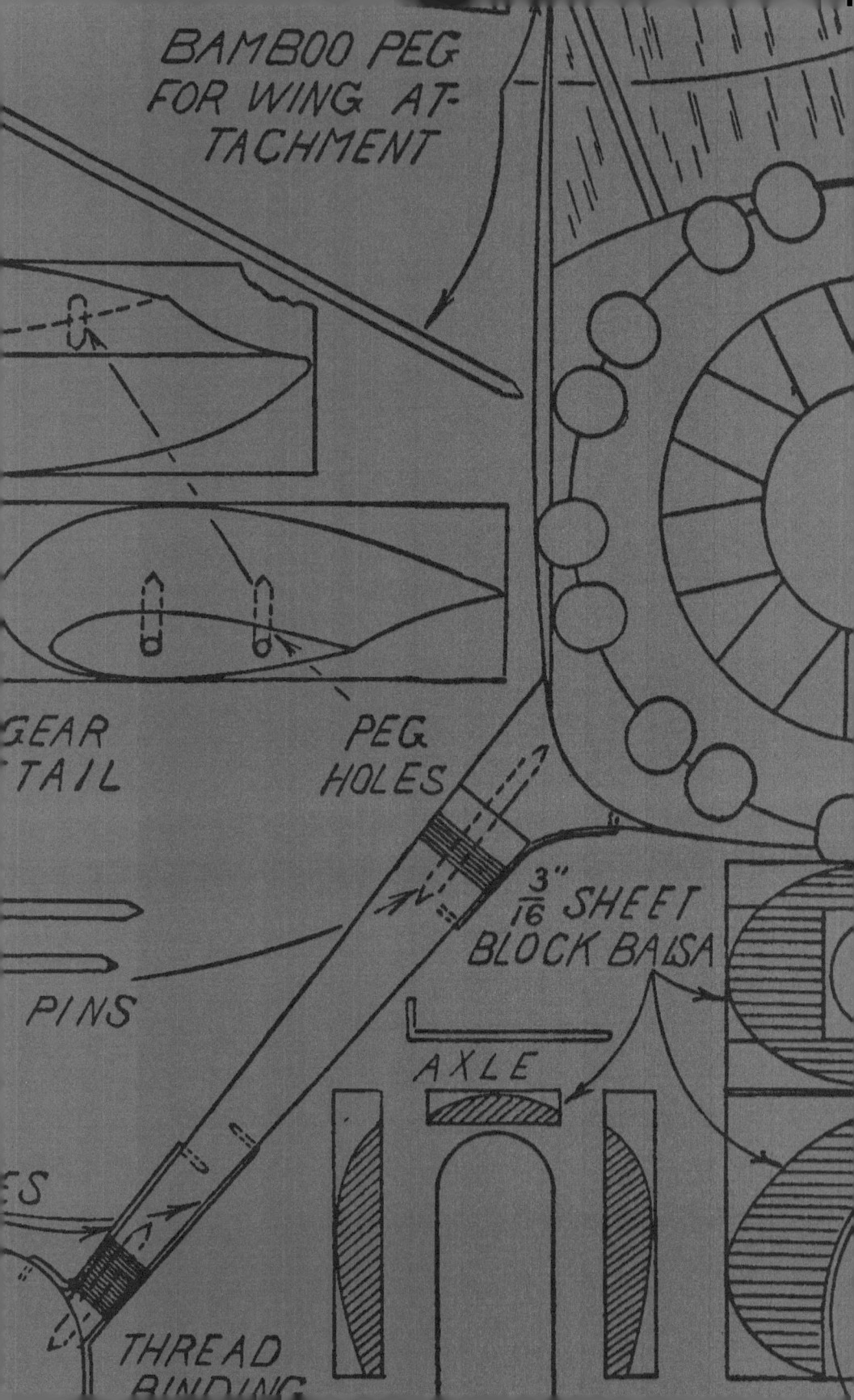

BAMBOO PEG
FOR WING AT-
TACHMENT

GEAR
TAIL

PEG.
HOLES

PINS

$\frac{3}{16}$" SHEET
BLOCK BALSA

AXLE

THREAD
BINDING

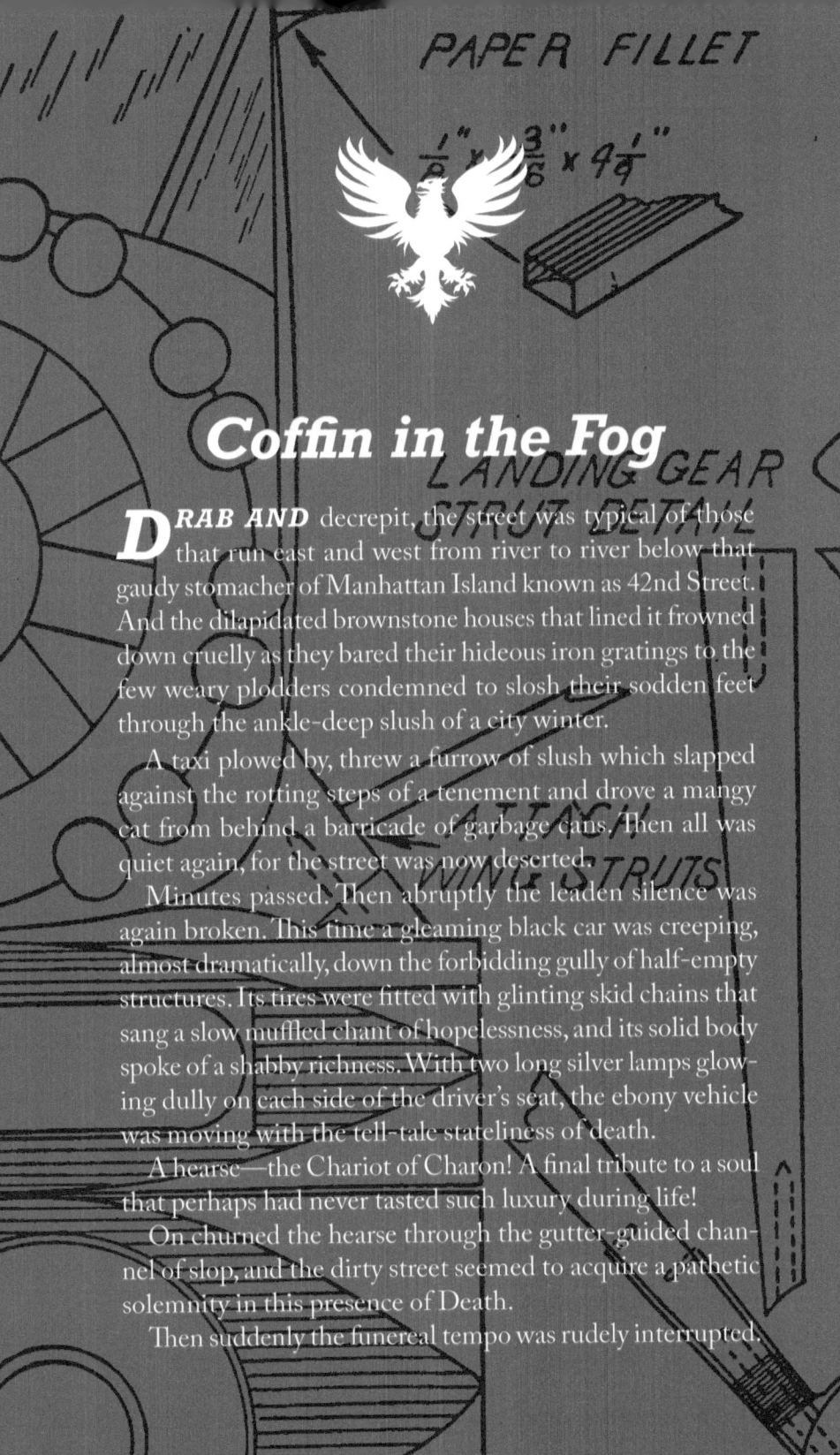

Coffin in the Fog

DRAB AND decrepit, the street was typical of those that run east and west from river to river below that gaudy stomacher of Manhattan Island known as 42nd Street. And the dilapidated brownstone houses that lined it frowned down cruelly as they bared their hideous iron gratings to the few weary plodders condemned to slosh their sodden feet through the ankle-deep slush of a city winter.

A taxi plowed by, threw a furrow of slush which slapped against the rotting steps of a tenement and drove a mangy cat from behind a barricade of garbage cans. Then all was quiet again, for the street was now deserted.

Minutes passed. Then abruptly the leaden silence was again broken. This time a gleaming black car was creeping, almost dramatically, down the forbidding gully of half-empty structures. Its tires were fitted with glinting skid chains that sang a slow muffled chant of hopelessness, and its solid body spoke of a shabby richness. With two long silver lamps glowing dully on each side of the driver's seat, the ebony vehicle was moving with the tell-tale stateliness of death.

A hearse—the Chariot of Charon! A final tribute to a soul that perhaps had never tasted such luxury during life!

On churned the hearse through the gutter-guided channel of slop, and the dirty street seemed to acquire a pathetic solemnity in this presence of Death.

Then suddenly the funereal tempo was rudely interrupted.

A dull red sedan shot out of a narrow driveway with the roar of low gear. It seemed to be out of control, for its chains were biting out gobs of macadam and throwing sprays of sparks toward a slush-splashed hydrant. Now the sedan skidded, jerked around, and threw its rear section across the street. Thus blocked, the hearse pulled up with a retching jerk.

The rest happened with the speed of light. Two men leaped

As the speeding Black Bullet curled over, four streams of
copper-tipped death spat from its Darns and Chatelleraults.
Forked by that withering hail, the port engine nacelle of
the diving Sikorsky disintegrated in a terrific blast.

from the rear door of the sedan and moved like wraiths toward the back of the hearse. Another came out from the front door, dashed for the closed driver's compartment, and swung open its door.

A pistol shot shattered the stillness—and the driver toppled out of the hearse to fall choking and gasping into the slush. He tried once to get up and grapple with his smaller opponent, but the man with the pistol brought the butt of the gun down on his head with a sickening thwack.

Meanwhile, the two men who had darted for the rear of the hearse were yanking the long pearl-gray casket out along its oiled rollers. They let it drop to the street with a cruel thud. Then, with a final glance about, they slashed at its sides with small hatchets and finally forced a long metal bar under its lid. There was a scrawnch of wood and metal, and the heavy lid crashed back and hung dejectedly on one portion of the hinge. Again the long bar was inserted and pried, whereupon the inner lid plopped up and flapped over.

It was but the work of another minute for the two men to lift out the shroud-covered object that reposed inside. Without a word they took it at both ends and slobbered through the slush to the dull red sedan. Unceremoniously, they shoved it inside, clambered over it, and wrenched the door to a crashing close.

Then the motor sped up and the sedan shot away—leaving the gaping casket still leaning against the open doors of the hearse.

The man in the street struggled to his feet, clutched at the air. "Lang!… Lang, you swine!" he gurgled. Then he fell forward on his face, as a patrolman dashed toward the scene.

The sedan raced on down the street, turned north, and disappeared amid the maze of elevated pillars on Ninth Avenue.

AT THE same instant that the gleaming black hearse had been hi-jacked of its silent load, a black amphibian was racing at high speed south from Philadelphia. The man at the controls was dressed in a black coverall and wore a scarlet mask of silk and rubber under his service helmet. He was handsome in a cold determined way. His lips were drawn in a hard line, but there was a hint of a smile at the corners. He stroked his controls, peered ahead toward the long pie-shaped sliver of water known as Delaware Bay.

After a careful inspection of the instrument panel and another adjustment on the throttle, he spoke over his shoulder to the man huddled under the rear gun mounting.

"You needn't go to sleep now," he said. "You'll see some fun any minute."

"Ye've been promisin' me thot all the way down. But faith, it's nothin' I've seen as yet except the blink o' airway beacons."

"Well, don't take any chances on anything. These yeggs are likely to turn up at any second. And they'll stop at nothing."

"So you decide to get in their way. And what was that gag you pulled the other day about an iridescent force meeting an uncomfortable object?"

"Oh, when that happens you get a carnage cocktail—served with potato chips."

"Well you'd be better off if you spent more time worrying about that guy Lang. He'll get you yet."

"I've been thinking of him," said the man in the scarlet mask. "You're right, Pulski, I've got to do something about the redoubtable Drury. He's just dumb enough to get in the way at times. Yes, we shall have to put some salt on that bird's tail, and—"

Abruptly, there was a scuffle behind as the man addressed as Pulski, whirled like a Dervish to get out his guns. The man in the mask quickly pushed his throttle, instinctively brought the black amphibian up into a smart climbing turn.

Just in time!

For a lather of hell suddenly bubbled all about them. Two bursts of fire smacked against the dural sides of the Black Bullet and a splash of cold flame half-blinded the gunner guy.

"Holy Mither o' Moses! They're using a *howitzer* on us this time!" he yelled.

The high echoes of the heavy armament almost deafened them. Again, from somewhere above, that hellish weapon coughed. Two times hefty slugs slammed past them with a whine of acidy hate.

BR-RONG! BRR-RO-OOM!

The man up front was tense now. He was fighting a mad battle to get clear of that terrible gun that was belching upon them.

"Yes, those devils have a cannon aboard!" he cried.

He tried to give orders, but Pulski had already opened fire with his .50 caliber Brownings, causing the covered cockpit to vibrate with a bedlam of clatter, rattle, and concussion.

A shell now blazed through the wing, snapped its graze fuse, and exploded with a battering roar. Flame blinded them both for a few seconds, but the pilot managed to dance the black amphibian away with a series of snap rolls and jerky dodges.

Again Pulski's guns clattered and in reply came another salvo of 37 mm. stuff that threatened to blast the Black Bullet out of the sky.

"What kind of a ship is that?" the man up front demanded.

"Can't tell, Ginsberg," came the reply. "Looks like a Sikorsky of some sort—two engined job with some foreign markings on the wings. Anyhow, they're certainly lousy with guns. Let's get out of here!"

"Nothing doing! We've got to put 'em down." And the pilot settled back for business. He gave the flap gear a couple of turns, cut out the Skoda muffler, and the Black Bullet climbed like mad. Behind, the gunner guy continued to pour burst after burst into the nose and sides of the big ship above, and in a moment it was apparent that his scourge of lead had either silenced the cannon or the crew manning it.

The Black Bullet flyers now took advantage of their lead

by climbing past the level from which the big twin-engined flying boat was working.

"It's an S-43 Sikorsky," the gunner screamed between his bursts. "As far as I can make out, that concentric circle insignia of hers is green, yellow, and blue. Yes, that's it! She's got the same colors on the rudder."

"I thought so. It's one of those S-43s sold to the Brazilian government."

"That's that country down south that they say just went Fascist?"

"Righto! Keep them off now until I get another 500 feet."

"The divils," bawled the man called Pulski.

He hammered another blast of heavy fire dead into the S-43 and then almost went out through the open cockpit top when the pilot suddenly slammed over in a dive.

The man in the mask worked fast. He set every gun in front of him and gave her the juice. With a scream, the Black Bullet braved the return fire of the Sikorsky and rocketed into a daring loop. Then, as the speeding Black Bullet curled over, four streams of copper-tipped death spat from its Darns and Chatelleraults. Forked by that withering hail, the port engine nacelle of the diving Sikorsky disintegrated in a terrific blast!

Relentlessly, the masked pilot held his gun trips down, slammed on through twin streams of gunfire that continued to rage from a special turret set just aft of the trailing edge of the Sikorsky's thick wing.

As they shot by, the gunner behind the masked man got in a final burst. But his shots were not needed. Weakened by the engine explosion, the left wing of the amphibian now tore away with a nerve-racking screech. The Brazilian-marked ship staggered, screwed up into a struggling zoom, then rolled over on her back.

The two men in the Black Bullet watched the plummeting wreckage as they circled in an easy spiral. It went down in an inverted flat spin, righted itself momentarily, then screamed into the water below.

"Okay! Get ready to take over," the masked flyer said calmly. "We're going down and see what she has aboard."

"Don't pull that line," came the reply. "Ye know what she has aboard!"

THE WRECKAGE of the Sikorsky had hit near the shore. Beyond, lay a sluggish marshy area that crawled away toward Cape Henlopen. The pilot of the Black Bullet circled carefully, drew a lever that lowered the retractable pontoons, then cut in the Skoda mufflers again.

With care and delicate skill he brought the Black Bullet down on the bay, then let her skim gently up to the tumbled wreckage which lay high in the water, indicating it had hit on a shallow bar.

He moved out of his seat and clambered out on the wing, while the man called Pulski moved up, took the control seat, and kept a careful watch behind. Then with a light movement he boarded the wreck, made his way to the open gun turret, and slid through. With a handy pocket torch he studied the interior a minute. Below him against the angle of the wall and floor lay two men, obviously foreigners. Both were dead.

Next, he moved up into the control pit, studied the Madsen air cannon mounted there, jotted down the gun numbers, and finally fingered through the pockets of the dead pilot and the still-breathing gunner.

The papers, books, and maps he gleaned from this ghastly inspection were quickly stuffed into the large thigh pockets of his black coverall. Then he made his way past the rear gun turret and kicked open a small compartment door. His torch brought to light that which he sought—a fairly large wooden crate, carefully bound with steel straps and bearing the official government marking of the United States Army. In addition, the torch brought out the stenciling:

Aberdeen Proving Ground
To Be Opened Under Official Orders Only.

Ordnance Department
U.S. Army

"Perfect," muttered the man in the scarlet mask. Then, after placing a small white card under a handy wall clip, he pocketed his torch, lifted the crate, staggered out with it, and shoved it up through the opening in the gun turret.

"Better come and give me a hand," he called to his aide who had shut off the Black Bullet's engine.

"Phwat in the name of all that's holy hav' ye got there?" came the query.

"You'll find out when we get back. Make it snappy!" And together they managed to get the crate along the pontoon, over the wing, and into the rear portion of the cockpit.

Then came the roar of oncoming engines!

"Let's get moving!" barked the masked flyer.

The man called Pulski forced himself under the crate which was leaning against his seat, and the pilot shoved the Black Bullet clear. Then, diving into the pilot's seat, he started the engine, kept the Skodas in, and eased her away. Once in the clear, he gave her the gun, lifted her up on the step, climbed into the sky—and flew smack into a three-ship formation of Army Douglas O-43-As!

Without a signal of any sort, all three opened fire on the Black Bullet.

The masked pilot darted the sleek black plane away. "You're too late," he sang out. "You birds missed up on this one."

The Douglas observation ships continued to blaze away from every angle, but once the masked pilot had retracted his pontoons, their speed was insufficient to overtake it. Soon they were left far behind.

Within an hour the amphibian with its mysterious load was gliding down to a landing a mile or so off the east shore of Long Island, and when it had taxied up on the shore, a hidden switch was pulled and the fake rock garden of Graylands opened wide to reveal a hidden hangar. In no time at all the sleek amphibian was tucked away and the mysterious doors closed.

The Griffon had returned to his lair.

IT WAS ten o'clock next morning when the flyers of Graylands were aroused by the thud of knocks upon the front door. A disreputable old Packard of questionable vintage stood on the icy driveway, coughing its objections to a thundering race under forced draft.

John Scott, head of the F.B.I., New York division, had no illusions of his own grandeur, and he was loyal to this car that had been true to him so many years. It would have been very hard to replace, for it had been taken from a pre-repeal gangster who had had the foresight to equip it with armor plate. Said gangster had also provided shatter-proof glass and many convenient and secretive spots where the odd Tommy gun or pineapple could be stowed. A small but effective short-wave radio set was also included.

John Scott was a phlegmatic, heavy-set man jovial when at ease. He had won his present position through dogged courage, his ability to think in one channel for days at a time, and his dauntless belief in himself. True, he was not a spectacular operator, and he often seemed to be attacking a case from the wrong end. But somehow, John Scott always managed to fight down the lawless opposition.

He hammered at the door again with the butt of a heavy pistol and then listened to the pad of footsteps coming down a stairway. John Scott grunted, wondered by what form of magic a man who was supposed to be busy could afford to lie in bed until 10 o'clock in the morning.

Barney O'Dare finally opened the door, peered out. He had a copper tea kettle in one hand and wore a disreputable bathrobe of garish green.

"Where's Keen?" Scott said without further ado—and pushing Barney aside, he made his way in.

On seeing the gun, Barney nearly threw a left hook, but he quickly restrained himself when he recognized the visitor. "He'll be down… in a minute," he sputtered. "He's had a late night."

"I don't care anything about that," cracked Scott. "Get him down here fast. This can't wait!"

"Come into the library," invited the Mick. "But say, what's the idea of the gun?"

Scott plunked himself down in a leather club chair, gazed at his heavy black weapon as though he had never seen it before, then somewhat embarrassed he tucked it away in his big pocket.

"I'd forgotten that," he admitted numbly.

Barney tittered, then stepped aside as Kerry Keen entered.

"Don't get up," smiled the bathed and shaven Keen. "But what on earth got you out here at this time of the morning?"

"I couldn't get you on the phone. I've been trying all night."

"Matter of a little switch," explained Keen. "No want bother, just flick switch, as the Chinese might say."

"It's a good idea, of course," agreed Scott staring at the broadloom carpet. "But it's hell on your friends." Then he pulled out the gun again and shoved it toward the young ballistics expert.

"That's Lang's," he said bluntly.

"Keep it. I don't want my finger prints on it. Okay, it's Lang's. So what?"

"That's the gun that killed Regan Hatcher last night!"

"And who was Regan Hatcher—and why did Lang's gun kill him?"

"That's just it," came the reply. "We don't know who Regan Hatcher really was—and what's more we don't know what happened to Lang."

"Let's have it from the beginning. I can't stand this jerky-sentence business. Put the breakfast here, Barney," Keen continued, "with an extra cup for John. He looks as though he needs it."

"Thanks," said Scott, getting up and crawling out of his monstrous ulster. "I'll say I do! I didn't get to go to bed last night. Anyhow, I repeat that Lang's been missing ever since we found the hearse!"

"Hearse?" gasped Barney, almost dropping the coffee pot. "Phat the divil is this?"

"They got Hatcher, stole the body in the coffin, and... well, read it here in the morning paper."

Keen waved the paper aside: "I want it straight. Not the way it's dished up for circulation in the Ninth Precinct. You tell it, Scott."

"Last night just before midnight, this guy Regan Hatcher is driving a hearse up 38th Street carrying the body of a guy named Granville Hubbardstone. He's taking it to Grand Central to have it shipped back to some place in Massachusetts... Hubbardstone's old homestead, I believe."

"Is Hatcher an undertaker?"

"No, that's what's screwy about it. The hearse belonged to a guy named Dooling—an undertaker over on the West Side. Dooling had the case and the body was all ready for transfer to the station. In other words, this guy Hatcher swiped the hearse and the body—and was bumped off on the way to wherever he was going."

"And the body?" asked Keen, frowning.

"They knocked off this Hatcher, broke open the casket, and took the body. If that makes sense, you ask the questions."

"But Lang's gun?"

"That's the rest of it. The police got to the dying Hatcher just in time to hear him babbling something about Drury Lang—and there was Lang's gun in the gutter. Here's the bullet that killed him. You figure it out."

KEEN TOOK the gun and the heavy lead slug. Then he went across the room, stuck the muzzle of the pistol into the opening of a long green metal box, and pulled the trigger. There was a muffled report and a thud somewhere within the box.

Scott sipped his coffee while Keen opened the firing

box and fumbled with his long fingers through the cotton wadding. He finally found the slug, and brought it out, and inspected it carefully for some moments.

"I could have done that on Center Street," said Scott with a mournful mien, "but I wanted you to do it. What's the story?"

"First off, it's a .38 caliber Special 'Super-Police' cartridge slug. A 200-grain soft-lead bullet. A lovely 'stopping' slug, no question about it. Yes, and it's Lang's bullet that smacked that fellow!"

"For Lord's sake, don't say it that way!" growled Scott. "I didn't come here to be told that. I came… I came, well, I don't know what the devil I came for."

"Lang's gun and Lang's bullet," taunted Keen. "He seems to have been the fellow who shot the guy. At least, he could have shot him."

"Sure he could. But why? We've got no such guy as this Hatcher on our crook list. And what the devil would he be doing with a dead body?"

"You can sell them… to medical schools," suggested Keen. "Have another cup of coffee?"

Scott held his cup out without answering.

"If Lang were only here," went on Keen, "you might get some idea what it was all about. But I suppose he's on the lam, as the boys say, since the murder."

"You're a big help," snarled Scott.

"That man, Lang," broke in Barney, "is capable of anything. I niver liked him at all—niver."

"No, and he never liked you. So you're both even," cracked Scott.

"He even thinks I'm the Griffon," said Keen in an injured tone. "He *still* thinks I'm the Griffon."

"Well, that's understandable. You're a queer guy, you know, Keen."

"But I don't go around shooting phony undertakers and swiping dead bodies."

"You don't *really* think Lang did that, do you?" asked Scott pathetically.

"Of course I do," answered Keen in the decisive tone of a stage villain. "But I suppose he'll slip out of it, like he does everything else. When he gets in a jam, he usually has the luck to be helped out by that Griffon guy. I wouldn't be surprised to learn some day that Lang himself is the Griffon!"

John Scott gasped.

"That reminds me," he said jumping up. "Where's that newspaper? See this—the Griffon again!"

"What's he been up to this time?" asked Keen with a disinterested air. Then he read:

THE GRIFFON STRIKES AT OUR AIR SERVICE
Sky Ghost Downs Brazilian Sikorsky
Patrol Planes Fail to Stop Robbery Of Anti-Aircraft Secret

The body of the story gave an account of the finding of the Sikorsky amphibian and also a somewhat sketchy report on the loss of a new secret anti-aircraft predictor instrument used in range-finding.

"There you are! Lang is missing and the Griffon strikes again," said Keen tonelessly.

"I wasn't going to say anything about this anti-aircraft mess," Scott said, "but now it's out, and you might as well know something about it. That thing was supposed to have been stolen more than a week ago. Now they report that it was stolen last night. Furthermore, this Brazilian plane seems to have been mixed up in it."

"Um," mused Keen. "Perhaps they've stolen *another* one. They leave those things lying around all over the place, I suppose."

"No," said Scott. "They have only built one. And after testing it out, they were going to seal it up and stow it away—for a rainy day. Anyhow, it don't make sense. That thing was reported missing about a week ago."

"Lang was working on it, I gather," said Keen with a queer

sniff in his voice. And when Scott nodded, he continued: "Well, go on and tell me about it."

"Oh, the anti-aircraft business? Well, we got the first report on it about a week ago. I'll have you know, too, that this business is a bit complicated. There are really two parts to this A-A gimmick, and—"

At that, there was an audible gasp from Barney who was lolling near the fireside.

JOHN SCOTT looked around quickly, but Barney covered up by slapping at an imaginary spark. Still, Keen caught the drift of it and gave the Mick a quick and knowing glance.

"These two parts," the big detective went on, "are equally important. One is the predictor, a device which somehow automatically gauges the height of a target while the other sets the fuses on the shells as they are fed into the gun. It's far above my head. But anyhow that's the general idea."

"Was the predictor stolen a week ago?" asked Keen with a moderate touch of interest.

"Predictor?... Golly, I don't know. One of the parts was swiped then, but I can't say which one it was. All I know is that it had a certain number on it and was bound up in a long canvas bag."

"Then if they stole another A-A gadget last night, it's quite possible that it was the second important part, eh?" Keen asked.

Scott nodded and peered toward the fire: "That's the way it sounds now. Yes, I'll bet that's what happened."

"And now Lang goes and gets himself in that hearse-and-coffin mess and leaves you completely in the lurch! Nice guy!"

"That's what I really want to talk to you about," Scott now cracked.

"The anti-aircraft thing?"

"No—Lang. You know, the old fool really likes you, Keen. Anyway, I wish you could give me a hand in locating him and getting him out of this mess."

"What? After that?" Keen snapped—pointing to the gun and the two slugs. "He's guilty, Scott. I want no part of it!"

Beads of perspiration appeared on Scott's brow. He started to get up but finally slumped down again and thrust his great hands into his pockets.

"Oh, well," Keen said opening the subject again, "maybe the case deserves my attention. True, I'm very busy. But if you want, I'll see if we can do something about it."

"We?" moaned Barney. "Leave me out of it! If that guy had the chance, he'd slap us into the klink so fast we'd never know what happened to us! So I don't wanta take—"

Scott scowled. Then Keen went on without mercy:

"I really think Lang is mixed up in something phony. Barney's right. But for your sake, Scott, I'll have a whirl at it—provided we have a free hand and you ask no questions. By the way, is there any money attached to that anti-aircraft thing?"

"Well, if someone accidently found it and turned it over to the right people, they might get a few bucks. But you just see what you can do about Lang—and I'll see that he lays off you in the future."

"All right. But no questions asked, remember. And when you get back to your office, look up the reward allowance on those anti-aircraft parts. We might be interested in that."

That brought a suspicious gleam to Scott's eye. But there was nothing he could do about it, so he nodded glumly and said:

"I don't know what the devil you are getting at, but never mind. You do something for old Lang, and I'll see that you are taken care of. I need that old bluffer, and they're not going to railroad him up the river for bopping off a guy who goes around swiping hearses."

"—And dead bodies," added Keen.

With that, he helped Scott into his ulster, packed him out the door, and returned to his breakfast.

"Hooray!" beamed O'Dare. "Now we've got Mister Lang where we want him!"

"Yes, but those crooks have apparently nabbed the predictor. We've got to get that before the companions of the late Mr. Haines try to get away with it."

"Haines? It was a bird named Hatcher who was killed."

"Of course. But I'm sure Haines and Hatcher were one and the same. Haines was the man who called me up about the cartridge they use in the predictor. He wanted me to figure out the ballistics of it. At that time, I didn't realize his crowd had swiped the part."

"Smart gag, getting it away in a hearse. But who did waylay this Haines-Hatcher guy?" asked Barney with a puzzled frown.

"Well, it was Lang's gun," said Keen without answering the direct question. "And I have a hunch the old guy was on the right trail. But if so, where is he now? And where is the predictor?"

"Find Lang and you get the part, eh?"

"Exactly!" said Keen. But then his expression changed. "Still, I'm not so sure," he added. "This gun business has me worried. Let me think."

And so, after Barney left Keen and went upstairs to dress, the ballistics expert went on thinking aloud: "Lang might have trailed me to Hatcher's place, and then in turn trailed Hatcher. Suppose he stumbled into the mess when Hatcher was about to drive off with the hearse and the body, or whatever it was; suppose Lang stumbled into that—and was picked off. They might have left him there, or they might have got rid of him. They *were* near the river!"

He pondered on for several seconds, then leaped to his feet.

"Step on it, Barney," he yelled. "We're leaving for the city in half an hour!"

ALL THE way into New York City, Keen recited his plan to Barney and instructed the Mick in the role he was to play in it. And by the time they were crunching up the slush of 38th Street, the Irishman had his part letter-perfect.

They finally pulled up beside the funeral parlor of Mathias Dooling, whereupon Keen left the Mick beside the car and approached the door of the establishment. The undertaker had set himself up in the lower portion of an old red brick building. There were two wide windows on the street level, one presenting a stark display of cheap caskets, the other decorated with two weary palms in cheap tin pots together with a faded sign explaining that a private chapel was available on the premises.

Keen went in and was greeted by a whiskery man of grayish complexion who was in unlaced shoes, a pair of greasy black trousers, and a shirt which was sadly in need of buttons and a visit to the laundry.

"I'm from the Department of Justice," explained Keen, stretching the truth a little. "I'd like to talk to Mr. Dooling about this business last night. Can I see him somewhere alone?"

"I'm Dooling," the man said with a challenging curl of his lower lip. "It's a foine business whin a man can't even call a hearse his own, eh?"

"The whole thing was very unfortunate, of course. But you should consider yourself lucky. You might have been—well, pretty badly handled had you been here."

"But what can I get for all the inconvenience and the damage to my business. For nigh on forty year now I've been in business here, an' niver have I had a'thing like this happen to me."

"I can appreciate the embarrassment," agreed Keen, thus winning the old guy at once. "Have you found the body of— of this Mr. Granville Hubbardstone?"

"Nary a trace of it," moaned the mortician leading the way into a small room on one side.

"As a matter of fact, Dooling, you never even *saw* the body of this Mr. Hubbardstone, did you?" said Keen closing the door.

The Irish undertaker sniffed, gulped—then accepted the expensive cigar Keen handed him. He sniffed it, lit it, and took a long pull before he answered: "No, as a matter of fact, mister, I niver did. You see, the body was brought here—with papers, of course—and I was simply ordered to put it on a train for someplace up in Massachusetts. I was to ship it this morning, as matter of fact."

"Now we're getting somewhere," smiled Keen. "I'm afraid there was no Mr. Hubbardstone, Dooling. But that was not your fault. It was a trick to 'move' something—something outside the law."

"But where does that let me out?" cried the Irishman, sucking on the cigar again. "I face a lot of expense repairing that hearse up. She was banged up plenty."

"We'll see that all that'll be taken care of. But in the meantime I'd like to look over the store-room from which the casket was taken. First, though you will let me see those papers you refer to? You have them here?"

"They're right here in this file," Dooling grunted. And fumbled through a wad of papers for a minute or two, then brought out a medical certificate and a corpse movement order made out to one Eitel Haines and signed by a medical officer connected with one of the small New Jersey towns across the river.

"This is faked, of course, for it does not bear the town seal," said Keen. "But I'll take a copy, just to get the addresses and names. Do you mind?"

"Not at all. I niver noticed that there was no seal. We get these things all the time, and we seldom bother much about checkin' 'em. But say, I won't get in a jam for that, will I?"

"How can you? There was no body—you were just tricked into shipping a casket."

"But there was *something* inside. What was it, Mister? 'Snow'?"

"Hardly. That much cocaine would be worth a couple of million, I guess," smiled Keen. "We don't know what it was. That's just it—we'd like to find out."

Keen copied the details from the shipment papers and put the paper in his pocket. "Now let's take a look at that storeroom of yours."

THEY GOT up and Dooling led the way back to a closed-off rear portion of the building. They entered through a small door and Keen recognized the usual morgue-type of room used by many undertakers. There was one long compartment with four small square doors, each bearing a number. He sensed that this was the "icebox" where bodies were kept prior to embalming.

Keen then noticed that a small side door led out to a tiny yard where several funereal-looking vehicles were near an open shed. From there he could see a covered driveway which evidently led to the street.

Dooling stood staring down the room, the cigar between his pudgy fingers sending up a trailing streamer of blue smoke.

"Thot's queer," he said.

"What?" asked Keen, shifting his gaze to the back of the room.

"Thot casket—over there. The lid has been taken off!"

They walked over to where a pearl-gray casket stood on two saw-horses. The lid had been removed and stood on its edge near the wall. Dooling was a very puzzled man.

"What's wrong? Nothing missing, is there?" asked Kerry Keen.

Dooling went up to the casket, stared inside. The white satin was badly rumpled. The pillow was jammed up into one corner, and at the lower end the lining had been ripped from the sides and badly torn.

"Another corpse of yours has escaped, eh?" queried Keen.

"There's bin somebody lying in there," gulped Dooling. "Phwat the hell is this, anyway?"

Keen studied it all a minute, then kicked aside some severed cords that lay on the floor. Dooling, who did not see this move, was breaking into another torrent of blasphemy.

"Look here," said Keen hurriedly. "Leave all this just as it is. I'll be back later. Don't touch anything!"

And with that he hurried out, passed through the shop, dashed out the front door to the car, and clambered in.

"So you found him, eh, Barney? Now get moving—to 55th Street."

Beside the Mick chauffeur sat Drury Lang, a weary-eyed devil with a day's growth of whisker on his chin! His lips were dirty and slobbered. He was rubbing his wrists which were almost raw.

"Found him snoozing in a casket, of all places," growled Barney letting in the clutch.

Lang did not speak. He was plainly exhausted, and he lay back while Keen found a flask in the door of the car and placed it to his lips.

"A little O'Doul's Dew ought to make him talk," grinned Barney, turning into Eighth Avenue.

"I'll talk... I'll talk," gasped Lang. "And I'll ask you guys how... how the hell you knew I was there."

"You talk too much, Lang," warned Keen. "And now we're going to turn you in! You're wanted for murder!"

"Murder!" gasped the detective.

"That's it. Now lay back and keep quiet. Maybe we can get you out of it—but I certainly doubt it."

"MURDER?" screamed Lang.

"Sure! Your gun killed a man named Regan Hatcher. I checked the bullets. They found him lying in 38th Street last night."

"But I was tied up... all last night in... in that box."

"Sure... Sure," said Barney out of the corner of his mouth. "But how you gonner prove it?"

"Fer cripe's sake! Didn't you just come in there and get me out?" Lang gurgled, reaching for Keen's flask.

"What of it?" both Keen and Barney barked together.

The bewildered detective turned his head slowly from one to the other: "But you're ribbing me," he finally said in a pathetic tone.

"Wait until you see the papers," taunted Keen, his eyes steely.

"It'll be the hot squat for you, Lang. It's about time they got some of you gun-toting coppers," added Barney.

"But you just pulled me out of a box back there."

"That's right. But we don't know how long you were there, do we?" Keen went on.

"Good Lord!" gasped Lang.

"You said it," added Barney.

"ALL RIGHT, Lang," said Keen after they had smuggled the Department of Justice man up to Keen's penthouse apartment and made him reasonably comfortable. "Now let's get it all straight."

"We can do with a nice chunk of reward money," taunted Barney.

"And there's two ways to get it," cracked Keen. "One is to turn you in."

"What's the other?" Lang almost whimpered.

"Scott was telling us something about a stolen anti-aircraft gun… or something."

"Yeah. That was what I was working on when they biffed me."

"Okay, let's have the details. Maybe we'll be able to recover the A-A gun, or whatever it is," Keen said smiling.

"Well," said Drury, "I was trailing this guy Hatcher—the guy you say is murdered."

"With your gun!" Keen broke in.

"I don't know about that. Anyway, Hatcher had been some kind of a writer on military affairs. He had been trying for weeks to get inside at Aberdeen to see this new A-A development. But he was always chucked out. They were suspicious of him, you see."

Keen nodded and took a drink from the tray presented by Barney.

"So," Lang went on, "when an important part of this new gun business was swiped while it was being moved from the Ordnance Department in Washington, they immediately thought of this guy Hatcher. And I was ordered to tail him."

"And wound up in a nice clean casket," jibed Barney.

"Well… yeah. Anyhow, I tailed Hatcher to Dooling's dump—and walked straight into a mob of guys swiping a hearse. They biffed me around plenty, then tied me up, gagged me, and tucked me away in that wooden overcoat. I guess they figured I'd be quiet for some time."

"They took your gun?"

"I guess so. I know I don't have it now. But they did leave the lid reasonably loose so that I could get some air, otherwise I'd never be alive to tell the tale."

"What do you know about this Hatcher?" asked Keen.

"Very little. He has been a military writer, all right. But he turned nosey and went into the business of selling armament secrets."

"Where does he live?"

"But you said he was *dead!*" bellowed Lang.

"All right, then—where *did* he live?"

"He was a floater. One place he hung his hat was over in Hoboken with some German people. Then he had another place over here in the New Century Hotel. That's where I picked him up—his trail, that is."

"All right. But what do you *really* know about him?"

"Nothing!"

"You're a big help," asserted the ballistics expert. "In other words, then, someone got away clean with this portion of an important weapon—hidden in an ordinary casket."

KEEN THEN explained the business of the fictitious Mr. Hubbardstone, while Lang nodded, his eyes on the broadloom carpet.

"You'd better think hard," Keen continued, "and see if you

can't remember something that will help us get that gun thing back. It's the only way you can get out of the mess you're in. If we can prove conclusively that this Hatcher was actually swiping this A-A part, we're in the clear. If you don't, and the gun part is still missing, you're going to be in hot water for a long time."

"But you say there is no such guy as Hubbardstone," wailed Lang.

"No, but that does not justify your shooting Hatcher—which is what they all believe you did. We've got to find that gun part and prove that Hatcher is the culprit."

"Yeah," agreed Lang mournfully. "But I can't give you any more info. They're probably on their way out of the country with it by now."

"I doubt it. Did Hatcher have a car of any sort?"

"Yeah, a new Graham—a red one with a supercharger."

"He would," said Keen. Then he sank into a blue study of deep thought. Both Barney and Lang were silent... as silent as the late afternoon that was creeping down on the city from above. A thin yellowish vapor was now streaking the windows with a murky film.

Fog!

Both Barney and Keen exchanged knowing glances. Fog—the thick unrelenting enemy of the airman—swirled its cape of death against the windows. Barney sniffed, went over and turned on the radio.

"A red Graham," muttered Keen.

"Yeah, a red Graham fitted with a supercharger," repeated Lang.

The radio then got into the conversation after a crackle of static:

... mechanics said the three men drove up in a red auto, a new Graham sedan. The airliner had been standing by in hopes that weather conditions would improve. The mail consignment had been removed, and only one mechanic was near the ship.

"What the deuce is that?" said Keen jerking out of his blue study.

"A news flash. Something about an airliner," Lang gagged, getting up to stick his thick ear near the speaker.

The announcer went on in that high-pitched, dramatic tone deemed so necessary by the radio fraternity:

Authentic information is lacking, so far; but it's said that the three men slugged the mechanic, then carried a fairly long and somewhat bulky parcel or package aboard. The engines were started, and before anyone realized what had happened, the plane bounded away into the mist, barely clearing the top of the new hangars being erected there at Newark Airport.

"That's it! That's it," Keen cried. "They hid in Hoboken, then drove out to Newark Airport and stole a plane. There goes the gun part, Lang!"

The radio blatted on:

... officials of the Trans-Nation Airways are perplexed by the incident. They say that weather conditions all over the country are particularly bad and that all flights east of the Mississippi have been cancelled indefinitely. The plane's fuel at the time of the robbery was scarcely enough to get it to a safe landing area outside of the storm-bound territory.

Keen sat staring at the radio set while the announcer added official warnings to all airport operators and others who might see the plane. The license numbers were given as NO-17821.

"You stay here, Lang," ordered Keen. "We're going out to Newark Airport and check on that red car. Don't try to contact anyone, and don't leave here. As a matter of fact, you better crawl into bed and stay there—you need some real sleep. We'll be back later, and in the meantime you can figure out how you can get that reward for the gun part switched over to me."

Keen and Barney had their overcoats and hats in their arms before the Secret Service man could protest. They were out of the door in a flash.

IT TOOK Keen and Barney well over two hours to get out to Graylands so vile was the visibility. Of course, they really had had no intention of going to Newark Airport. That had been just a gag—for Keen was certain that the three men who had held up the hearse the night before were the same three men who had stolen the Trans-Nation airliner. It was the stolen plane that mattered—not the red Graham.

"Anyone who takes off in soup like this must be mad," said Barney when they pulled into the Graylands driveway.

"Well, you ought to know. *We're* taking off, too!" cracked Keen.

"What for?"

"To get that airliner. They're heading out to sea on the northeast leg of the Newark beam. I have an idea where they're going, too."

"You mean to say that we're going to take off this afternoon?" demanded Barney unbelieving.

"We are," said Keen, darting through the door and into the kitchen of the house. "Get moving. In this fog we can get away without being seen."

"We're both nuts," said Barney. But he got out, closed the garage doors, and hurried to the underground hangar that housed the Black Bullet.

In five minutes they were ready. All damage to the ship had been repaired the night before by the indefatigable Barney, who never went to bed until the sky charger was ready for business again. They opened the great doors and Keen ran the ship out into the yellow mist.

The wings were opened and locked in place, then the rock garden doors were closed. Barney now settled down in his cockpit while Keen let the plane roll gently down into the water. Once off shore, he set the pontoons for a take-off and let the silenced Avia move the craft into the clear beyond the boathouse.

After a last glance around, Keen opened the engine and

let the Black Bullet hurtle up into the blank wall of fog that hung out over the Atlantic.

"You keep your set tuned to the night airline frequency, Mick," he said over his shoulder when they attained the 3,000-foot level. "And keep listening for a call for a bird by the name of Schlessor from someone using the name Blackie Berndorff, Mike Farrow, or Granville."

"Where'd you get those names?"

"Out of that wrecked Sikorsky. They leave things around like that. It's a chance anyway, so we'll give it a whirl. In the meantime, I'll be looking for that Newark beam. Now keep your ears open—and don't switch to Amos an' Andy!"

Keen now settled back to fly on instruments, plugging in his headphones meanwhile on the beam set. He first picked up the "A" signal of the quadrant, then swung over farther toward the east until the signal merged into a single tone and he knew he was dead on the northeast leg of the Newark beam. He had figured that the men who had stolen the airliner would hug that signal all the way out to sea. It was evident that they were taking one long chance to make their get-away—and in doing so had shown part of their hand. They were attempting to contact someone!

"Flyers who know enough about a Douglas to take it off that way," muttered Keen to himself, "know enough not to try to land it in soup like this. Very likely they have reports that weather conditions were better somewhere out at sea."

He sat tight, listening carefully to maintain his position on the beam. He knew the stolen airliner had a big start on him, but that might not mean anything. He was hoping that the thieving flyers would have difficulty in making whatever contact they had in mind. He now sensed, however, that the weather was even worse than the radio announcement had intimated.

Barney sat behind him with the dumb expression of a haunted sheep. He stared mournfully at the Western Electric set bolted into a wall panel and listened to the dull terminology of the airlines. Then suddenly he reached forward and moved the wave-length lever up the band to the day frequency of 5.5 megs. Then he glanced toward Keen with a guilty expression.

Like a shot, the first tell-tale words of a poignant sentence came from the set:

... calling Farrow... calling Farrow... Bretaigne.

Barney stiffened, listened again. Yes, whoever was calling was operating on the airline day frequency!

"Hey, who is 'Bretaine', or 'Brettain'?" Barney bellowed at Keen.

" 'Bretain'? I don't know. What is it?"

"This guy 'Bretain' is calling a bird by the name of Farrow. But wait a minute—"

Barney listened again, caught:

Schlessor on Bretaigne calling Farrow... Schlessor calling Farrow. Come on in, Farrow.

Barney quickly relayed the news to Keen.

"Schlessor? Yes, that's the guy. But what is 'Bretain'?" the puzzled ballistic expert queried.

Barney listened again and heard the message repeated.

Keen pondered on it all then suddenly slapped Barney on the shoulder.

"Fake a call number—any call number—and contact the Nantucket Lightship. She has a radio-beacon and can get a cross-bearing on that call through the Pollock Rip Light. Make it snappy!"

Barney flipped the transmitter switch, put through the message. He made the contact within a few minutes.

"Hello, Nantucket," he called, "can you get me a bearing on signal coming through on 5.5 megacycles? Operator named Schlessor is calling someone named Farrow."

The unsuspecting Nantucket operator accepted the message without question and said he'd call back.

Barney nodded to Keen, turned the set back to "Receiving," again listened to the calls of the man named Schlessor.

Then suddenly in response came a wailing cry:

Calling Bretaigne… Farrow calling Bretaigne. Hurry, Schlessor. We're running out of petrol!

A frantic answer followed:

Get through! Get through! Someone's trying to get our bearings through Nantucket. Get through, somehow, Farrow. Where are you?

The frenzied reply to this was:

About four miles from your position, at 6,000 feet. We've been waiting hours up here for you.

And then Barney caught their message from the lightship:

Nantucket calling W2AID… calling W2AID… Position of call was 41:36:15 North by 68:12:22 West. Got it?

Barney repeated the message and thanked the Nantucket operator. Then he handed the scribbled bearing up to Keen.

Keen took it and nodded. They apparently were somewhere near the Douglas, so there was no time to ask for a bearing on their own position. Moreover, the flyers on the airliner had stated they were within four miles of their contact base, whatever it was.

THEN SOMETHING suddenly swooshed past the Black Bullet. And both Keen and Barney ducked low in their cockpit, barking the same words:

"The Douglas!"

Immediately, Keen set his nose after the dim shadow and fired a few desultory bursts.

"Keep on that set and listen closely!" he bawled to Barney.

For several minutes they chased madly through the murk. And at times the flailing prop of the Black Bullet seemed virtually to be fanning the great tail of the Douglas.

Keen watched his altimeter which was dropping fast now. The Douglas was going down onto the sea to contact with something which, according to Barney, was called 'Bretain.'

" 'Bretain… Bretain'?" muttered Keen, holding the Black Bullet dead on the misty shadow of the Douglas. "Now I get it," he suddenly cracked. "That must be that French Loire long-distance flying boat—the *Bretaigne!* It was supposed to have been lost last year on the South Atlantic run. That's it, the Bretaigne! They've swiped it to contact this guy Farrow, whoever he is. And they're going to try a water crack-up landing with the Douglas to make the change. Smart stuff—if they get away with it!"

Keen kept watching the eerie shadow of the Douglas, his eye on the altimeter. The airliner was in a slow glide now, and the outline of its wings took on a heavier silhouette. They now had the flaps down.

The needle of the altimeter dropped lower and lower. Keen rammed the steel lever forward, put his retractable pontoons down. Then, as the murky waves began to appear through the swirling mist, he opened fire with his Darns and Chatelleraults!

The Douglas went straight on for what seemed minutes before anything happened. But then Keen gave her another heavy burst, and this time she rolled badly, dipped a wing, momentarily righted herself with a jerk—then plunged nose first into the water!

There was a dull thud and a great wall of water and spray was thrown in the air. One of the ill-fated ship's engines canted hard, went swirling up in a crazy arc, then fell back near the wing-tip. The tail of the airliner now came up, hesitated a minute, then flopped back into the sea.

"Get up on your feet and get a gun ready," Keen yelled to Barney.

Then curling around in a tight circle, he brought the Black Bullet around and managed to put her down gently on the water. He watched closely all around him as he churned the amphibian up to the wreckage of the Douglas upon which there were no signs of life.

But just as he was about to ease the Bullet up, the sound of gunfire came from across the water. They both turned, saw emerging from the mist the long silver prow of a great flying boat.

"Give it to them, you dumb Mick!" bawled Keen.

Another burst of fire crackled across the water from a gun mounted in the control cabin of the huge Loire.

Barney answered with a well-aimed burst from his Brownings that silenced the fire at once. There was a jangle of glass and the low scream of a man. The engines of the big flying boat then opened up. She churned forward with a roar and passed close to the wreckage of the Douglas. Barney gave them another burst as a send-off, but it was hardly needed, for it was apparent that the Loire had had enough.

As soon as the big flying boat had cleared, Keen was out on the wing of the Black Bullet and throwing a grappling iron toward the wreckage of the Douglas. He caught a battered cabin window and drew the Black Bullet in close. Then with a quick movement, he was over the leading edge, down on the pontoon, and across to the back of the Douglas. Barney watched for a few minutes, then gave a low cheer when Keen emerged with a fairly large package tightly wrapped in stitched burlap.

Keen shoved the ungainly package over the wing, and the Mick took one end and guided it into the cockpit. In no time at all, it was stowed away, whereupon Keen went back for a further check-up of the wreckage. He returned in a few minutes dripping wet, for the wreckage was sinking fast now. He had found that the men aboard the Douglas had been killed in the terrific crash.

Then he loosened the line, shoved the Black Bullet clear, and taxied away just as the once-sleek Douglas plunged beneath the surface with her cargo of death.

Without taking a second look, Barney huddled down under the covered cockpit and let Keen take the Black Bullet off. The clock on the instrument board read 8:15 p.m.

Keen made a quick calculation, climbed her fast, and leveled off. They were on their way home!

EXACTLY FORTY minutes later, Keen picked up the first dull gleam of Montauk Light. He had tobogganed in on the Newark beam until he caught the dull glare of Fire Island Light, then he had turned north again, cut in his Skoda mufflers, and groped his way up the shore of Long Island. Finally, he identified a marker buoy, and with a grin back at Barney, he eased the Black Bullet down. The fog and mist were still as thick as ever, but by skillful use of his navigation instruments he had brought the speedy amphibian back to her secret hangar.

They quickly ran her up on the shore inside, whereupon Keen hoisted out the long burlap-wrapped bundle and placed it beside the one they had taken from the wreckage of the Sikorsky.

"Nice gun shooting, Barney," said Keen as he slipped out of his black coverall.

"Nice sky-bootin' bringing th' Black Bullet through that fog," answered O'Dare. "Why even the sea gulls musta been walking tonight!"

"Yeah," laughed Keen. "And now get into your street togs and load this stuff aboard the Dusenburg. We're going to raise a corpse—for the benefit of one Drury Lang. But we'll have to work fast."

In fifteen minutes they were racing back to New York with the two mysterious bundles in the rumble seat. Again the trip took nearly two hours, but instead of heading for 55th Street they crawled through the midtown traffic to 88th Street.

Though it was after 11 p.m., there was still a dull gleam of light in Dooling's small office, so Keen barged right up and rang the bell. Dooling was sleepy-eyed when he let them into his drab establishment.

"Well, I'm back," said Keen. "And now may I have your assistance for a few minutes?" he queried, laying two crisp one hundred dollar bills down on the dreary wicker table to emphasize his request.

"You *are* a Secret Service man, aren't you?" old Dooling quaked.

"Pick up the money and leave the rest to me," came the

reply. "If you don't trust me, you can call this number—head-quarters of the New York Division—but I'd rather you didn't. I've got to work fast."

"I guess I understand," nodded Dooling.

"Fine! But remember that this is very important, hence you must keep your mouth shut. We are working to trap a gang of international spies who have been trying to obtain possession of an important military secret. You can under-stand now that I am being very confidential with you."

Dooling was highly impressed. He folded the crisp bills with enthusiasm, nodded like an automatic doll.

"Now first," said Keen, "we want your hearse together with that casket we were examining when I was here before—the one with the lid off."

"Ye can have anything, sir—anything if it'll help get them dommed spies!"

"All right. We'll take the casket out and place it in the hearse now. Then your part is done. The rest will be carried out by my assistant," he added, indicating Barney.

The three of them then went in the back, lugged the disar-ranged casket out, and placed it in the hearse. The lid was left off.

"That's all," explained Keen. "Now you and I will go back into your office and smoke a cigar. Pulski here will take care of the rest of the business."

"Pulski?" gasped Dooling. "I thought he was a County Cork man by the look of his mug. But ye niver can tell, huh?"

"No, you never can tell," agreed Keen as he walked away with the little mortician. He gave Barney the wink and the Mick went out to the Dusenberg.

"Now, Dooling," explained Keen. "Your hearse will be brought back early tomorrow morning. And remember that you know nothing about this regardless of who questions you."

Dooling nodded, smiled, and sucked on the big cigar Keen had just given him.

"For one thing, a fussy guy named Lang will no doubt drop in. He'll ask a few dumb questions—but you can pass them off. He's only a half-pint operator who's trying to get along. Your story is that the hearse was taken again last night, and that you don't know anything about how it happened."

"But my hearse—it will come back?" Dooling asked.

"Positively! I'll see to that. If they are not here with it by 10 a.m., report the loss to the police in the regular way just to cover up."

"I get you, Mister… Mister…."

"Ginsberg," filled in Keen. Then he winked, and Dooling winked back.

Now they heard the hearse rumble out through the driveway, and Keen got up to leave.

"Remember now," he warned, "you're not only doing me a big favor—but you are being an honest citizen who is helping the cause of law and order."

"Thot's me ivery time, Mr. Ginsberg," assured Dooling as Keen joined Barney on the front seat of the hearse.

IT WAS a well-satisfied pair of "operators" that let themselves into Keen's pent-house apartment twenty minutes later. They had left the hearse a short distance up the street from the canopied entrance of the building and then went upstairs together—after Keen had had a confidential word with the doorkeeper.

They found Lang was huddled up on the couch with a silk comfortable around his shoulders. He jerked into a sitting position with a start when Keen and Barney came in.

"What happened?" he cracked, obviously worried.

"Nothing. The Graham car got away—clean," explained Keen, sitting down with a feigned gesture of weariness.

"I bin listening on the radio—news flashes on it. I guess we're sunk."

"You mean *you* are," said Barney. "Still, it may only be a life sentence."

Lang shoved his fingers through his stringy hair. "I'm

gonner give myself up," he said. "They can't plant *all* this on me."

"If you could only prove that Hatcher was at the bottom of that anti-aircraft gun business and then get the A-A gun gadget back, you might get away with it," mused Keen, staring at the ceiling.

"That's what you birds were gonner do for me—and what happens?"

"We did our best. We wanted the reward money on that gun, you know."

"Yeah? An' I'd have got it for you, too."

"How?" said Keen looking at his watch.

"It can be done, you know."

"I don't believe you. I'll bet if that thing was laid in your lap right now, you'd grab it, take all the credit, and hang onto the dough yourself," Barney broke in.

"How can I? I'm a G-man. I can't take rewards."

"No. And neither could you see that we got it," Keen went on with another look at his watch.

"I'd like the opportunity to try," snapped Lang. "Just give me the opportunity. I can tell a good story, you know—if I get the chance."

At that instant the house phone rang.

Keen arose, took up the receiver. "Lang?" he cracked into the mouthpiece. "Drury Lang...?"

"Don't give me away, Keen," Lang pleaded.

"Yes," went on Keen. "Yes, he's here. But how did you know... What's that?... Why it sounds like a practical joke."

Lang was on his feet now, and Barney stood with his mouth open, a glass in one hand, a bottle in the other.

"Right. We'll be down immediately," Keen said, and then he hung up. "Here's a pippin," he explained. "Someone has just left a *hearse* downstairs for you, Lang. The doorman took the message and just called up."

"Somebody's trying to pull a fast one on me," bellowed Lang.

Keen was climbing into his overcoat again: "I don't care what you think," he said. "I'm going downstairs."

Lang stood by dumbly, whereupon Barney joined the excitement and went for his coat.

"Come on, Lang," Keen said. "You have nothing to lose. Apparently, the fact that you're here is no secret any more."

Finally Lang gave a weary wag of his head and followed them to the elevator. They went downstairs and found the doorman reading an early morning edition of a tabloid.

"Yeah," he explained with little interest. "He just left. Said his name was Ginsberg and that he didn't know what the hell you wanted with a hearse, but there it was, and will you see that the guy gets it back in the morning?"

"Come on," cried Keen. "This is a beaut!" And they hurried out and made their way to the hearse.

Lang immediately clambered into the seat and stared around dumbly. "I get it," he said with an air of resignation. "Here it is!" And from the slit between the horn button and the top of the steering wheel, he took out a card. On the pasteboard in neat black letters was printed *The Griffon*.

"How do you like thot!" gasped Barney.

"Let's look in the back of this bus," said Keen.

"I know," growled Lang. "We'll see that Douglas airliner inside this stiff wagon. Do you know any more funny jokes, Keen?"

"Wait a minute, Lang. This is the same hearse that Hatcher had. You're not going to plant this on me," Keen snapped, getting down. "We try to help you out, we worked all day at Newark, we try to trace Hatcher's gang—and you try to plant this on me. All right, then," Keen added. "I'll drive it down to John Scott and tell him the whole story. Come on, Barney, we'll give it a whirl."

"Wait a minute! Wait a minute!" said Lang quickly. "Let's have a look and see what's in back there."

"I knew you'd see it our way," Keen said with a growl. "I'll bet there's a tie-up here with the A-A case—and you'll claim the reward now, I suppose."

"Listen, Keen. If there's anything to this, I'll see that you get what's coming to you. But I still think it's a rib!"

BARNEY HAD the rear doors open by now. He let out a gasp: "Sure, an' it's another corpse!"

Keen shoved him away, drew the casket partly out of the interior. "You open it, Lang."

Lang gave Keen another puzzled look. He figured he was caught now, but he was not quite sure how. He climbed inside and began to twist the bronzed thumb-screws until the lid was free. Then he looked inside and found a long canvas-wrapped bundle together with a wooden crate bound with steel straps. He peered at them for a moment, then let out a low whistle.

"Put that lid back on, Keen. I'm getting out of here," he said in a husky voice.

"What is it?" gagged Barney. "A corpse? It sure looks like—"

"No… It's the gun parts… two of 'em."

"The anti-aircraft gun?" queried Keen hiding a smile.

"Now how the hell did you do this?" said Lang. "One of these parts was put aboard that airliner this afternoon."

"And the other was stolen last night from the Aberdeen proving ground, wasn't it?" added Keen.

"That's right," said Lang hollowly, putting the lid back on and screwing two of the lugs down. "That means that you *couldn't* have planted it!"

"Of course not. We were at Newark airport. It must have been that Griffon guy, Lang."

"Yeah, the Griffon guy!" Lang echoed.

"There goes our reward," moaned Barney. "That's what we get for trying to get Lang out of a jam. The Griffon puts it over while we are trying to clear this mug."

"Listen, you guys. I'm winning in this game, but I'll see you get what's coming to you. If you two hadn't brought me to this dump, I never could have had it planted on me. And they won't ask too many questions when they get this stuff back. They gotter keep this quiet now."

"Oh, well, somehow you always win, Lang," said Keen helping to shove the casket back.

"Yeah, I win. But you guys always get the dough."

"Well," said Keen, "I'd like to know how you're going to phenagle that reward for us. But if you *don't* get it for us, I suppose I'll be obliged to go to Washington and—"

"You leave that to me," broke in Lang, fearful at what he still figured Keen had on him.

"Take this bus away, then. I'm beginning to smell like a hearse," growled Keen, brushing his coat.

Lang, beaming with smug triumph, was glad to. He went up to the front, climbed in—and took it away.

"DID YOU plant the rest of the stuff—the papers I took from the Sikorsky crowd—on Lang?" Keen asked Barney under his breath as the hearse rolled away. "That would give the poor old devil enough to put his case over."

"Ay, I put 'em in—maps and everything," said Barney as they went up in the elevator. "An' now suppose you tell me what this is all about—how you caught onto it, and all."

"On a promise," said Keen, leading the way into the apartment, "that you make me a hot toddy to wipe out the taste of that hearse—with a noggin of grog for yourself, of course."

It did not take Barney long to return with the order, and soon they were comfortably seated before the fire which Keen had replenished.

"All right," said the ballistics expert, "where do you want me to begin?"

"Right up front. I've niver got it straight since you went off on that crazy trip down below Philly."

"All right—from the start it'll be." And Keen lit a big cigar, sat back, and began:

"Hatcher was the representative of a foreign agent group in this country. As you know now, his name was really Haines.

I first got wind of what he was up to when he called me up and tried to wheedle some ballistics information about a queer cartridge. I knew, you see, that that cartridge was one I had helped devise for the Army. It was to be used in a special range-finder bit, the details of which would be over your head. Anyway, I knew what had happened—they had stolen the range-predictor part of the new gun. But I did not know where it was."

"But why did we go to Aberdeen?"

"I knew the Army figured something was wrong. They had a patrol flying over the proving grounds day and night, and I figured they felt that the other part—the special speed-check instrument—would be swiped next. I didn't know how Hatcher's gang would work it out, and so I made the 'mistake' of leaving on Hatcher's desk a small note-book in which I had carefully jotted details of the Black Bullet and information on the Griffon."

"But what for?" gasped Barney.

"Well, you see, I figured that if they got away with the second part by air—and I had every reason to believe they would—then I wouldn't know what sort of a plane they were using. So I gave Hatcher that bait on the Bullet, figuring they'd attack the ship if they saw it. That move on their part would tell me what ship was being used to swipe the part."

"You always seem to do things backward. Fancy making those guys tell you who and where they were—when you didn't even know who *they* were."

"Well, I had to do that. Now about Hatcher and the coffin business."

"Yeah, straighten that one out."

"Very simple. Hatcher knew I had some idea about the gun part, and he must have known Lang knew something about it, because I kept tipping him off that a guy named Lang was looking for some one who had stolen a secret gun part. I played that up so much that he finally got Lang on the brain. Then when those lugs knocked him off in the hearse business, he could only think of Lang. That's why he died barking about Lang."

"But why did those birds knock him off? That's the part I can't figure out!"

"Because they knew Hatcher had been in contact with me; but they didn't know why, because apparently Hatcher was saving that cartridge detail part for himself."

"They thought he was double-crossing them?" asked Barney.

"Of course. Then the coffin gag was pulled to hide the gun part for a few hours in Dooling's place. They had no particular idea of sending it to Massachusetts. That part of their plan was just a stall; until the time came for them to get the part out to that flying boat."

"You mean, they were not going to take it to Massachusetts?"

"Oh, they could have done so, of course, and then picked it up with the proper papers and brought it back here again. But as you've just said, they figured Hatcher was double-crossing them, so they bumped him off, took the gun part, and left a scene that looked as though Drury Lang had killed a hearse driver and swiped a body."

"Poor old Lang. He'll be months getting over this," laughed the Mick.

Keen went on:

"Then, as you know, Lang got caught. He followed Hatcher and his mob to Dooling's and they nailed him, not knowing *what* to do with him, they tied him up and stuffed him in a convenient casket. Then Hatcher, supreme in his belief that all was clear, drove off. The rest of the gang then hopped into that Graham, cut him off a block or two away, bumped him off, and took the gun part out of the casket. I have an idea Hatcher was simply moving it to a place where they could quickly transfer it to the plane they intended to steal at Newark airport. But, of course, he never got out of 38th Street. Another reason for doing away with him was to grab his share of dough for themselves. Incidentally, Lang hadn't let on who he was when he was caught by the gang. A good agent never does—and this time Lang was good. So Hatcher was still worried about Lang even after they'd put him in the casket, for he didn't know it was Lang they'd caught. And Hatcher didn't recognize the Graham when he was hi-jacked because of the poor visibility that night."

"Then the casket gag was only pulled to hide the gun part for a few hours when they sensed that either you or Lang were really on their trail?" asked Barney.

"That's right and it was a swell idea, too. Who would have thought of looking in a casket for that gadget? We might have nailed Hatcher and his mob—but we would never have found the part, even though they went to jail. They would have tipped some one else off to pick up the coffin in Massachusetts, and that is all there would have been to it."

"I think I'll mix you another toddy. That yarn is worth it," said Barney getting up and taking Keen's glass. "That casket gag even had me fooled."

"Make it a double-grog, Barney," came back Keen.

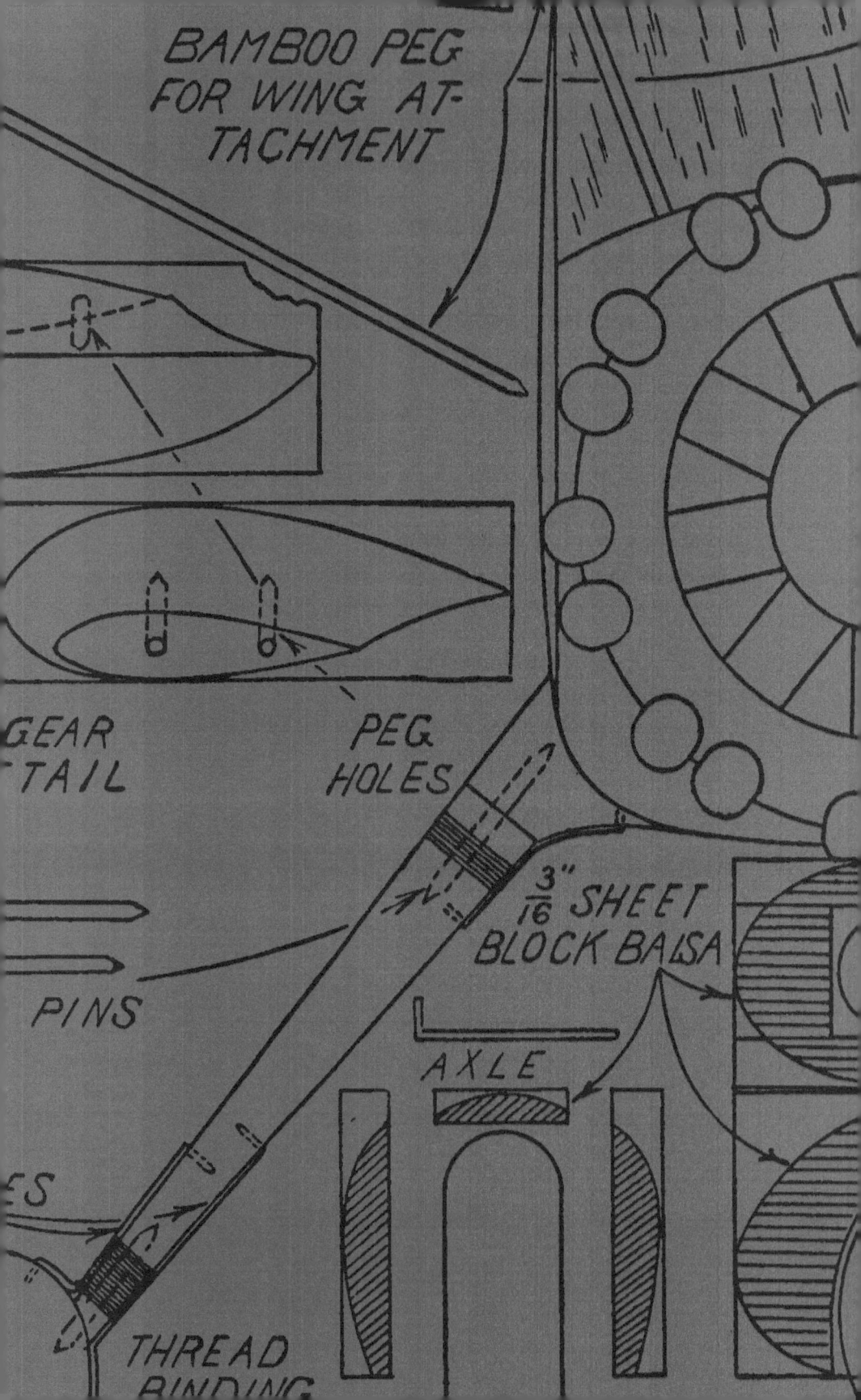

BAMBOO PEG
FOR WING AT-
TACHMENT

GEAR
TAIL

PEG.
HOLES

PINS

ES

$\frac{3}{16}$" SHEET
BLOCK BALSA

AXLE

THREAD
BINDING

Death Haunts
the Clipper

IN THAT snug, comfortable room at Graylands the air was tense. True, the solid maple panels gave off a warm and cozy glow. And a pleasant log fire threw cheerful dancing reflections over the walls and along the glass doors of the bookcases, while now and then a sputter of sparks leaped out of the charred embers and fluttered up the yawning chimney.

It would have been a scene of complete comfort had it not been for that air of excitement which permeated it—a queer nervousness centering about a man who hunched in a strained attitude before the black panel of an expensive short-wave radio receiver.

He was a trim figure. And his neat herringbone business suit failed to hide the supple muscles beneath. He fingered the dials deliberately with tapering hands that bespoke strength and skill, and now and then he paused to listen carefully through his rubber-cushioned ear-phones.

A second man—a brusk-looking Irish individual—sat watching the other with a tired and puzzled mien. He wore heavy shoes that were badly laced, a pair of greenish dungarees, and a grimy leather jacket. His face might have been carved from a squarish chunk of muddy beeswax for all the color it boasted. He had the ease of a rustic, the slackness of a tramp—and yet there was a bright gleam in his close-set eyes.

With a doleful wag of his head this man in the dungarees

The proud Clipper staggered, fell off in a sickening side-slip—and Kerry Keen knew no time was to be lost. Gritting an oath through his clenched teeth, he hurtled the Black Bullet directly into that preying flock of Macchi M.C. 77s!

now changed his position slightly, reached for a tall glass, took a healthy swig, and said: "You've tried every European station, you've had a whack at the ship-to-shore telephone band, and you've listened in to every squeal on the aircraft segment. Tell me, what the divil *are* you looking for?"

"Messrs Lang and Scott are worried," the man at the radio said evasively.

"Begorrah, them mugs is *always* worried. And what is it now?" the guy in dungarees champed.

"They're not quite certain themselves," was the reply. "But their guess is that some one is about to pinch a Clipper ship—one of those big Martin babies. Anyhow, it's got 'em worried."

"I'm a little worried about somethin' meself, Mr. Keen," the Irishman said, shifting his position.

"Shut up, Barney, and let me worry for a change. I've got all I can handle without listening—"

"I know—but this is different," returned the other insistently.

Kerry Keen, the noted ballistics expert, ignored him and went on: "I'm looking for a radio clue. And since the Martin

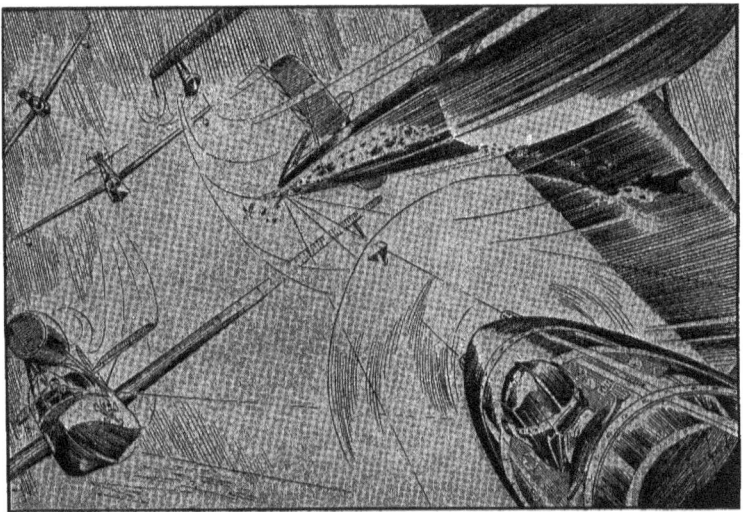

company has built a giant flying boat for the Soviet government, it's possible that—"

"I'm gettin' sick of hearin' about that plane. What I wanted to tell you was—"

"Never mind. It can't be important. Now the stealing of a giant flying boat would be a whopper. And Lang and Scott have a hunch that some one is going to pinch it when it's flown up from the Martin plant to New York for shipment abroad."

"If it's so good, why don't they *fly* it to Russia?" the Irishman said. "But now let me tell you about—"

"The contract calls for shipment to Russia, meaning they're taking no chance with it. But still Lang and Scott are worried—as well as the Martin company— because a lot of queer things have been happening down there at the Baltimore factory. You see, some one has made two attempts to get away with it already."

"I don't think that's as important as this matter I wanted to—"

"It *is* important," stormed Keen. "Now look here, you dumb Irishman. We're going to stop those thieves, because if that job gets into wrong hands, there'll be a devil of a mess. What's more, I have a hunch that the trouble will start soon."

"Why? Is the ship flying up tomorrow?"

"No. They're sending up an ordinary Clipper—just for a try-out to see if they can make these crooks show their hands."

"All right. But what can we do about it?"

"We can be on the sidelines to see—" Keen abruptly broke off his sentence, leaped to his feet, and stared across the room.

"Who in Heaven's name…" he began. But he could not go on. He simply stared.

IN THE doorway stood an apple-cheeked old lady dressed in a sleezy alpaca skirt and a faded blue sweater. Her thin gray hair was parted uncompromisingly in the middle and drawn back over her gnarled ears into a knot at the nape of her neck. She stood there with her head cocked a little to one side in a manner that would have been thought coy were she fifty years younger.

"It's me gran'mother from Clonakilty—me Granny McShane from Ireland," bleated Barney O'Dare.

Kerry Keen was speechless. The idea of a woman in Graylands was too much for him.

"But, Barney," he finally managed to say, "you should have *told* me. Why on earth did you bring her here?"

"I was tryin' to tell you," cracked the Mick. "Anyhow, I had no other place to bring her." Then he turned. "Come in, Granny… Come by the fire, me love."

"It's not me that's a'wantin' to be a bother, Barney, me lad," the old woman cackled, shuffling toward the fireplace. "Indeed, if yer gintleman can't abide the likes o' me, I'll be shiftin'."

"No!… No!" protested Keen. "Please don't misunderstand me, Mrs…. er… Mrs. McShane. I was only wondering whether you would be comfortable out here. Don't you think, Barney, that she'd like it better in New York—at the penthouse."

The little old lady bristled: "It's no penthouse ye'll be a' puttin' me in. I saw one once in the cinema at Skibbereen. I don't want to mix in with yer fancy ladies who drink cocktails, with niver a soul knowin' whether she'll be kissed under the piano or on top o' the gintleman's bureau."

That said, Mrs. McShane smoothed her skirt with a haughty flourish and spat into the fire.

Keen was too amazed to see the humor of the situation. His mind was vibrating like the snares of a trap drum. He figured Barney must be raving mad to bring this woman—any woman—here.

Barney tried to explain. "I didn't know she was coming meself," he said. "You see, I found her in a saloon—"

"A saloon? What the deuce are you talking about? Give me that bottle of O'Doul's Dew. You must be going screwy."

"Yes, it was in a saloon on Second Avenue—Mickey Flarety's old place."

"Saloon, is it?" the old lady bristled again. "In Clonakilty we call 'em public houses—an' better beer they serve, too."

"How did she know *you* would be there?" probed Keen.

"Where else would an O'Dare be?" the old lady demanded.

"You see, it was like this," Barney explained. "I dropped in there, like I usually do, when I was in town today getting—"

"—I know, getting another case," Keen snapped.

"Anyhow," went on Barney, "Mickey Flarety says to me, 'There's an old lady bin in here lookin' fer ye, an' she says she's from Clonakilty.' And I says, 'What's her name?' An' says he, 'She says she's your grandmither and the name's Mrs. McShane.' In a few minutes in she comes. And she *is* my Granny McShane—me auld mither's mither," mooned Barney, sentiment oozing out all over him.

"Are you *sure?*" demanded Keen. Then without pausing he asked, "How did she get here?"

"You chatter like a pair o' parrots," spoke up the old lady. "I came on the *Empress of Ireland.* What ither boat would I come on?"

"Oh, then you came by way of Canada—through Montreal?" said Keen.

"Sure, an' I did. Straight from Queenstown. It's still Queenstown to me, even though De Valera wants us to call it 'Cobh'," Granny McShane replied, smoothing her skirt again.

At that, Keen seemed to warm a trifle: "Well, now that we have it straight we shall have to make you comfortable, Granny. You take her along to the west guest room, Barney, and see that she is fixed up. Then tomorrow we'll see what other arrangements can be made for her."

Barney looked at Keen with a puzzled stare, being flabbergasted by his change in attitude. But then he helped the old lady to her feet and guided her out of the room.

"Make sure she gets something warm to eat in the kitchen first; I'll be with you in a minute or two," Keen said.

FOR SEVERAL minutes after the pair had gone, Keen sat staring into space. Then his glance fell on the telephone. He frowned. Then making a quick decision, he got up, carefully opened the door, slipped out into the luxurious hallway, and darted into the small reception room on the other side. Here he switched on a small light and stood contemplating the telephone set there for several seconds. The instrument was dusty, and there were tell-tale marks on the receiver portion. He started to pick it up, then noticed that it was placed on the bracket with the mouthpiece toward the right.

He nodded, then said to himself quietly: "Some one was talking through this phone—and when he was suddenly interrupted, he fumbled with the receiver and in his anxiety placed it on backwards."

Satisfied with this explanation, Keen glanced at his watch. It was 9:20. Then with a quick move he went across the little reception room, opened a small door set into the blocked panelling, and inspected a small machine inside on which was fitted a wax cylinder. He immediately noted that the reproduction arm of this recording device had moved almost half way down the cylinder.

Keen quickly removed the cylinder and placed it on a reproducing instrument. Next he pulled on some lightweight ear-phones, snapped a switch, and listened intently.

Two male voices came to his ears, and when he heard their conversation, he emitted a low whistle. Quickly he "played" the cylinder over again to get every word, then he put a fresh cylinder on the recorder and closed the panel door.

"We have about an hour to pull it off," he muttered to himself as he glanced at his watch. "And now we must take care of Granny McShane."

BARNEY WAS fluttering about the kitchen like an anxious mother, preparing a meal for Granny McShane when Keen came in. He had put golden and buttery toast, a hot pot of strong tea, and a large platter of frizzling ham and eggs before the old lady.

"… an' I can see ye need a woman about this place," the old lady was saying. "Men and boys are all right in their place— but it takes a woman to run a house."

"And you're just the person we need to run it," beamed Keen. "Of course Barney's all right on outside work and around the garage, but in the house here he's inclined to shove the dust under the furniture."

Barney frowned. He wondered what Keen was getting at.

"And now, Granny," Keen went on with enthusiasm, "I'm going to make you a warming noggin of grog to put you to sleep. For you must have had a hard day."

"Not *that* bottle," cried Barney, seeing Keen reach up high on the shelf and snatch out a tall green bottle. "That's the— the Irish whiskey."

"An' who has a better right to Irish whiskey?" the old lady beamed, pursing her thin lips. "Let the gintleman make me a noggin o' grog, an' I'll drink to ye and to the O'Dares o' Clonakilty."

"But ye don't want *that* bottle," Barney tried to say again.

"We know the *auld crater* when we see it, don't we, Granny?" laughed Keen, pouring a good dollop into a glass. "A lemon, Barney, and the brown sugar. I'll get the boiling water."

The Mick obeyed orders like a man in a dream, and in three minutes the glass of grog stood steaming before the old lady. She had already dropped her knife and fork in anticipation.

"An' ye'll not join me?" she queried.

"No," replied Keen. "Barney and I must go out at once. We'll see you comfortable and set for the night before we go, though. You'll be all right then."

"We're going *out?*" gagged the Mick, still in a dumb daze.

"Yes, Barney. I just got a call from Lang. They have a little job for us, and we'll need all the money we can get now—if we're going to entertain Granny here in the style to which she is accustomed."

But Granny was gulping the grog with keen relish, swigging the hot liquid down as if well-experienced. Having finished it, she smacked her lips, nodded pleasantly, and went back to work on the food.

"You see her upstairs as soon as she's done eating," ordered Keen. "I'll be downstairs getting the car ready."

Barney wagged his head and gave Keen another blank stare. He was utterly at sea, but for the first time he was beginning to realize the seriousness of the situation. Suppose Granny McShane saw what was going to happen outside. Suppose she caught on to the relationship of Kerry Keen and the Griffon. How would they be able to explain the nocturnal movements of the Black Bullet?

Puzzled, scared, and totally unnerved, Barney hovered over the old lady until she had finished her meal. Then with true Celtic gallantry he urged her to go to her room and get to bed.

Strangely enough, the old lady displayed no desire to remain and tidy up the kitchen. She seemed very sleepy and was thankful to be shown to her room, which looked out over the front of the house.

"Ah!" she smiled, sitting on the bed. "It's a long day it's bin, Barney, me boy, and it's tired I am. I'll get right into bed, and ye can trot off and take care o' yer gintleman. An' a very foine gintleman, he is, too. He knows a good grog when he sees one, eh, Barney?"

"The light switch is over there when you're ready, an' ye'd better open this window here."

"Just leave me, me boy. I'll be all right." She yawned. "I'm very, very sleepy."

"I had an idea you would be," said Barney with a strange tone in his voice.

HE HURRIED back downstairs, found Keen in the study, already attired in a black coverall, with helmet, goggles, and a scarlet mask in his hands.

"What's the idea o' putting that particular grog into the old lady?" asked Barney as he reached inside a panel for his own coverall. "That stuff was doped."

"I know it. But we've got to be sure she goes to sleep, haven't we?"

"But we can't be doing that every time we run the Bullet out."

"That's right. We'll have to try some other game. By the way, are you really sure she's your grandmother?"

"Of course. She had a passport issued by the Irish Free State, and she has photographs of me old mither."

"But what's she doing over here? None of it makes any sense to me."

"She's the only one left; all the rest are dead. So she sold her little dairy farm and came over here. All the Irish do."

"She knew you were in New York?"

"Sure. All the Irish are in New York!"

Keen snickered. "There's one or two in Boston, and I've heard of another one in Jersey City."

"Well, she figured she had to take a chance. And she thought of New York first."

"But it still seems strange to me that she should go straight to the one gin mill that you honor with your presence."

"She tried them all in that section, and finally found one where they knew me. That's the Irish way of doing things."

"Well, you should have had more sense than to bring her here. What the deuce are we going to do with her?"

"I never thought of that."

"We'll probably have to shoot her," smiled Keen leading the way down the stairs to the wine cellar.

Barney stifled a low cry, then followed his master.

They went through the secret panel and entered the underground hangar. Barney, still muttering, started the big 1,000 h.p. Avia motor while Keen inspected the cockpit and controls. Finally the Mick pulled the switch that opened the big folding doors, whereupon Keen ran the well-muffled ship out into the open. After closing the fake "rock garden" doors, Barney opened the folding wings of the black amphibian. Then he climbed into the back seat, closed the sliding hatch, and sat quiet as Keen guided the ship past the sheltering grape arbor and down onto the packed sands alongside the boathouse.

Once the Black Bullet had reached the water, Keen drew back the lever which set the pontoons for a water take-off. Then he glanced about, waited for the rotating beam of Montauk Light to swing away—and gave her the gun. With the Skoda mufflers deadening the roar of the Avia to a low purr, he let the Bullet streak out past his mooring buoy and well on into the darkness before he let her get away.

Finally she cleared the drag of suction, took the air, and climbed steadily until they were well out to sea, where, at a 4,000 foot altitude, Keen swung her around and headed back almost due west toward the glowing tip of Manhattan Island.

"What's the game now?" prodded Barney as he finished the last of his buttoning and buckling.

"You'll see. And you'd better be on your toes, because Lang and Scott had a real hunch. Right now, my friend, we're looking for a Martin Clipper which is being flown up to Port Washington."

"Where'd you get all this dope?"

"Off the record," answered Keen with tantalizing vagueness.

"Okay, Al Smith. Have it your way. I'm just along for the ride."

"And believe me, you're going to get one."

That seemed to satisfy Barney for the time being, for he began busying himself with the rear gun mounting, dragging it out and testing it, changing the ammo boxes, and the like. But while this business was imperative and important, he could not help but think of the old lady who had so suddenly blossomed into his life. For the life of him, he could not understand now what had made him bring her to Graylands. The gravity of the situation had finally dawned on him. With Kerry Keen playing his amazing dual role—a young ballistics expert and man-about-town by day, and the crafty, cool Griffon by night—it was impossible to have a third person about the place. Keen had spent years planning the secret details of Graylands' rooms, equipment, study, and hidden hangar. And with an old lady pottering about, as old ladies will, it was obvious that sooner or later she would stumble on to some of the betraying evidence of Keen's nocturnal activities.

He peered out, saw that they were cutting wide of the Fire Island Light and swinging in a quarter circle around the lower portion of New York Bay. He noted that Keen was anxious now, for after keeping clear of a south-bound airliner that was heading for Newark Airport, he scoured the sky in all directions—for what, only Keen himself knew. Rain came, impeding vision.

Suddenly he turned south again and headed for the bulbous light of Ambrose Lightship. Barney felt increased tension now. He got to his feet, peering about.

"A Martin Clipper, did you say?" he husked over Keen's shoulder.

"A Clipper—and the rest," nodded Keen, crouching low.

"There it is!" Barney suddenly barked. "Off to the east! See her riding lights? Through the rain?"

"I see plenty! Look high above her!"

BARNEY PEERED up, caught the knifelike glint of silver wings. There were six pairs of them spread from trim, boat-like fuselages above each of which were mounted egg-shaped engine nacelles. In front, like gleaming Cyclopean eyes, bristled domed gun turrets.

"Whew!" whistled Barney. "And take a gander at their nose insignia—skull and bones!"

"Sure, Captain Kidd has sprouted wings. And how do you like it?"

There was no time to answer. Keen had ripped out the Skoda mufflers; and the Avia, free of any back-pressure, leaped into wild action. The Black Bullet swept into a mad climb, and Keen bit his top lip in anxiety.

The fleet of black raiders—they proved to be Macchi M.C. 77s—were sweeping down on the helpless Martin Clipper like the hawk of doom, and their six sets of Breda-Safat guns were already pouring a converging blast of nickeled-lead into the giant flying boat. The Macchis flew like gulls, holding their tight positions with such skill that it was impossible to see any change of course, except as a six-part unit.

The Clipper frantically carried on. But after holding to her course for several seconds, she staggered and seemed to lose control of herself.

This was enough for Keen. Gritting an oath through his clenched teeth, he hurtled the Black Bullet directly into that preying flock—spraying lead from every forward-firing gun.

The rush pried apart that trim sky pirate formation, and Barney came through with a series of skillful snap shots that split them wide. Keen swung the Bullet up again, whipped her over hard, and glared at the skull-and-crossed-bones insignia painted on the nose of the Macchi flying boats.

"This is an outfit that *is* an outfit," he growled. "I wonder where the devil they got those ships and who's in back of them?"

He steadied the Black Bullet now and let drive at the leading Macchi. Twin streams of heavy caliber stuff slammed into the motor nacelle of the silver flying boat—and the craft exploded in midair. Barney let out a wild yell of triumph, slapped a heavy burst full into the side of another. That ill-fated Macchi seemed to stiffen from nose to tail. Then it climbed up slowly, rolled over on its back, burst into flame, and went down in a flat spin with a pin-wheel of flame chasing its forward gun turret.

Two Macchis now converged on the Bullet forcing Keen to zig-zag his way through a bitter torrent of lead. Then he tried to find the Clipper, but he first had to engage another Macchi with his forward Darns and drive it out of its attack dive.

Barney slammed away at the others, made them sheer off and reform about a quarter of a mile away. The Clipper was circling below them now, and Keen sped the Bullet in close and watched the giant flying boat go down to a shaky landing near the Ambrose Lightship.

"Keep your eye on those Macchis," ordered Keen. "I'm going down to make certain the Clipper boys are Okay. We may have to give them a tow to the lightship mooring."

"Say, you're getting soft in your old age," growled Barney.

"Maybe. But we can't leave them floating about like that. They might sink. Anyhow, cover that mug of yours with a mask, the same as I've done, or you'll give the game away."

And with that, Keen muffled the Avia, lowered the retractable pontoons, and set the flaps for landing. The Clipper was down wallowing in that rainspotted sea about half a mile from the lightship. Keen put the Bullet down gently while Barney watched the still-circling Macchis.

As Keen began to taxi up toward the Clipper, the Macchis came down again hammering leaden death. The Mick stiffened, let one knee drop, and took careful aim. His double spray caught the first Macchi full in the nose, but it kept coming on. He winced, swung the gun mounting a trifle, and gave a second a heavy powdering that made it swing up in a screaming zoom. But that first Macchi kept coming.

Keen reacted fast. He gave the Avia the gun, kicked a rudder pedal, and let the Black Bullet skid over the sea in a water-loop.

And he was just in time—for a terrific thud and splash followed as the lead Macchi hit the water directly over the swirl of foam left by the slithering Bullet!

THE REMAINING three Macchis managed to clamber back into the sky with Barney's guns whipping at their high tails. Behind them, flicked the surface flame of the burning Macchi wreck. The fuel had sprayed out and spread a fiery blanket over what was left of the Italian fighter.

Keen gave the Bullet the gun again and got clear. He steered her toward the floundering Clipper, then yanked back his hatch. Cutting the engine down to idling speed, he hailed the flying boat.

"Ahoy! Do you need assistance?" he called.

"Plenty! We're in bad shape. Captain Pierson, the pilot, is seriously wounded. I'm the co-pilot and am in command now."

"Stand by. I'll toss you a line and tow you to the lightship," boomed Keen again.

"Thanks. I don't dare use my engines. My wing tanks are leaking badly. I'll come forward and take your line."

Keen nodded to Barney, who got out a long line and clambered onto the right pontoon with it. Then as the Bullet came around, the Mick heaved it true. A man in a blue uniform bobbed out of the Clipper's forward gear-hatch, caught it, and snubbed it around a cleat.

Then with the Avia at low speed they began the heavy

task of towing the huge ship toward the bobbing lightship. Ahead they could now see a small power boat chugging toward them.

Keen bellowed over his shoulder: "Cut that line the minute they get anywhere near us. We're taking no chances now."

"What about the Macchis?"

"They've had all they want."

"But aren't you going after them?" asked Barney.

"Time's too short. We have to get back to cover ourselves with Lang."

"Wait a minute," said Barney. "That Clipper pilot is hailing us again."

"Thanks for the tow!" they heard the Clipper flyer yell. "Who can we report aided us?"

"Tell him 'Ginsberg'," said Keen. "And cut that line."

"Ginsberg!" yelled Barney.

"Come again. I didn't get the name."

"Ginsberg—the firm of Ginsberg and Pulski," yelled Barney.

"Isn't that the Griffon's Black Bullet?" the man hollered.

"Tell him to stop reading cop-and-robber comic strips," said Keen.

Instead, Barney turned and barked back over the water: "What do you think?"

At that sally, the Clipper co-pilot disappeared back in his cabin, whereupon Keen gave the Bullet the gun, took off with a roar, pulled up his pontoons, and headed hell-bent-for-election back for Graylands.

IN TWENTY minutes they were home, running the Black Bullet into her secret hangar. There were no lights anywhere in the house, and both were satisfied that Granny McShane was deep in slumber.

They hurried through the secret panel in the wine cellar, and dashed up the stairs just as the telephone rang in Keen's study.

The ballistics expert sat down with a low sigh, slipped off

his mask, and took up the instrument. "Hello," he said in a weary tone. Then on hearing the answering voice he nodded up at Barney who stood over him with an expectant gleam in his eye.

"Yes… Yes, this is Keen. That you, Lang?"

There was another period of silence while Keen listened.

"Tut tut," Keen suddenly spoke up. "Barney and I are here entertaining Mrs. McShane. That's Barney's grandmother from Clonakilty—you know dear old Clonakilty, don't you?"

Lang's voice bellowed back:

"Stop the gagging. Where have you been?"

"Right here with Granny McShane," insisted Keen. "If you don't believe me, come on out and we'll introduce you to her."

For a minute Lang was stumped. Then he asked:

"Is that on the up and up?"

"Why not? Someone has to entertain her."

"Now look here: You remember that business we was telling you about the other day? Well, some one got a Martin Clipper tonight, though it wasn't the big one built for Russia."

"Talk sense! What do you mean someone 'got' it."

"Just that. They forced it down near Ambrose Light, according to a message we just got from the lightship. But that Griffon guy drove off the beggars who done it."

"That's me," laughed Keen. "Always around when there's anything going on like that."

"I said it was the Griffon drove the thievin' birds off," Lang bawled back.

"What 'thievin' birds'?"

"The guys who shot up the Clipper!" screamed Lang, now beside himself.

"Oh, I thought you meant the Griffon shot the Clipper down," replied Keen winking at the grinning Barney.

"I don't know why I'm wasting my time with a mug like you for," moaned the weary Secret Service man.

"I do."

"Yeah? Why?"

"Because you think I'm the Griffon—so you wanted to make certain I wasn't home. That Griffon guy, whoever he is, is certainly putting it over on you."

"He drove those guys off the Clipper," barked Lang.

"You just said the Clipper was shot down," taunted Keen.

"It was… but… but the Griffon flew up in a black plane, actually shot a couple of them down, and gave the Clipper a chance to get down safe. One report even has it that the Griffon gave the Clipper a tow over to the Ambrose Lightship."

"That's Robin Hood stuff. You don't expect me to believe that, do you?"

"But I'm only telling you what the reports are!"

"All right—but don't overdo it. Now can we go back to entertaining Granny McShane?"

"You can. But Scott wants to see you in the morning. He'll have some machine gun slugs for you to look over—some foreign stuff."

"Okay, I'll be down—about 10 o'clock. And now, goodnight, Lang. And regards from Granny," closed Keen, as he leaned back and suppressed a chuckle until the instrument was down on the prongs.

"NOW LOOK here, Barney," Keen said before they retired, "we're in a bad spot with this Granny McShane business. You'll have to make other arrangements for her."

Barney gave Keen a quizzical look. "Ye don't like me gran'mither, do ye?"

Keen took time to light a cigarette before he answered. He was thinking of the two men's voices he had picked up on that recorded telephone conversation. He was trying to fit them in with the tangle of Granny McShane who said she had come from Queenstown on the *Empress of Ireland.*

"She's me Granny McShane, all right," Barney insisted. "I'd know her anywhere."

"But you haven't seen her since you were a kid, have you?"

"No—not since I was twelve. But a man knows his own flesh and blood, don't he?" argued Barney.

"I'll find that out in the morning. In the meantime, you'll have to stick close here and keep an eye on her—until other arrangements are made."

"Don't worry, I will. In fact, I'm afraid the O'Doul's won't hold out unless I do."

"All right. And now shove off to bed. I've got some work to do before I turn in."

Barney took the hint and trotted upstairs. Keen sat quiet, studied the flame that trickled along the logs in the fire. Finally, he reached for a paper pad, laboriously wrote out a lengthy message, and addressed it to the Chief Police Commissioner at Dublin. Then he picked up the telephone, called Western Union, and read out the message which asked pertinent information on a certain Mrs. McShane, late of Clonakilty, County Cork. Lastly he also gave his New York City address, to which the reply was to be sent.

Then after hanging up, he folded the written message and slipped it into the leather corner of his desk blotter. There was a smile on his face as he again settled himself before the fire.

IT WAS nearly nine a.m. when Barney barged into Keen's bedroom with a steaming breakfast and gave him the nod that his bath was ready.

"And how's Granny McShane this morning?" inquired Keen.

"She's foine. Says she slept like a top. And she's bin up for a couple of hours, busying about and cleaning up. She's bin through that study of yours already and has it lookin' like the office of a Wall Street broker."

"I had an idea she would," said Keen. "I think she's interested in me."

"She'll be a big help around the house here," Barney went on. Then not getting an immediate reply from Keen, he continued: "What's the matter? You don't like her?"

"Sure. I like her all right. But I think you took an awful chance bringing her here. She's too close to the Bullet and the rest of our secrets."

Barney was silent a minute. Then he said: "I guess you're right. I'll move her downtown this evening after you get back."

"All right," agreed Keen, heading for the bath. "But don't let anything slip up while I'm gone. I'll be back in midafternoon."

With that warning, Keen went through his morning ablutions, came back glowing, and sat down to his breakfast. Then he dressed and went down to his study.

Just as Barney had boasted, the room was painfully trim. Books had been placed back in their proper positions on the shelves, pictures had been straightened out, closet doors were closed, and the desk was as neat as a bride's kitchen.

But though the sheet of folded paper—the message he'd sent to the Police Commissioner at Dublin—was right where he had left it, there was something about it that caught his eye. It was now tucked in with the folded edges inward—whereas, Keen had been careful to place it with the folded edges *outward!*

Without a second glance toward it, Keen went across the hallway and slipped into the small reception room. Silently he crossed to the wall panel again and peered in at the recording instrument. The indicator arm, showing how far the record had been used, was still in the same place. That meant the telephone had not been used since the night before.

Taking a heavy blackthorn stick, a jaunty felt hat, and a light camel-hair top-coat, Keen sauntered out the front door, stepped into the garage, and backed out his Dusenberg. Then as he rolled down the gravel drive he glanced up toward Granny McShane's window.

The old lady stood front and center, one hand holding back the cretonne curtains, the other waving a motherly farewell.

Keen slapped the horn button and gave her a cheery toot. "I'll be seein' you... I'm afraid, Granny," he muttered to himself.

THE RUN down Long Island was mechanical—for Keen

was now so absorbed in his thoughts and contemplations that he did not consider either the countryside or his speed. He was trying to figure out just why Granny McShane had come to Graylands and what the story was behind the two mysterious men who had talked on his reception room telephone the night before. Then there was the puzzle of the Macchi pirates who had shot down the Martin Clipper ship. What connection, if any, did all these unrelated events have to the proposed flight of the giant Soviet flying boat?

But before he knew it, he was swinging up to the curb before the unpretentious office of the New York Division of the Department of Justice. He got out, flipped the brim of his hat, took out his walking stick, and strolled into the building.

Both Scott and Lang were waiting for Keen when he wandered in. They were sitting at their desks glowering with the anxious looks of weary bloodhounds that had lost the scent.

Keen flipped his hat on a nearby chair and dramatically announced: "The Griffon is here!"

"Sit down," growled Lang.

Keen sat down, grinning.

Then without more ado, Scott tossed over three copper-jacketed slugs. "We had these picked out of that Clipper," he said. "What are they?"

"Um… twenty millimeter stuff," said Keen weighing the slugs in his palm. "And they have the initials 'B.S.' moulded into the base."

"We figured that meant 'Bofors, Sweden'," said Lang.

"No, the Bofors gun is a 25 mm. job. This is Italian—Breda-Safat stuff."

"Yeah? Well, what were they fired from?"

"A light aircraft cannon. Nice, eh?"

"You *would* know," barked Lang. "I'll bet a buck you were somewhere around."

"Just a gambler at heart, aren't you, Lang. Bang goes your buck on a long shot."

At this point Scott broke in again:

"Never mind all that. What we want to know is, who has any such gun in this area?"

"Well, there's one in a glass case up at Grant Hall—that's West Point. But I wouldn't know about any others. Anyhow, why bother me with this stuff?" argued Keen. "What's the story? And where do *I* fit in?"

"Ever hear of a guy named Eligio Pozzolo?" asked Scott.

"Sure, on a box of ravioli. It's advertised on all the subway billboards."

"No!... No!" growled the Secret Service man. "This guy is supposed to be a foreign correspondent for some European newspaper service. He's been pestering the Martin outfit for a ride on the new Soviet Clipper, but they kept him off it. Finally he got pretty nasty and wrote some goofy stuff about the plane, whereupon Martin tried to get him and straighten him out on the facts. All that made him sore."

"And Pozzolo took a shot at the other Clipper to get even?" grinned Keen.

"We don't know. But about a week ago, as we told you, Pozzolo disappeared and a lot of queer things happened down at the Martin plant. The ship has been on a ramp for some time, you know, getting its final touching-up. Well, about four days ago, some one actually tried to swipe the thing. They got it down the ramp and into the water—but somehow couldn't get it *off* the water. From what I understand, the Martin people have some sort of a control-locking device, and only their pilot who has the key can fly it."

"Don't you know who tried to steal it yet?"

"No. When the thieves realized they were licked, they jumped overboard. And apparently some one was nearby in a motor boat to pick them up."

"Well, where do I come in?" asked Keen selecting another cigarette.

"You know this Griffon guy, don't you?" snapped Lang. "You *must* know him."

ment to his ear, glaring at the young ballistics expert. Then he hung up.

"Swell stuff! No one answers. Where'd you get this Granny McShane gag, anyway?"

"Don't worry. It's on the level. Barney must have taken her for a walk."

But it was evident that Keen himself was now worried. He stared back and forth from Lang to Scott, tried to read their minds. For a moment he was afraid Granny McShane had been planted on him by the two Secret Service men.

Finally he decided to take the bull by the horns: "Did you fellows hook that old woman on me?" he asked bluntly.

"No—but it's an idea," grinned Lang. "And now what about the Griffon? That new Clipper is coming through tonight, you know."

"And she's got to get through, Keen," chimed in Scott. "If you know the Griffon, you'd better make sure that he sees that she gets through."

"What's the matter with the Army—or the Navy. Can't they escort her?"

"She's a commercial job, so that's no business of the military services. All we are worrying about is that she actually gets to Russia—and not into the hands of some one who can use her for something else. Of course, the Coast Guard could try to get her through. But after what we heard about last night, they wouldn't stand much chance against that pack of fighting planes with the ships they have handy."

Keen saw the reason in Scott's words. But he was still worried about that telephone call that was not answered.

"What in the devil are you worrying about, anyway?" said Lang suddenly as he saw the expression on Keen's face.

Keen did not answer. He was biting his top lip and peering into space.

"We got him this time, Scott!" Lang barked.

THE YOUNG ballistics expert only smiled and reached for

the telephone. He then called his New York apartment building and got an answer from the doorman at the entrance.

"This is Mr. Keen," he explained over the wire. "I'm downtown on business. Can you tell me if any important messages have been left for me this morning?"

The doorman's voice came back:

"There's a cablegram, Mr. Keen. It just came in. I signed for it—is that Okay?"

"Sure, Pete. Now open it and read it to me, will you? It may be important."

And while both Scott and Lang stared at him, wondering what the message was, the doorman at Keen's apartment read:

"It's from Dublin, Ireland, Mr. Keen—the office of the Police Commissioner. And it says—"

"Read it slowly," advised Keen, glaring at Lang.

"It says: 'Mrs. Maggie McShane, widow of the late Patrick McShane of Clonakilty, County Cork, is at present an inmate of the Bandon Workhouse where she has been since May 1932. No record of Free State passport having been issued to anyone by that name in past twelve months—A.M. Hearne, Deputy Commissioner, Dublin.'"

Beads of perspiration were trickling down Keen's forehead by the time the doorman had finished.

"Thanks, Pete," he said in a husky voice. "Keep that cablegram in your pocket and don't turn it over to anyone but me. I'll be up there in half an hour."

"I'd give ten bucks to know what that message was," smirked Lang.

"I'll sell it to you tomorrow at noon for a century note," laughed Keen. "And now I'll be toddling."

"I'll take that message for a century, at that," said Lang.

"It's a deal!" Keen agreed.

"And don't forget that Clipper," warned Scott. "And, say— you're a little worried about Granny McShane, huh?"

"Well, you know what these old ladies are," parried Keen.

"Yeah. They talk too much—and you're afraid of that, eh, Keen?" said Lang, as Keen hurried for the door.

"You let me alone for twenty-four hours, Lang, and I'll see that you get that message. And maybe the flying boat *will* get through Okay."

"It better!" warned Lang.

KEEN HURRIED north to his 55th Street apartment and retrieved the cablegram from the doorman. Then he hurried upstairs, grabbed his phone, and called the Graylands library number.

For three minutes he sat with the instrument glued to his ear—but there was no answer. Then he decided then to call the other number—the phone in the reception room.

Almost instantly there came an answering *"Hello"*—and it was in an unfamiliar voice.

Then Keen took a long chance: "This is Pozzolo," he husked, using a mid-European accent.

"Good!" the strange voice replied. *"Quick! Give me the dope."*

"Here you are," gutturaled Keen. "The Clipper leaves tonight!"

"All right, Pozzolo," the other voice replied. *"I've got everything clear here."*

"Okay. And be sure the rest of the plans go through on schedule," Keen answered, holding the disguise in his voice. Then he hung up.

"Whew! Now we *are* in for it!" he gasped, wiping his brow. The full realization that Granny McShane had been planted on them struck him with its full force. Knowing Keen was in close touch with the Secret Service department, someone had smuggled Granny McShane into Graylands to watch him—to trap him.

"Well, Mr. Keen," he muttered to himself, "get yourself out of *this* one!"

His first thoughts were to get to a bank, draw out as much money as he could lay his hands on, and get aboard a boat.

But then he remembered Barney—something had to be done about Barney.

So Keen sat back and calmly planned a campaign of action.

BUT AS he schemed, a gripping scene was being enacted at Graylands. The library was now a shambles. Keen's desk had been shoved unceremoniously into the bulge of the fireplace and the heat was scorching the finish so that it gave off a pungent odor.

Before the desk, Barney O'Dare stood groggily staring at the bulky figure before him. Down one side of the Mick's face streamed a pennon of gore. Before him, crouching with a short leather billy in one hand, stood "Granny McShane."

A startling change had taken place. "Granny" was now a cruel-faced ogre with arms like a gorilla, and "her" movements belied the venerable garments "she" wore.

"Ye thievin' County Cork spalpeen!" screamed Barney.

"Can the chatter, O'Dare. This is my party," the masculine voice of "Granny McShane" boomed across the room. "I'll split your skull next time."

Barney lunged. But half blinded by blood, the two short hooks he threw at the figure in the old lady's costume were wide. "Granny McShane" skillfully stepped inside the swings and brought a knee up hard.

O'Dare let out a low-pitched groan and toppled forward gasping for breath. Then with a quick twist "Granny" broke clear and again swung at Barney with the billy.

THOCK!

The leather-covered weapon flattened itself against the Irishman's skull and he dropped to his knees, his eyes glassy. Then his body twisted and he sprawled across the floor leaving a reddish smear where his bloody face hit the parquet flooring.

"That should hold you, O'Dare," the erstwhile "old lady" said. "Next I'll get that other mug—Keen."

Thereupon "Granny" calmly undid something at "her" waist and stepped out of the alpaca skirt. Next a tight-fitting wig was yanked away, disclosing a closely-cropped bullet head. And the man who had been Granny McShane then turned down the folds of his trousers, slipped out of a seedy velvet blouse, and drew out the collar of his soft shirt.

The transformation was now complete. "Granny McShane" was a thick-set man with a face that might have been considered intellectual were it not for a cruel sneer that distorted one side of his face and the hooded effect given to his eyes by the heavy lids.

Kicking his discarded clothing under a chair, the man pulled the desk away from the fireplace. Then he rolled O'Dare over, carefully bound his arms behind him, and shoved him into a corner.

"That will hold you for a time, anyway. Now for another look around before the other guy gets back. This place has me stopped."

He went out into the hallway and continued his careful search of doorways, panels, stairways, and closets—a search which had been suddenly interrupted by Barney a short time before.

But his investigation was fruitless. And now, as it began to get dark, he wound his way back up the stairs from the cellar below, weary with frustration. For more than four hours now he had gone over every inch of the house and cellar seeking secret rooms—especially one that he figured contained a plane. He had tapped walls, taken out panels, and followed the course of laundry chutes from top to bottom. But nowhere could he find a trace of the sleek Black Bullet.

He now returned to the embattled library determined to make a final effort on O'Dare. But when he lurched into the room with a heavy black automatic in his hand, a cry of amazement escaped him. His victim had disappeared!

"W-why!" he gasped. "I thought I'd flattened that Mick for hours. Where in the devil did he crawl to?"

Before he could make another move to look, the crunching of tires on the gravel outside caught his attention. Nervous now, he slipped into the shadows behind the heavy portière. In a moment the car stopped, a door slammed, and then the measured strides of Kerry Keen were heard in the hall.

The man behind the portière waited cautiously until Keen approached. He hesitated a moment when he saw that a .38 automatic gleamed in the young ballistic expert's right hand. But then he shrugged, drew a short bead with his own gun, and pulled the trigger.

There was a thudding explosion, and Keen's gun, blasted out of his hand, smashed against the wall near a dark corner.

"That's all, Keen. Put on the light," the man behind the portière ordered. "And it won't be healthy if you make me shoot again—for I'm quite handy with a gun."

"So I see," answered Keen, rubbing his right hand which still tingled from the shock. "But what have you done with Barney—Mrs. McShane?"

The man started at Keen's recognition of him. But then he smiled. "Your man's put away to cool. Now come on in—I want to talk to you." And he flicked the gun barrel, indicating that Keen was to enter the library. The shambles inside told Keen all he wanted to know—Barney had been cruelly disposed of… somehow.

"Now talk fast, Keen," the man said. "I don't have much time to waste. Where's that plane of yours?"

"Let's see… haven't I seen you somewhere before?" Keen parried, staring at the man in the low warm light of the library. "You look a lot like a man who was once known as—as Justin… Justin something or other."

"That's right. I'm Justin Devereaux, the actor. At least, I *was* an actor until things went bad."

"You mean until you were unable to keep your fingers out of the funds of the Actors' Equity, of which you were treasurer," taunted Keen.

"That was the beginning, yes. But now that's all past and done with. I do acting of another kind now, Keen. In fact, both you and I put on the sock and buskin now and again. Right?"

"What is it you want?" said Keen, avoiding the inference.

"I want that black sky job of yours. It's a beaut of a plane and we can use it tonight."

"You, Eligio Pozzolo, and that mob?" Keen asked with a gleam in his eye. "You're after the big Clipper. Is that it?"

"Yeah. We can use that ship—because a certain party is ready to pay us plenty for it with no questions asked. Our little gang deals in stuff like that, you know."

"That Russian job would carry quite a few bombs, eh, Devereaux?"

"More than enough for the people that want it."

"Your Macchi seaplanes—I suppose they're the ones that were hi-jacked on the way to Spain—wouldn't do for your client, eh?"

"They might—but we need those planes for our own work."

"Let's see now," said Keen. "If you pick up the Soviet Clipper near the Ambrose Lightship—"

"Wrong. We're picking her up off Smith's Island—that's in the lower end of Chesapeake Bay."

"Um…I see."

"Yeah, and there's a lot of queer places down along the North Carolina shore where we can hide her temporarily. In fact, we got a beaut of a place down there."

"It wouldn't be Ocracoke Island, would it?" smiled Keen.

"You bin down there, too, huh? Nice little hideout I call it. Them natives down there are so dumb they still think the country is owned by the British yet. We got 'em thinking we're a new outfit belongin' to the Coast Guard."

"Very interesting. And from there you'll head south quite a way—you'll go somewhere south of the Mosquito Gulf and then a certain freighter will pick up the plane."

"Sure. Them Japs—and now I've gone and told you who wants it—will pay real dough for that job. But let's quit gabbing and get down to business. We want your Black Bullet to help us nab that Russian boiler. That's where you come in. You're flying me down to somewhere near Smith's Island and then we'll take her over."

"You're wrong. I'm not turning that ship over to you. Now tell me where Barney is."

"He's on ice with a billy-bash on his noggin. I had to beat him up to make him behave."

"Where is he?"

"You worry about that. Now come on, where is that ship?"

"I'm sorry. You don't get it."

"All right. You asked for it. We'll see how long you can hold out. You'll come through—or you'll never walk out of this dump again."

"I doubt it," said Keen.

"Come on—down this way!" ordered the ex-actor. "There's a cozy little chamber down here that will give you a swell time."

FORCING KEEN to walk ahead of him, he shoved through the door that led to the cellar. At the bottom, a beam from a flashlight guided him toward a small door that led into a root cellar. Inside Devereaux set the flashlight on a low bench and its beam reflected off the whitewashed ceiling.

Then Keen realized that his captor was carrying something that looked like a gas-mask.

"There's a box over there—sit down on it. I picked this place just for the job. Now we'll see how long you can hold out."

And with that, Devereaux pulled on the gas mask, adjusted the nose piece, and glared through the large goggle lenses at his victim. Keen looked about. The door had been closed and he could see that Devereaux had tacked wide strips of weather-stripping around its edges. The root cellar was practically air-tight. On the opposite side were two musty windows cut into the solid stone foundation that were about chest high to anyone standing in the cellar.

"Now sit still, Keen," said Devereaux out of the side of his face mask, which he held open with one finger. "And when you're ready to talk, get up and nod your head. Understand?"

Keen did not answer. He was trying to figure out the man's game. Then suddenly he got it. Devereaux set the flashlight steady and walked across the room, still covering Keen with his gun. Then with a quick movement he took a large wrench from somewhere in his voluminous pockets and swung hard at a small gas bracket that protruded from the wall.

Devereaux intended to asphyxiate him!

Where was Barney? Could he hope for any help from him?

Already the fumes pouring from the broken bracket were nauseating. Devereaux, grinning behind his mask, now stood with one elbow leaning on the window sill. He was calmly contemplating his victim.

But Keen's mind was working fast. Breathing only when he found it absolutely necessary, he looked about and made a quick mental calculation of the size of the room and the amount of air it originally contained. Then he glanced up at the broken bracket and tried to figure the amount of gas that was pouring into the room. Already his head was reeling and his eyes were watering. But somehow he maintained his mental faculties.

He glanced up at Devereaux who was still leaning on the wide sill, his eyes gleaming and taunting. Keen knew he was waiting for him to surrender. Instead, he let himself sway giddily on the box that was his seat—then abruptly he toppled onto the floor.

Devereaux looked down at him, unable to make up his mind. And at that instant, Keen took his long wild chance.

With a quick motion, he rolled over, shielded his head in the crook of his left elbow, and reached in his pocket with his right hand. Then with a low prayer, he snatched out a cigarette lighter and pressed the lever!

BRR-R-R-OOM!

The roar was a thunderous one. And immediately after it a box-shaped billow of flame flashed off the ceiling, and two tremendous jets blew out the two windows. And the door also went out in the terrific blast.

Keen gasped as the concussion crossed the small of his back. And felt a sweep of heat as his hair was singed from the back of his head. His ears rang with the explosion, and he was half blinded. But he managed to crawl across the floor and throw himself into the main cellar.

Illuminating gas, being lighter than air, rises. And he had saved himself by lying on the floor.

Then someone came out of the blackness and lugged him to his feet. It was Barney, still covered with blood and still struggling with loose ends of bindings that fluttered from one elbow.

"Quick! Cut off that gas line, Barney," screamed Keen. Then he staggered to a crate, sat down, and stared inside at the jet of flame that still blossomed from the broken bracket.

"I certainly timed that one right," he said as an electric light went on over his head.

Beneath the broken window he could see the terribly mangled body of Justin Devereaux. The unscrupulous actor had taken the full force of the blast when it blew out the glass pane. All that was left of him was a mangled mess of clothing, rubber, and seared flesh.

Keen thanked his stars he was alive as he watched the spurting bracket flame slowly die down and finally go out with a low pop.

THE MICK came staggering back, still unable to comprehend what had happened. But he had brains enough to lift Keen, carry him upstairs, and lay him on a couch.

"Boy, you look funny," he gargled. "You won't need a haircut for a month. What happened?"

"Get me a drink and I'll tell you."

And while Barney poured out two stiff noggins of brandy, Keen related what had occurred.

"The louse!" spat the Irishman. "He nailed me when I caught him going through your stuff in the reception room. He finally knocked me out, and left me tied up here in the library. Then when he wasn't watching me, I crawled out, went down into the cellar, and hid in the hangar. I had just managed to slip out of the bindings when I heard that explosion."

"What's the time?"

"About 8 P.M. Why?"

"We're leaving in half an hour. Get that sky boiler ready downstairs, put what's left of Devereaux on a pontoon, and let me rest for about twenty minutes. Then we'll get going again."

"You're nuts to try anything in your condition."

"Don't argue, Barney. This is really serious. Go dab that noggin of yours with iodine, slap on a bandage, then see that we've got plenty of fuel. We're in for a night. On your way now!"

In twenty minutes, Keen staggered to his feet, and climbed into his Griffon kit. Barney came in with a bowl of hot gruel and another drink, and Keen gulped it all down and said: "Let's go!"

In the hangar, Keen noted that Barney had already followed his instructions regarding the actor's body. They were set to go, so he climbed in, started the motor, rolled her out carefully, and ran her down to the water. Barney quickly joined him after he had closed the rockery doors.

"We're on our way to Smith's Island. You remember Smith's Island—the place where we hid out one week-end. The Macchi tribe is holed up nearby at Ocracoke. They're going to nail the Russian Clipper somewhere in the lower end of Chesapeake Bay and then run her back there."

"But I still don't get the gag."

"It's simple. From Ocracoke they'll fly south, contact a Jap freighter, and turn her over. The Nipponese are going to give 'em a nice piece of jack for it."

"And now that bunch knows who the Griffon is—and where he hangs out," said Barney.

"Exactly! That's why we have to do this little job ourselves—to make certain it is done right!"

"Leave it to me," the Mick said, spitting on his hands.

The Black Bullet was already hurtling through the skies on her southern course.

"Let him go," growled Barney, referring to the gruesome bundle they carried. "We can't keep those floats down all night."

Keen nodded, quickly hoiked one wing up, and they sensed that the battered body of Justin Devereaux had taken its last curtain call. Well weighted, it would sink after hitting the water 3,000 feet below.

"Even so," spoke up the Mick, "I left one thing in his pocket."

"What?"

"A Griffon card."

"Where did you acquire the dramatic touch, O'Dare?"

"I get it from me grandmother," sarcastically cracked the Mick as he settled back for a long cold flight.

THEY WERE at 11,000 feet over Smith's Island at 10 o'clock, cruising at three-quarter throttle. It was cold. But both were alert.

They circled back and forth between Smith's Island and Point Lookout to make certain they would not miss the Clipper as it proceeded down the bay toward the mouth of the Potomac.

Barney hung over the radio recessed into the cockpit wall on his right. He swung the wave-length lever back and forth, tried to pick up something on the Clipper take-off.

"Here she comes," he boomed. "She's off at 2,000 heading for Cedar Point. They'll be along any minute now!"

"Any minute?" roared Keen. "Here's Pozzolo's bunch now."

Before Barney could rip off his earphones, three Macchi fighters dropped down out of nowhere. Flying in orderly array, they took up a position behind the Black Bullet—and waited.

Barney had his double Brownings out, but he held his fire. "They act dumb!" he called to Keen.

"Hold it—and act dumb, too, until they make a move. They think Devereaux's in charge here."

Then the weird four-ship formation started up the Bay, seeking the giant Clipper ship. And with the fighters behind them, Keen sensed his hackles standing up on the back of his neck, expecting any minute that a burst of heavy Breda-Safat fire would blast through his backbone.

"They're signalling with a lamp from the front bus," Barney yelled.

"Okay. They're looking for a password—give it to 'em!"

Barney, only too pleased to oblige, let drive with a torrent of fire that javelined into the turret nose of the Macchi dead behind them. Then he raised his dual muzzles a trifle and sped another burst across the windows of the pilot's cockpit.

There was a short splash of return fire, then the metal power-egg of the Macchi broke away from its dural tubing legs and started to roll along the top of the wing. That did the damage. A flash of flame leaped out from a wing tank and the craft blew apart.

With a yell, Barney swung his guns toward the Macchi on his left.

But a converging fire from the remaining Macchis was crossing a few feet ahead of the Black Bullet's nose and Keen had to yank her up hard. Barney poured a burst dead into the top of one Macchi while Keen climbed the Bullet.

Finally he flashed the sleek craft over into a half roll, then nosing down he set his steel beak on a floundering Macchi and pressed all his trigger bars.

The Black Bullet trembled with the recoil of six guns, and Keen kept her dead on his target until it seemed that he must slam right through the M.C. 77. But at the last second he pulled her out, executed a wing-over, and gave Barney another shot as they cartwheeled through a Niagara of lead from the Macchi that was still holding its own.

Barney again steadied himself, hosed a double stream of lead dead into the pirate plane's fuselage. And this time the flying boat faltered and swerved sharply into a flat spin.

"Hold her a minute!" the Mick bawled. "Give me another whack!"

Keen banked hard again, cut in fast. Then Barney drew a cruel bead on the flying boat, let her have half a box—and watched the port wing fold back and foul the tail assembly. Then she snapped her head hard, like a rowelled stallion, heeled over, and went down a tangled mass of smoking dural.

"That's enough!" yelled Keen. "Let me take the last one!"

"It's all yours!"

The Black Bullet swerved over, nosed down, and raced after the remaining Macchi. Keen caught the floundering bus in three minutes, came up under her with a scream of slipstream, and slammed a heavy burst of Darn gun fire deep into her greasy hull.

He held his trips down for seconds, then cleared as the pirate ship belched a plume of smoke, added a splintered design of yellow flame, then exploded with a dull yellow and blue death-fan of smoke.

They saw three helpless figures thrown clear, to plummet down through the night sky—figures that went all the way down without benefit of parachute and hit with foam-flecked thuds into the black sea.

Keen sped the Bullet away as the Macchi wreckage slammed into the sea and disappeared. And he found himself wheeling full into the course of the oncoming Martin super-Clipper.

Keen cut it close, waved an arm, swung wide of the Clipper's tail—and headed north with everything wide open.

TWO HOURS later, an excited Drury Lang was talking over the phone to a very calm and world-weary Kerry Keen.

"It was the same guy, Keen," he blurted out. *"They say he*

came out of nowhere again and shot three black flying boats down before they got anywhere near the Clipper."

"How nice!" returned Keen.

"Nice? It was perfect! And the Coast Guard found the body of one of those guys—that Eligio Pozzolo fellow."

"Dead?"

"I said the body, didn't I?" bawled Lang. *"And the Clipper just got in at Port Washington a few minutes ago. Now tell me—did you tip that Griffon Guy off?"*

"Me? Don't be silly. We've had troubles of our own."

"Whatta ya mean, 'troubles'?"

"I mean that 'Granny McShane' business. It seems Granny was a phoney—and now she's missing!"

"That woman you had up there—the old lady supposed to be O'Dare's grandmother?"

"Yes. You see, the real Granny McShane is still in an Irish workhouse. I got the full dope in that message you're going to pay me one hundred bucks for, Lang. I'll be down with it in the morning—so be sure to have those one hundred skins ready."

"But what the devil, Keen? What was she up to?"

"I don't know. Just burglary of some sort, I guess. I'll tell you all about it in the morning."

"Okay. And if we can do anything for you, don't be afraid to ask."

"I will—I'll ask for that century," laughed Keen, hanging up. "And we'll send it across the sea to the real Granny McShane, eh, Barney?"

"She'll only buy whisky with it," replied the Mick. "I know them McShanes."

"You didn't know *that* one," laughed Keen, reaching for the bottle which was clutched in O'Dare's horny fist. "But how would *you* know that the *Empress of Ireland* does not touch Queenstown? She takes the northern route and hits Belfast. That was what gave Granny McShane away."

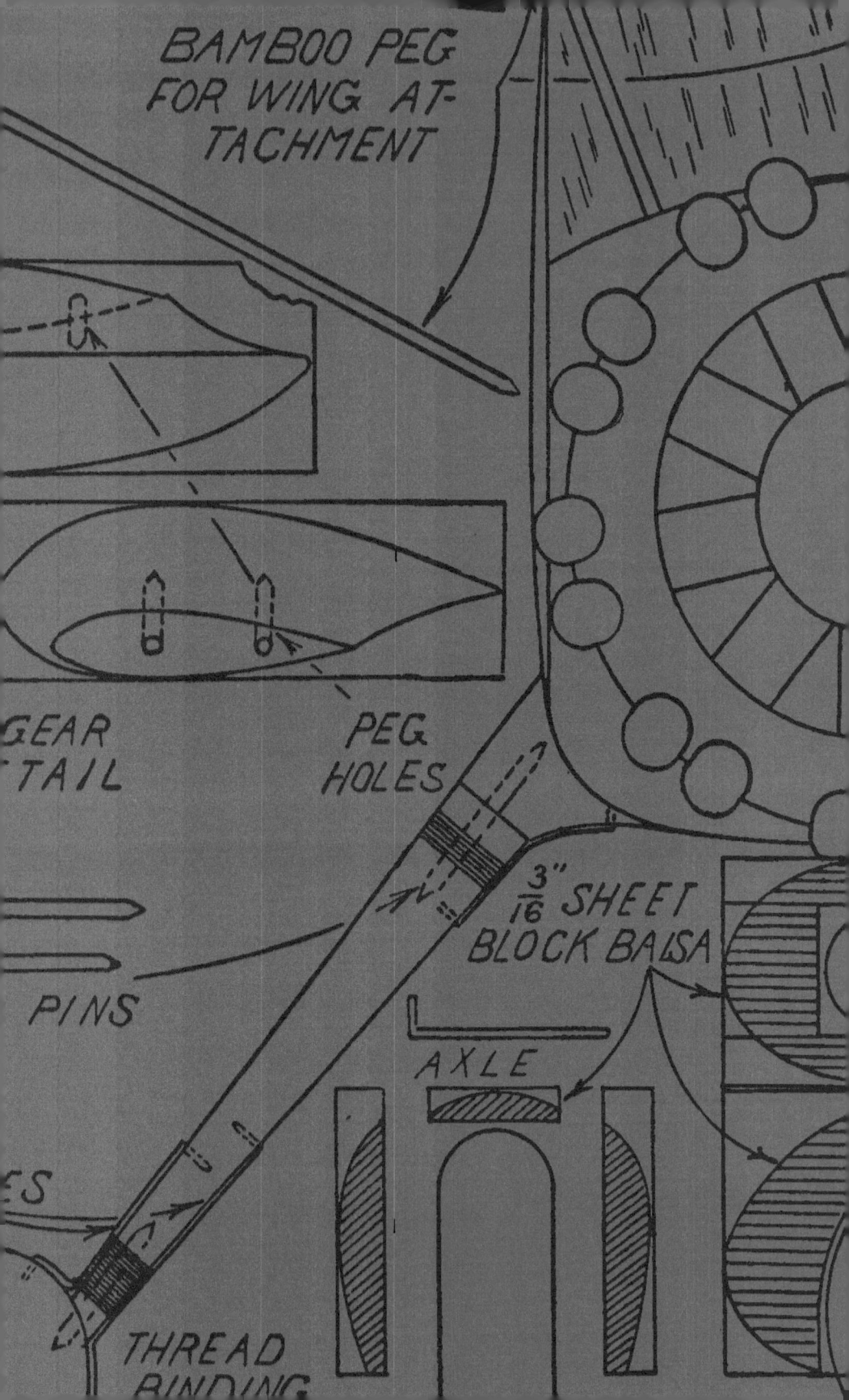

BAMBOO PEG
FOR WING AT-
TACHMENT

GEAR
TAIL

PEG
HOLES

PINS

$\frac{3"}{16}$ SHEET
BLOCK BALSA

AXLE

ES

THREAD
BINDING

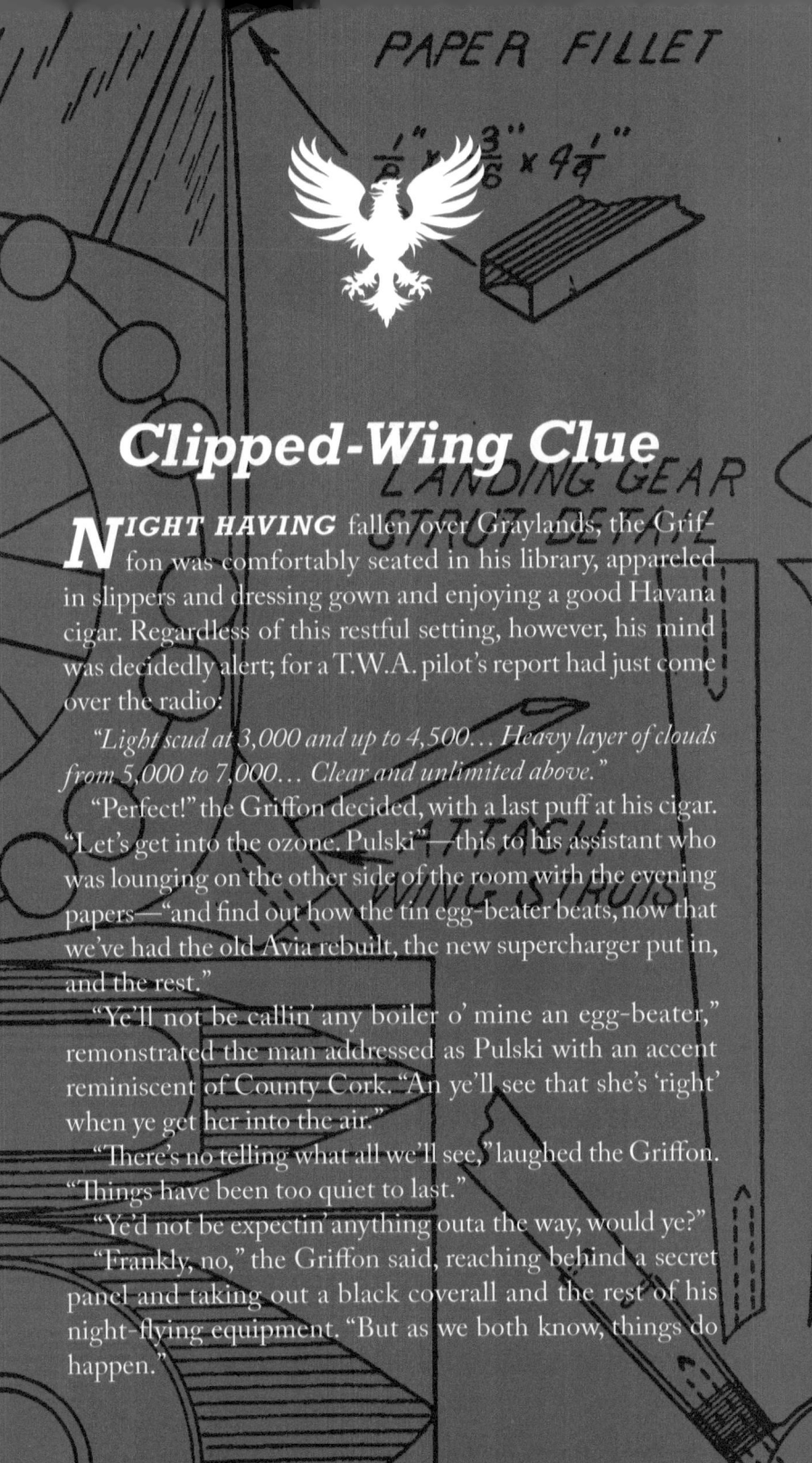

Clipped-Wing Clue

NIGHT HAVING fallen over Graylands, the Griffon was comfortably seated in his library, appareled in slippers and dressing gown and enjoying a good Havana cigar. Regardless of this restful setting, however, his mind was decidedly alert; for a T.W.A. pilot's report had just come over the radio:

"Light scud at 3,000 and up to 4,500… Heavy layer of clouds from 5,000 to 7,000… Clear and unlimited above."

"Perfect!" the Griffon decided, with a last puff at his cigar. "Let's get into the ozone. Pulski"—this to his assistant who was lounging on the other side of the room with the evening papers— "and find out how the tin egg-beater beats, now that we've had the old Avia rebuilt, the new supercharger put in, and the rest."

"Ye'll not be callin' any boiler o' mine an egg-beater," remonstrated the man addressed as Pulski with an accent reminiscent of County Cork. "An ye'll see that she's 'right' when ye get her into the air."

"There's no telling what all we'll see," laughed the Griffon. "Things have been too quiet to last."

"Ye'd not be expectin' anything outa the way, would ye?"

"Frankly, no," the Griffon said, reaching behind a secret panel and taking out a black coverall and the rest of his night-flying equipment. "But as we both know, things do happen."

"We ain't heard from old Lang in weeks," Pulski added.

"Another reason why anything can happen. The calm before the storm, you might say."

Then, with a last glance around the library, they snapped off the lights, walked into the corridor, and hurried down the stairs.

"Nothing doing," the Griffon warned his man as they passed the wine cellar. "Lay off that O'Doul's Dew until we get back. It's not that cold... upstairs."

With a guilty gesture, Pulski wagged his head and continued on into the Griffon's underground hangar.

Then with practiced skill they prepared the Black Bullet for action. The Griffon slipped into the front seat and tuned the Avia motor. Pulski stood nearby until he got the nod from the pilot, then snapped two more switches. One doused the lights, the other put into motion the great doors.

In three minutes, the Black Bullet had been run out into

Battered by the strange stub-winged craft and
hammered by the diving Seversky, the Black Bullet
was trapped—trapped in a leaden vise of death!

the shadows of a heavy grape arbor, whereupon the great doors were closed from the outside. To all outward appearances the hangar had assumed the innocent lines of a garden rockery.

With quick decisive moves Pulski then opened the folding wings of the Black Bullet while the Griffon snapped in the king-pins. The Avia, muffled by Skodas, purred like a contented tiger as it was run quietly across the turf of the sheltered lawn to the hard packed sands near the boathouse.

Then the Griffon let her run down into the water, drew a steel lever back three notches on a quadrant, and the pontoons assumed a normal water take-off position.

"All clear," Pulski muttered as he slipped into the back seat and drew up the sliding hatch.

In a hundred yards she was well clear and climbing fast toward the west. And soon they were above 4,000, racing through a strange, filmy drapery of scud that hung from the upper cloud bank like gossamer props of some fantastic stage setting. Indeed, for several minutes they swept through this fairy-like medium.

"Queer, eh?" the Griffon said reflectively.

"Yeah, queer. In fact, it gives me th' willies," said Pulski. "It looks like somethin' outa a banshee story me Granny McShane used to tell me."

"Not *the* Granny McShane?" taunted the Griffon.

Pulski emitted a queer bellows sound—something like the pathetic gasp of a punctured football bladder—and sat down.

But no sooner had Pulski relaxed when a chunk of dural slammed across the tandem cockpit and banged a jagged hole through the opposite side and scarcely five inches from his chest!

ANOTHER CRASH sounded somewhere behind, and Pulski turned like a mechanical doll and stared back. A great gap had been battered through the fuselage about two feet ahead of the main tail-section bracing.

Almost at the same instant, the Griffon hurled the Black

Bullet over on one wing-tip and drew the stick back to zoom the craft away.

"What was that?" he yelled.

"Look, over there!" cried Pulski. Then his hands automatically brought his guns into play and he sent a full salvo of .50 caliber stuff full at a strange, clipped-wing ship that had suddenly appeared.

But though his aim had seemingly been good, nothing happened!

"What the devil!" he roared, giving the strange plane another deluge of leaden hail.

"If you can't do anything with that," roared the Griffon, "hold tight and let me have a smack at him."

Pulski stood behind his guns and peered at the unique machine as it raced through the gossamer curtains of cloud film. It was a small projectile-like craft with wings hardly four feet in span apiece. From the windows of the well-streamlined cabin, flecks of flame spat out at them, indicating that these strange attackers had two high-caliber guns.

"What the deuce?" Pulski growled as he watched the Griffon wheel the Black Bullet around and poise for an attack dive.

"This *is* one for the book," the Griffon snarled. "It's smaller and racier than some of those trick jobs we saw at the National Air Races. Yet there seem to be two—maybe three—men in it."

And now the Griffon opened up with everything he had, and they could see four scarlet streaks battering toward the tiny ship.

But still nothing happened! There was something peculiar in the ship's motion that threw off their aim.

Amazed, the Griffon hoiked the Bullet up on its tail and screamed into a vertical zoom just as two explosions threw a double-yolk of flame at their tail, and chunks of shrapnel again crashed through the dural of their wings.

Pulski took his cue, leaned over the tail, and poured

another torrent of lead toward the upper portion of the tiny fuselage, and this time a few of his bullets struck the craft.

But just then two more shells bashed out with loud *B-R-R-OOMS*. To evade them, the Griffon swept over into a reverse turn, then stared down and tried to figure out what kind of enemy they had run into. The little clipped-wing fighter was now streaking along to the left, doing sharp turns to avoid the Black Bullet's fire.

"We didn't bring that O'Doul's Dew, did we?" Pulski asked over the Griffon's shoulder.

The Griffon was in the process of another dive. "No," he answered. "But somehow I wish we had."

Again the Black Bullet went down, and once more two double streams of fire poured toward the little ship. But now she slithered into another series of turns, stuck her nose up slightly as if in derision, then shot through a curtain of filmy cloud and disappeared into the heavy cloud bank above.

"What *is* this?" the Griffon muttered. Then he opened his eyes in stark amazement. "Look!" he said, pointing off to the right.

But hardly had Pulski noted the tiny scarlet parachute that had attracted the Griffon, when there was a blinding flash of light, a tremendous crash of concussion—and the Black Bullet was blown over on her back. The Griffon tried to right her, but another concussion and an earsplitting crash echoed out a short distance ahead. The Bullet went over again—right side up.

The next few minutes brought a bedlam of concussion and horror.

More scarlet parachutes came down, oscillated lazily, then blew to bits under the force of tremendous explosions. But the Griffon finally managed to get the Black Bullet's nose down into a full-power dive. Above him raged the deluge of dangling destruction as he eased out at about 1,500 feet and swung out to sea again.

A cold perspiration trickled down his temples and a

strange taut feeling constricted the muscles of his back. Gradually, however, his terror changed into a kind of tingling courage and he turned back and shot upstairs again. For he was unable to ignore the fascinating attraction of that danger above.

For about a quarter of an hour he cruised about, darting through layer after layer of cloud trying to find the answer to the mystery. But no tangible clue remained to explain the mystery. There was only the tangy stench of picric acid and the irritating smell of burned explosive.

"When you gonner get down out of here so I can get cleaned up?" a voice suddenly boomed over his shoulder.

The Griffon turned, stared into the bloody mug of his gunner.

"What's the matter? You hit?"

"No… don't think so. Just a bad nose-bleed, I guess, from the concussion. But what the devil was that, anyway?"

"You've got me. Some kids playing pranks with their gas models, I guess. No wonder the Washington boys have started to license them," laughed the Griffon.

"Yeah? You ain't kiddin' me. You're scared, too—an' you know it."

"Scared? This isn't even me talking."

And with that reflection, the Griffon put the beak of the Black Bullet down and didn't pull it up until she was a few hundred feet above the water.

Then he cut in the Skoda mufflers again, cruised about carefully and finally caught sight of two Coast Guard cutters racing at high speed on a north-east course.

"They're looking for the cause of all the bang-bang," smiled the Griffon, "we'll have to be careful."

Thereupon, he cut wide of the C.G. ships and raced for Graylands.

THE BLACK BULLET skipped the rollers for about twenty yards and finally settled down on her pontoons. The

Griffon glanced about in all directions, adjusted the angle of the pontoons for land movement, and ran up the beach.

Pulski was out in a flash, still dabbing at his gory face with a handkerchief. Then once they were in the shadows of the arbor, he drew back the folding wings and started to dart for the hidden switch that would set the Rock Garden mechanism working.

But he went sprawling on his face before he reached the base of the fake rockery.

"What the…?" he started to say. Then he turned swiftly from a kneeling position and hurled himself at the prostrate form of a man that lay on the grass. He reached for the fellow's throat and held him taut for a minute. But then he sensed that the man was offering no resistance. So, puzzled, but wary, he eased up and stared down into the man's face.

The man was cold—stone dead!

Pulski, his face white, dragged him clear, then went over and yanked the switch set under a flat rock. The great doors opened and the Black Bullet was eased inside.

The Griffon crawled out through the open hatchway "What's up?" he asked, sensing that something was wrong.

"You'd better come out here and take a look at this guy," Pulski said in a hollow voice.

The Griffon gave Pulski a strange look, then went back out on the lawn. Pulski pointed to the strange relaxed figure.

"Let's carry him inside. We can't do anything here," said the Griffon.

Together they lugged the body into the hangar. And under the lights they noted that the fellow wore a flying helmet, a face mask, and rubber cushioned goggles of strange manufacture.

"Whew! What is it? Something out of Buck Rogers?" cracked the Griffon, observing both the man's fine build and queer mask.

Pulski now turned the body on its face and disclosed a strange piece of equipment set in a light canvas harness. It

"I used to know a guy named Ginsberg," parried Keen.

"Never mind that line. This Griffon fellow undoubtedly knows *something* about this mess. He certainly knew that Clipper was coming through as a chunk of bait—and outside of me and Scott here, you were the only one who did know about it. You must have tipped the Griffon off!"

"And the Griffon plays Robin Hood. He appears over the Ambrose Lightship, saves the Clipper from destruction by shooting down a number of mystery ships, then tows the disabled Clipper to the Lightship and disappears again," prattled on Keen. "That's good stuff, Lang. You ought to be writing movie serials. I've seen worse."

"Yeah? Well, how did you know the Griffon towed the Clipper to Ambrose Light?" barked Lang getting to his feet.

"I can read the papers."

"What papers? That ain't in any papers."

"No? Well, you said something about it last night, didn't you?"

"No! I said there were *reports* that he did. I didn't say that it actually happened." Then Lang turned. "This guy knows more about it than he'll admit Scott," he bellowed, working himself into a fury.

"It so happens, Keen," said Scott in a low tone, "that the Griffon *did* tow the disabled Clipper toward the Lightship, then let her drift again when the lightship sent out aid."

"Well, I must have gathered that much from what Lang said last night," pressed Keen.

"So you were entertaining that Mick's grandmother, eh?" sneered Lang over his shoulder as he paced up and down the room. "I wish I was sure of that."

"You could call up and ask Barney—or Granny McShane herself."

"I think I will. What's your number out there? I forget it."

Keen gave him the number of his library phone. Lang called it, and for three minutes he sat holding the instru-

seemed to be carried over the shoulders like a small rucksack and its main parts were long slender cylinders about two inches in diameter and approximately ten inches long. The Griffon snapped the small flaps up and pointed to two metal tubes that led from the cylinders to a kind of valve device attached to the strange helmet. Plainly, this was some sort of an oxygen mask of unusual design.

The coverall was made from some gray-green material of particularly fine texture. The man's pockets were empty and no marks of identification were to be found anywhere on the outside of the suit.

"Take that stuff off him," ordered the Griffon, starting to get out of his own flying kit. "Let's have a real look at him."

"We'd better fill him full of flat-irons and dump him out there in the ocean," moaned the perplexed Pulski.

"Don't worry. I will—after I find out what this is all about."

For fifteen minutes the Griffon and his homely assistant went over the corpse. They noted that the man's face was distorted, as if by some fear or pain. But there was no indication of any physical violence whatsoever.

"If he had been thrown out of a plane," the Griffon muttered, "he would be quite battered. But there isn't a bruise on him."

"Okay, then how did he get here? Walk on the water?" queried Pulski.

The Griffon simply went on with his examination. The man was about thirty and appeared to be a military type. He had a wind-burned face, a small neatly clipped mustache, fine teeth, and a healed scar over his left eye. His clothing was well-pressed and expensive, but there were no labels on it of any kind.

"What are you planning on doing with him?" demanded Pulski.

"Leave him down here for tonight and see what happens by tomorrow."

"You're taking an awful chance."

"I know it. But first we must try to find out who he is, where he came from and what he was doing here."

So they deposited the body in a corner, covered it with a piece of burlap, and snapped off the lights. Then they went upstairs.

"Well, Mr. O'Dare," smiled the Griffon, addressing his man by his correct name, "what do you make of it all?"

"You've got me, Mister Keen," answered O'Dare getting the situation back to normalcy again. "But I'll bet a buck Mister Drury Lang will soon be asking us a lot of questions."

HARDLY HAD he spoken when the telephone bell tinkled. Kerry Keen lifted the receiver languidly and breathed an easy "Hello."

"Hello, my eye!" snarled a voice from the other said. *"How long do I have to sit here and wait for you to report?"*

"Sure, an' it's Lang," said the O'Dare, his eyes on the ceiling. "Whenever the phone begins to rattle I know—"

"Shut up," ordered Keen. "No, not you, Lang—I'm just trying to quiet the Mick here. But what's up?"

"That's what I want to know!"

"Then we both might as well hang up, eh?"

"Now don't get wise. Tell me what the devil that battle is that's been going on up your way. They got half the Army out here," Drury Lang bellowed over the wire.

"Good practice for 'em. But what are you talking about, anyway?"

"That young war up your way. We've heard it all the way down here in the city. The radio stations are swamped with inquiries, and the Coast Guard is chasing all over the Bay."

"But I don't understand," argued Keen, putting a strained catch in his voice.

"Do you mean to tell me you haven't heard the racket that's been going on up there for the past hour or so?" Lang squealed. *"Why it sounded like a tall night in Barcelona. Something must have been bombed somewhere up that way."*

"I've been reading," said Keen lamely. "Have you heard anything out of the way, Barney?"

The Mick looked at him surprised, then answered in a low tone: "Are you nuts?"

"No, Barney hasn't heard a thing, either," Keen continued into the phone. "He's starting to learn to read. He's just got hold of a copy of *Black Beauty*, and there's no chance of shaking him away from it."

"Okay, wise guy. You heard it all right. And you probably know what it's all about, too. What's more, you'll hook yourself one of these days," growled Lang.

"Now we're getting somewhere. You're in a threatening attitude, and I feel better now, Lang," laughed Keen. "So let's have your story."

Lang was silent for a minute. Then he burst out with: *"Do you know Booth Talbot?"*

"Booth Talbot, the engineering chap? Out at Melville? Yes, I know him. As a matter of fact—"

—*"As a matter of fact, you were consulted by him on a ballistics problem a short time ago,"* broke in Lang.

"Right! What's up? Some one swipe the thing?"

"Not yet. But they've made two tries, and Booth Talbot called us up to see what we can do about it."

"And so you called me to see what I know. Well, you have certainly drawn a blank this time. I tell you, I have been teaching the Mick to read."

"Stop it! Stop it! That mug can read, and you know it. He can read labels on whisky bottles a block off. Anyhow, there's something screwy going on up there at Melville and I'd like you to go down there in the morning and see what you can make of it."

"And suppose I don't feel like it?"

"You'd better. If you don't I'm going to make an inquiry into why you've been in such close touch with a Swiss armament firm. Yeah. Maybe you'll tell me just what the devil you want with parts for an Oerlikon gun, Keen?"

"Oh, I use them for den decorations. I'm collecting things

like that. You know me—Kerry Keen, young man about town, expert in ballistics, and 1937 champion at tossing the—"

"At tossing the bull," Lang interrupted. *"But,"* he bawled, *"you'll go up to Melville tomorrow, or I'll know the reason why. And another matter we might inquire into are those Dutch cheeses delivered to you a day or so ago. What are you doing? Going into the sandwich business?"*

"We got them for mice bait," answered Keen. Then he suppressed a laugh—for he had imported them purely because he liked Dutch cheese.

Lang was quite incensed now. *"Are you going up to Melville tomorrow, or not?"* he snorted.

"I might—now that I think of it. I'm interested in that business—from a public spirited point of view, of course."

"Don't make me laugh. You public spirited—and buying Dutch cheeses! Why don't you buy good American cheese, if you must have cheese? Public spirited my eye! You won't do anything unless there's a bunch of money in it," stormed Lang.

"Ah, yes," said Keen. "That reminds me—just how much is there in this Talbot gun business if I uncover something?"

"Dear old public spirited Mister Keen," taunted Lang. *"There's nothing in it for anyone. But Lord help you if anything happens to that business up there. If that mobile anti-aircraft unit is damaged or pinched, Mister Keen, you're gonner wind up eating bread and water with that cheese of yours—in a Leavenworth cell."*

"Good heavens!" Keen replied. "You are in a flutter, Mr. Lang. You'd better go to bed and sleep it off before you have a complete collapse. I'll drop in tomorrow and take your pulse, eh? Nighty-night!"

"You'd better drop into the Talbot Engineering test ground tomorrow first, though," barked the Secret Service man as Keen hung up.

Barney was moaning. "He's slowly catching up on us, ain't he?"

"He gets an idea now and then," admitted Keen.

OUTSIDE THEY could hear the tell-tale drone of aircraft engines as Naval, Coast Guard, and Army planes hummed over in a search patrol. It was evident that what Lang had said was the reason for their activity. The explosions of the parachute aerial mines had been heard for miles. And now the radio was giving out a mad cacophony of wild rumors.

Barney, still showing the effects of his concussion shock, went to bed predicting a dire end for the two of them. Keen packed a heavy briar, put a match to it, then hoisted his feet up on a table and let himself simmer off into a dark blue relapse of reflection.

But nothing he thought of clicked or fitted into position, so he finally decided to follow Barney's example and go to bed. He set the library in order—then abruptly stiffened as he sensed a door being opened somewhere. He listened for a minute, then got a gun from a desk drawer and went out into the corridor. There he snapped on a light.

Puzzled, he searched about. Then he found that the front door was open, bringing in a slight breeze that ruffled the tails of two coats that hung on a rack near a long pier mirror.

He walked quickly to the door, looked out across the wide lawn and satisfied himself that it had probably been left open carelessly by the Mick. He closed it, snapped the lock, then went back to the library and put the gun away.

"So some one's trying to swipe Talbot's new mobile anti-aircraft unit?" he said, resuming his reflections. "Well, you can't blame them. It seems to be the kind of thing they have all been looking for. But how the deuce could a spy expect to get away with a big piece of apparatus like that? He couldn't drive it through the streets. In fact, I don't see how he could get it through those concrete walls that surround the Talbot test field in the first place."

And with those problems to ponder on, he hied himself off to bed, determined, in spite of Lang's threats, to go and see for himself next day.

THE MORNING came and with it a sunshine-bathed world mellowed by the blue of the ocean which lapped the lawn beach of Graylands. Silver dew flashed from the lance points of the grass, and a soft, caressing breeze flapped at the chintz curtains of Kerry Keen's room.

He awoke, stretched, and grinned up into the sour-puss mug of Barney O'Dare who stood at his bedside with a broad tray of breakfast.

"Shove it on the table, Barney. I'll have a quick shower to get the cobwebs out of my brain and prepare for a great day."

"Begorrah, an' it will be a great day if you don't get that guy out of here," the Mick moaned.

"What guy?... Oh, you mean Buck Rogers downstairs. Don't worry, we'll take care of him. Stick a stamp on him and mail him to some worthy medical school. That's an idea, eh, Barney?" laughed Keen diving for his bath.

"I don't see anything funny about it," O'Dare muttered. "You getter get him out of here. When ya gonna do it?"

"First thing this evening when we go looking for that flying projectile with the stub wings that we ran into last night."

"Do you mean to say you're gonner take a chance like that again tonight—with the sky full of Air Service guys all looking for something to shoot at?" boomed Barney. "Anyhow, I don't like it! I got a feelin' in me bones that something is all wrong."

"Go get yourself a drink. You're not yourself. In fact, when we get this mess cleaned up, we'll barge off on a vacation—and just sit for a while."

"Thot's an idea," agreed the mournful Mick.

Keen, tingling after his brisk toweling, slipped on a light robe and dropped into a chair before the gleaming breakfast tray. He poured himself a cup of coffee, selected a golden slab of toast, and sat back to plan his day.

But he had hardly finished his first cup of coffee when he heard the pounding footsteps of the Mick. Keen twisted in his chair, a sudden fear gripping him. Like a tidewater flood, the memory of the open door of the night before made his body tingle.

Barney barged into the room breathless.

"He's gone!" was all he could gasp.

"Who?... What?" Keen said, gripping the arms of the chair.

"That guy downstairs—the dead guy!" the Mick answered, practically whispering.

"You're crazy!" the young ballistics expert said. "He was dead!"

Nevertheless, Keen slipped his feet into his slippers and hurried down the stairs, throwing inspective glances about as he made for the hidden hangar.

"We certainly put our chins out for this one," moaned Barney.

"Shut up. The man was dead. He couldn't walk away."

"No? Well, perhaps he went on roller skates."

Keen ignored the statement. "Were all these doors closed when you came down?" he asked.

"Sure, and they was. Everything was ship-shape—but even so, the ghost walked!"

Once in the hangar, Keen walked over to the corner where the body had been rolled. The piece of burlap was there in a partial bundle—but there was no trace of the man. The coverall lay on the floor near by where it had been left. Otherwise the hangar was just as they had left it.

Keen stared about unable to fathom this new mystery. "Are you sure we left him in here?" he said finally, clutching at a last hope. "We didn't take him into the cellar, did we?"

"No. We left him here—took off his coverall and then dragged him over here. Look, there's the marks through the dust and oil."

There was no argument to that. "But did you go outside last night before you went to bed?" Keen suddenly asked.

"No. But why?"

"Oh, nothing. Only when I went upstairs, the front door was open."

"Wow!" boomed Barney. "What are we waiting for? If we move fast, we can get out and make Canada by tonight."

"What for?"

"Well, we're not going to sit here and wait for them to come and slap a big butterfly net down on us, are we? How long do you think it will take that guy to get to the authorities and spill the Griffon goulash?" demanded Barney.

"Why that man was dead! You saw that yourself."

"Sure he was dead—but he ain't here now. Some one must have come and got him."

"Wait a minute. That doesn't sound reasonable. If the man was dead, why would anyone take a wild chance like that? We searched him carefully. There was nothing on him to give him or anyone else away."

"Then the guy *wasn't* dead!" Barney said with a hollow tone.

"He couldn't have been," agreed Keen with a mystified grimace.

THEY WENT back upstairs to Keen's room where Barney poured himself a cup of coffee, spiked it with a stiff shot of cognac, and drank it off at a gulp.

Keen sat pondering on the situation for some time. Finally he got up and said: "I'm going to look for that guy. You stay tight—and I don't mean 'get' tight—here. And give this place a thorough inspection. That guy planted himself on us in some way, using the 'death' gag to get inside. Above all, go over that ship downstairs and make sure he didn't slip one over. He broke in here for some reason, you know."

"But where are you going?"

"To the Talbot place. I'm going to see if there's any connection."

Barney winced. "And leave me here to get picked up, eh?" Then he shrugged his shoulders disconsolately. "Well, drop around now and then and bring me a pack of cigarettes, will you?"

"Take it easy. There's nothing much to worry about—yet."

"Not *much*—only a dead guy who gets up and walks out on us!"

Keen dressed for the Talbot visit carefully and with silent reflection. He put on a neat worsted suit, a gay necktie, and a lightweight felt hat. He was not quite sure he'd be back—for anything might happen. But he hoped.

Barney had the Dusenberg ready when he got downstairs, and without further reference to the events of the night before, Keen slipped behind the wheel, let in the clutch, and crunched down the curved driveway. He whistled quietly to himself as he let in the high gear and whisked into the main road for Amagansett. From there on the Dusenberg hummed at an even sixty through Southampton, Hampton Bays, and Riverhead. Shortly thereafter, he was being passed through the heavy metal gates of the Talbot Manufacturing Company's experimental grounds.

He found Booth Talbot in his office, amid a maze of drafting boards, blueprints, and wooden patterns. He was greeted with sincere enthusiasm, and it was not for some time that Keen sensed the tense spirit that pervaded the place.

Booth Talbot was a tall, stoop-shouldered man of indeterminate age. He had a youthful but somewhat weary face, a mop of healthy hair, and deep-set eyes.

"What's up?" asked Keen when they were alone.

"What's up?" echoed Talbot. "I—I'm not quite sure. But I'm worried in a way. Why, have you heard about it?"

"Yes. This chap Lang, the Secret Service bloke, says you're worried about some one trying to swipe the business."

"Well, I called on Lang because the Government has practically taken the thing, and I don't want anything to slip up now. Various strange things have happened. That sky mess that occurred last night may have had some bearing on this case. And now come along. I want to show you something."

Talbot led the way through two small offices and into a well-lighted shop. In the center of the floor stood something that looked like a cross between a modern tank and a mobile anti-aircraft truck. It had a six-wheel tractor drive, with the front wheels fitted to perform the functions of steering. On each side were two long metal legs that could be swung out on pivots and planted down on the ground to provide a suitable base for the gun carriage. Above the two arms were stream-lined boxes from which portable microphonic devices could be carried for a certain distance from the main section of the truck.

Keen had had these latter units explained to him before. They were important parts of the range-finding equipment which enabled the operators to get a triangulation check on the target. Their findings were automatically transferred over an electric cable to the master range-finder in the armored portion of the car.

Nothing quite like this had been devised before, and Keen had recognized early that Talbot had a weapon far ahead of anything of its kind. He had seen it in action against test craft, and had watched the automatic rangefinder select a shell, set the nose fuse and aim the gun. Radio checks from the planes flying above had assured Talbot and the Government men who had observed it in action that these range-finders were startlingly accurate.

"This is what worries us," Talbot went on to explain when they were out of earshot of the mechanics nearby. "Notice at the upper corners of the gun turret sides—those two holes about two inches in diameter."

Keen looked carefully and nodded.

"Well, they worry us. They do not belong there, and no one seems to know how they got there."

"You mean some one drilled them in?" asked Keen, puzzled.

"Absolutely. And, as I say, they do not belong there, because the gun turret is supposed to be gas-proof."

"But outside of that, these holes do not damage the turret to any extent?"

"No, not in the least. That's what we can't make out."

"Um," mused Keen. "And now when are you continuing your tests?"

"Tonight. We want to see how it works out under night conditions. We also hope to simulate active service conditions with a smoke screen on the ground."

"I get it. And now when do you plan to commence operations?"

"I'd say about 11 o'clock."

"Do me a favor and make it exactly 11 o'clock, will you?" asked Keen in a toneless voice. "I might be around to see what happens."

"All right. And by the way, just what do you make out of that aerial torpedo business last night?"

"Well, between you and me, I do think you're the cause of it all," Keen said without taking his eyes off the gun device.

Talbot let out a low whistle: "You mean they were after this device of mine?"

"You can't tell. If I were you, I'd have some real ammunition handy—high explosive stuff suitable for long range work. Yes, you can't tell. You might get a chance to use this gadget of yours."

"I don't quite understand," Talbot said, his eyes drawn to slits. "What do you *really* know about all this business, Keen?"

"I only wish I knew half as much as Lang thinks I do," said Keen in a tone that gave Talbot the impression he was talking to himself.

"But what was that bombing business?"

"I don't know," Keen replied in a studied monotone.

A FEW mechanics now came up to the mobile anti-aircraft unit and began work on several adjustments, whereupon Talbot drew Keen away, saying: "Let's go back to the office. I want to talk to you about tonight. You've got something up your sleeve."

Keen smiled, wagged his head, and followed the inventor. His mind was a chaos of clashing ideas.

He was just following Talbot into the engineering office when a door opened on the other side and a man came through, striding with an aggressive tread, looking neither right nor left. He was fairly tall and good-looking. Neatly dressed, he carried himself with the air of a man who knew what he was doing.

But Keen saw none of this. He saw only the man's face—and that was enough!

With a quick move he slipped past Talbot and took cover behind the wall.

"What's up?" Talbot asked, some what startled.

"That man—going through the other office. Who is he?" Keen asked in a whimper. "No—don't call him. Just tell me who he is."

"That fellow who just passed through? Why, that's Stor-row—Eric Storrow, our pilot," Talbot explained. "Why? What's up?"

"Well," answered Keen, "I'd like you to take me inside your office and tell me more about him. I seem to have—to have seen him somewhere before."

Once they were seated beside Talbot's desk, the inventor quickly drew out a drawer and produced a bottle and a tumbler.

"Here," he said, "you'd better have a drink. You look like a man who has seen a ghost."

"Maybe I have," said Keen. And he had to force his smile as he poured himself a drink—for not twelve hours before Eric Storrow had been lying "dead" in his secret hangar.

"Storrow," went on Talbot, "is the man who has been flying a Seversky P-35 for us during the tests of my device. We got permission from the Army to use a P-35 to simulate modern maneuvers of an enemy plane in the air. It has speed and ceiling, and carries a two-way radio. Thus it fits our require-ments to a 'T'."

"I see," nodded Keen. "But who is this fellow?"

"He came to us through a contact we made with Colonel Tudorn, late of the Ordnance Department. I have an idea he's some relation to the Colonel."

"Colonel Tudorn? Why, I didn't know he was in the United States," answered Keen. "Wasn't he transferred to one of the Pacific outposts?"

"Colonel Tudorn? Why no. I met him some time ago in New York. I was conferring with him on the gun. Under cover stuff, you know."

"I should say it was," snapped Keen. "I think you've been sucked into something. And I'll bet you all the silkworms in Japan that Colonel Tudorn isn't within 3,000 miles of New York. I'm certain he was transferred for a two-year stretch out in the Philippines, or somewhere like that."

"My heavens! Then who the devil was it I was talking to?"

"I don't know. But you certainly ought to check it up. How did you contact this 'Colonel Tudorn'?"

"He contacted me. I got the impression he was under War Department orders. Anyhow, I never questioned the matter when he showed me his credentials."

"Has he ever been here when you staged any official tests?"

"No. He said he was the man behind the scenes for the Government. I just presumed he knew what he was doing and let it go at that."

"And he suggested this Eric Storrow?

"Yes. And Storrow's a good man, too. Knows what it's all about and has made several worthy suggestions."

"Does he know anything about the gun and the range-finding mechanism?"

"No. That is, he's never been informed of the triangulation system we use. Remember, he's just a pilot who flies that plane for us in these experiments."

"Well, keep him that way. And don't say anything to him until I give you the word. In the meantime, if it's Okay with you, I'll check this 'Colonel Tudorn.' He certainly is a phoney.

And I'll buzz off now. Meanwhile, you go out and keep Storrow out of the way while I'm driving out. I don't want him to see me here."

"You're acting awfully queer about all this, you know, Keen."

"Queer? Doesn't this whole thing seem queer to you? You fall for a Colonel Tudorn who isn't even in this country, you hire a pilot you know nothing about, and some one goes and drills holes in your gas-proof baby-carriage—and you think *I'm* acting queer!"

As Talbot wagged his head confusedly, Keen got up, reached for his walking stick, and gave Talbot a knowing glance. "Anyhow, you'll stage this night test as near 11 o'clock as you can, eh?"

"Just as you say. I'll go out and give Storrow his orders now. And will you be here tonight?"

"I might. But don't forget to have that live ammunition handy—just in case."

"We've plenty. But I don't see—"

"Neither do I—yet. But a lot of things can happen between now and midnight. In any event. I'd like to see that thing ready for real action. Understand?"

Talbot didn't. But he nodded just the same.

KERRY KEEN burned up the roads between Melville and New York City once he got into the clear. He made straight for the Battery, then took a ferry across to Governors Island and hurried into the office of the Corps Area Intelligence Officer.

Major Montrose gave him a warm welcome. And in twenty minutes Keen had satisfied himself that Colonel Albert Tudorn definitely was in the Philippines and had been there for the past two years. The information he was then able to give Major Montrose was enough to set the military dragnet for the man who was masquerading as Colonel Tudorn.

Keen was thanked and offered the assistance of the Intelligence Department should he feel the situation required it.

"I'll let you know in the morning," smiled the young ballistics expert. "The old gentleman may pull in too long a length of rope and save us all a lot of trouble."

Keen left with a grin. But he was still worried. Events were moving a trifle too fast for him now, and he sensed that he would have to step fast to keep up with them.

He hurried uptown, sauntered into Lang's office, and found that worthy in close conference with John Scott, district head of the F.B.I. Lang greeted him with his usual sneer and pointed to a disreputable club chair.

Keen sat down and took one of Scott's cigars from a desk humidor before he spoke.

"Well," he opened, "I've been up to Talbot's place."

"So?" Lang queried with another sniff.

"Well," came the reply, "some one's going to swipe that thing—unless they screw it down."

"Yeah? If they do, you'd better head for parts north—very north."

"Don't worry, I will," laughed Keen.

"What's the answer?"

"They have a lad there named Storrow—Eric Storrow—who might be the Ethiopian in the kindling. Anyhow, I don't like him."

Both Lang and Scott exchanged glances.

"No?" prodded Lang, "What's wrong with him?"

"He doesn't tick right. He got in there on the say-so of some phony who claimed to be a colonel in the Ordnance Department who actually is in the Philippines."

"Whew!" Scott broke in. "What are we waiting for? Why not pinch Storrow now before he does any damage?"

Keen laughed: "Just like a copper," he said. "Pinch him—and what have you got? Just a phony pilot!"

"Pilot?"

"Sure. He's flying the plane on which they make their experimental rangefinding tests. But you'd better not pinch him, yet."

"Why not—before he swipes the anti-aircraft thing?"

"Swipe it? How can he? He can't get it out of the place unless he can throw it over a concrete wall ten feet high. I don't see how—" But Keen suddenly stopped as a new idea crashed into his mind.

"Go on. Keep talking, Keen," Lang said with a curled lip.

"No, don't pinch him. Let's see what he tries to do. Maybe we can catch him red-handed," Keen said. But his thoughts were now wandering—wandering to those holes drilled in the turret of the anti-aircraft unit.

"Wait until he swipes it—and then try to get it back, eh? That's a smart idea," Lang growled sarcastically. "But, Keen, you just hesitated—meaning some idea has 'struck' you. And I'd give five bucks to know what you're thinking about."

"So would Mr. Storrow."

"But what are you going to do about it?" pressed Lang. "Talbot just called up. He's just about nuts now. You sure left him dangling in the air. And they're testing again tonight."

"Yes. You'd better be there, too. You might see some fun."

"Something like last night, eh?"

"Even better, I figure. But leave Mr. Storrow alone until I tell you to clip him," said Keen rising to go.

"Oh, so *you're* telling us what to do now?"

"You don't want anything to happen to that anti-aircraft unit, do you?"

"No. But if anything does, you and that Mick of yours will go into the jug—and it won't be no cream jug," Lang spluttered. "Besides, we might continue our little investigation on your cheese importations. You haven't talked yourself out of that one yet."

"Oh, we use it for axle grease, make glue out of it, spread it on—"

"Yeah, and you sure spread it on thick!" growled Lang. But Keen had already gone out of the door.

EFFICIENCY—STARK EFFICIENCY—WAS reflected in that cabin, which was built of glass, gleaming dural, and polished wood. Banks of dials were fitted into the V-shaped depression at one end, and the floor was neatly covered with gray battleship linoleum.

At the aft end, a polished wood table had been let down from a section of the dural wall and four men sat at light-weight swivel chairs that swung out from the lower portion of the wall. Slightly forward, a man stood at a large hand-spoked wheel, his eyes glued to three small dials mounted on a hinged panel.

A low tremor of even vibration purred through the structure, and the man at the wheel cast glances across the cabin at intervals at another man who stood before a gleaming binnacle.

Through the wide windows, nothing but a steely-blue haze could be seen, except when the moon broke through and cast a tell-tale shadow of long, pointed proportions.

Colonel Anton Tubuloff, wearing semi-dress uniform, decorations, and a Death Head Hussars tunic, sat in a hunched position at the far end of the table. A giant of a man, he appeared to have no eyebrows or eyelashes and there was a bluish-red rim to the edges of his eyelids. Still, he was a distinguished figure for all that, and the other three sat in rapt attention and listened carefully to everything that he said.

"So far," Tubuloff went on, after giving the bank of instruments a quick glance, "everything is working out splendidly."

"Then Storrow was able to fool this devil Keen?" asked Hans Berger, who wore the blue jacket of a German Naval commander. He was a small, chunky man who made strange nervous gestures at the end of every sentence. Beady-eyed and shifty, he provided a marked contrast to Tubuloff.

"He got down safely, as Janckert reported, from the lowered observation car."

"Yes, Keen must have found him when he landed after firing on Janckert and Wolff in the car," added the extremely thin Kolbein, who wore a captain's insignia braid on the sleeve.

"That was it. Somehow those swine escaped the air-mine barrage we put down and then found Storrow. As you know, Storrow had a small charge of—well, of that stuff we all carry in our special masks for use in case we make a mistake. It was well diluted, of course, and only gave him the appearance of death."

"*Gott!* That Storrow is a brave one!" the bland-faced Nils Blaut added as Tubuloff glanced up at the dials again. "That required more courage than anyone aboard this ship has."

"You speak for yourself, Blaut," snarled Tubuloff over his shoulder. "We shall see, some day, perhaps. Yes, an emergency may arise when we shall see who has—and who hasn't—the bravery to sniff from the small tanks in our stratosphere helmets."

Blaut closed his eyes and drew a set of heavy fingers across the lower part of his face. "Then he got inside?" he inquired.

"His plan worked beautifully! They picked him up—and he came to in a section of the cellar and found the plane there—with wings folded."

"Why didn't he betray this man Keen?" demanded Blaut suddenly. "There are police officials in New York who would give plenty to know that man's secrets."

"Don't be a fool, Blaut!" snapped Tubuloff. "There's no necessity to betray him—yet. Of course Storrow knew that Keen had to be checked. But he had no idea how to do it. His plan of getting inside—and getting out again—was the safest. If he gave Keen away, he would have to explain *how* he came to be there and *why* he happened to be suspicious of the man who had been called in to protect the Talbot anti-aircraft gun. That would have been very unpleasant. And besides, Storrow has his own methods of working. In any case, I—Tubuloff—rely on him explicitly."

"You have all this straight?" asked Berger with anxious eyes.

"Perfect! Here's the message he sent to us an hour ago when he went aloft to check his plane for tonight's flight," answered Tubuloff with a gruff gesture as he shoved a thin sheet of paper across the table. "Here it is just as it was decoded."

The other three read it and appeared satisfied.

"Then they begin at 11 o'clock, eh?" said Kolbein.

"Exactly, and you had better check the equipment again, Blaut, and see that the winch is working correctly, and that the hoist gear and prong tackle is correct with the original measurements. Nothing must go wrong this time, or—or, there's nothing left for us but to turn that little valve in the back of our stratosphere helmets. We have failed twice now—and this is the third and *last* time."

"And you are sure this fool Keen has been taken care of?"

"So Storrow says, and he should know. He has been in the man's secret hangar—and I wouldn't like to fly any ship on which Storrow had put unfriendly hands," snapped Tubuloff.

"I'd feel better if he had made certain of Keen himself," muttered Kolbein with a glance at Blaut. "That man has too many lives for us. Storrow should have finished him off. He could have done so if he really went into Keen's house."

"Do you doubt Storrow?" screamed Tubuloff rising to his feet. "Do you question the loyalty of one member of this crew. *Gott!* But I will report you when we return!"

Kolbein paled and looked to Blaut to back him up. But the blandfaced one figured he had troubles of his own.

"I do not doubt the man's loyalty," protested Kolbein. "But I do question his ability to plan clearly. He has made our position insecure. All we had to do, you say, was to go down to a prearranged altitude, lower our observation car and the hoisting tackle, then Janckert slides down the fifty feet of cable and adjusts the four hooks in the drilled holes. Then the Talbot device is hoisted clear, taken aloft, and placed inside our main hold. Well, I say that all that is too much—too much to hope for."

"It has worked four times already, hasn't it?" sneered Tubuloff. "We picked up that British amphibian tank during the Cotswold maneuvers, we stole the new French cold-light searchlight at Bruay, and we stole crates containing the jigs and dies of the new Czechoslovakian machine gun from a railway platform. Indeed, only a month ago we succeeded in picking up wholesale a complete mountain battery from the test grounds of our friends on the other side of the Alps. Can we make a mistake *this* time?"

"The other cases were clean-cut. There were no involved side issues as these which Storrow has brought on us," argued Kolbein. "There are too many risks involved here."

Tubuloff sat staring at Kolbein for several seconds, and now Kolbein's face began to blanch. He put his hands behind him, forced himself up to his feet. Fear made his elbows tremble and his tongue clove to the roof of his mouth. Tubuloff was slowly drawing a large black Mauser-Astra automatic pistol from a black holster at his hip.

Kolbein watched the slow movement of the great hand as it came clear. He tried to speak as he saw Tubuloff's thumb draw the hammer back. He could hear the release bolt move forward and insert a cartridge from the 20-round magazine—and he knew his doom was sealed.

But he was game. He regained control of his frame, stood erect and faced his master.

"*Herr* Commander. I will return to my post. My watch begins in a few—"

But there was a sharp report and he never finished the statement.

Tubuloff put his weapon away, then gave the others a pertinent glance.

"We will descend to 3,000 meters, Helmsman, long enough to unseal the cabin and dispose of the remains of this insubordinate somewhere out to sea."

The others stood up, clicked heels, and saluted while Commander Tubuloff—who had recently preferred to be known as 'Colonel Tudorn'—stalked back toward his private chart-cabin aft.

"And remember," he thundered as he left, "every man will be on duty from 10:30 on—and every man will remain at his post until our work is completed!"

Hands went up in salute, and parched voices responded: "Aye, Commander!"

"I'VE BEEN all over her. Nothing seems to have been touched," Barney said for the seventh time while Keen continued his intense inspection of the Black Bullet for evidence of sabotage by Storrow.

They had inspected king-pins, control cables, and wing-fittings. They had checked high tension leads and rollers of the distributors. They had blown out the feed lines and gone over every inch of the ship for file marks or soaped-in saw cuts.

If Storrow had damaged the ship in any way, he had certainly covered his tracks carefully.

And yet both Keen and Barney were certain that the man who had feigned death had not taken that long chance for nothing.

"The devil!" snarled Keen. "Let's go—before this thing 'gets us' and we quit cold." And he began to climb into his coverall.

Once attired for the air, they both hesitated—stared again at the Black Bullet, making a last effort to uncover the sabotage they felt sure was there. But the Black Bullet, as beautiful a bird as she was, could not tell them.

Keen got in the cockpit, then made a final adjustment on his scarlet face mask. He started the engine and with a last glance at his wrist watch gave Barney the nod. In five minutes they were out on the dark waters, thumping the pontoons on the rollers for a takeoff. Then they cleared and climbed the Bullet carefully, their cockpit hatches open as a safety measure in case anything went wrong.

They swung back over the island at 3,000 feet, and Keen

began to put her through a series of maneuvers to test her spars and controls. She responded beautifully. Yet still they were not satisfied.

"I can't figure it out," remarked Keen. "She takes everything nicely. Let's go through with it," he said with a glance back at Barney.

Then when the Mick nodded, he plugged in his headphone jack and twisted the wave-length lever to the band that had been allotted to the Talbot firm for its anti-aircraft experiments. Almost at once he caught the carrier hum of a portable set. Then a voice came through:

"... and I am now at 7,000 feet approximately over Bay Shore."

"That's Storrow," Keen muttered, swinging the ship around and climbing up to 7,000.

He listened intently as he sped along, but his sub-conscious mind was still seeking the evidence of sabotage, and a strange icy feeling crept up and down his spine.

Again Storrow's voice came over the air:

"I am now at 9,000 feet... over Brookhaven. How do we check?"

There was a jumble of instructions from the ground. Keen hoiked the Bullet higher. And then he almost leaped from his seat—for he suddenly spied the strange clipped-wing ship of the night before streaking toward them through the haze.

"Look!" he half screamed.

Barney twisted in his cockpit and glanced forward. Sure enough there it was again. And from below its teardrop fuselage, which carried no apparent landing gear, dangled a strange looped tackle of some kind. Moreover, the peculiar ship didn't seem to have a propeller.

Stunned with surprise, Keen let the little craft pass him, and then he curled around and followed it.

"Don't shoot—yet," he called to Barney. But his attempt to avoid a conflict went for naught. Because suddenly the flyers on the unique ship opened fire from two cabin ports and heavy slugs battered their way through the fuselage not three feet from Barney's knees.

"... *I am being attacked by a strange plane,*" Keen then heard the man in the still-unsighted Seversky report. And the ballistics expert quickly guessed the reason for that message. Someone had tipped Storrow off and he was using a fake attack story to get into the action against the Black Bullet.

"Watch out for the Seversky!" Keen yelled at Barney. But the Mick did not need to listen—for he was already drawing a bead on Storrow's sleek monoplane that now came lancing down at them from above. He pressed his triggers.

But from his Brownings there only came a short screeching burst followed by a dull explosion!

"What—what happened?" bellowed Keen.

Barney stood there holding the spade grips of his beloved guns, stared out with blazing eyes and saw that both barrel muzzles had burst! He pressed the triggers again, but there was no response. The Brownings had been spiked with "fixed" ammunition.

Battered by the strange stub-winged craft and hammered by the Seversky, the Black Bullet was trapped—trapped in a leaden vise of death!

Keen sensed that something serious was wrong aft, and he slammed the Black Bullet through a mad series of maneuvers to evade the withering fire. Finally, with a wild climbing turn, he managed to whip away from the clipped-wing craft. Then he sent the Bullet straight at the Seversky which was now curling away after her dive.

"Me guns are busted!" Barney was raging.

"Just sit tight," called Keen. Then he drew a fine bead on the Seversky, noting as he did so that Storrow was jerking his stick in an effort to get his monoplane fighter clear. Keen now drew his triggers, watched four streams of fire flash across the sky.

But then there was a series of low coughing explosions that jarred the framework of the Black Bullet! Keen swore—

for he knew it was all up. His own guns were out of commission now!

"The swine!" he growled as two more bursts fanged out from the clipped-wing ship which was now sweeping back on them. "Storrow slipped some heavy stuff in our ammo boxes and blew out the works. What fools we were!"

"Well, what are we waiting for?" yelled Barney. "Don't you know the way down?"

BUT KEEN had no intention of going down. He quickly glanced around at the little clipped-wing job, then curled the Bullet over on one wing-tip and roared through the sky at the Seversky. Skillfully he brought the Bullet along side Storrow's fighter and proceeded to outmaneuver him at every turn.

Gun-less though they were, Keen was playing his hand to the limit. "Come on, you rats in that flying torpedo," he yelled. "Fire at me now!"

Then the break came. The stub-winged plane slammed two heavy bursts at the Bullet just as Keen whipped up. Blinded by this move, Storrow sat petrified, fearful that the Black Bullet would sideslip into him. And it was his fear that brought his end—for as the Bullet curled over, a third burst from the clipped-wing job hammered full into the Seversky.

Keen saw that his coup had worked— saw the Seversky break in two as a jagged, flaming explosion burst its wing tanks. He heard Storrow scream his death knell into his microphone: *"Janckert... you fool... Oh... Oh...!"*

A tangle of dural wreckage, carrying a mourning plume of black smoke, went down to its doom somewhere beyond the shore-line of the Atlantic Ocean.

"Now what?" demanded Barney, "You can't make that guy in the flying shell-case shoot himself down, can you?"

"I'm not worrying about him. Put your heavy underwear on. We're going upstairs—to get the Big Guy!"

And with that Keen snatched up his radio mike, flattened his tongue to disguise his voice, and began to talk:

"Hello, Talbot station… Calling Talbot station again… This is Storrow, better known as the Griffon, speaking."

Immediately he got an excited *"Go ahead"* from Talbot on the darkened field far below.

"This is Storrow—the man known as the Griffon," went on Keen. "I am trying to block a plot to steal your anti-aircraft weapon. And I want you to do just as I ask."

Getting an anxious acceptance, he carried on in his faked voice:

"Somewhere above me is an unknown dirigible. From it has been lowered a special observation car bearing three men. The plan is to lower it on down to the ground under cover of a terrific bombing display like that of last night. And unless we stop them, the men in the car will fasten a hoisting tackle through those holes drilled in the turret of your mobile A-A unit, pull it up aboard the airship, and fly it across the Atlantic. So," continued Keen, "you must obey my orders and fire when I signal."

"Yes… Yes… Go ahead, Griffon," Keen caught. *"Go ahead. We have live ammunition ready."*

"Okay. Then set your range-finders on me—for you can hear my engine, where as the airship power plants are efficiently silenced so you won't be able to range on them. You must range on me. I'll take full responsibility for the chances."

"But my heavens, man!" Talbot answered. *"You'll be shot down yourself!"*

"It's a risk I have to take," answered Keen. "You won't see me or hear me again, anyhow."

"You're insane—but game!"

"Don't argue with me," Keen ordered. And he climbed the Black Bullet madly.

For what seemed like hours he climbed. And then at 15,000 over a thick layer of clouds he finally caught up with the great lighter-than-air craft. There was no denying it now. It hung there stationary, its great silver propellers just turning over.

"Here they are," he radioed down. "They are probably trying to draw up the car, now that they know what has happened. Range me at 15,700… correct your range for dirigible 100 yards to my left… and *Fire!*"

His heart in his throat, Keen then turned the Bullet in the opposite direction and gave her all she would take, praying that Talbot's gun had the accuracy claimed for it.

The slightest error would mean death for the Griffon!

Hardly a moment later, three great yolks of flame splashed out behind the racing Bullet. The bursts had come slightly below the huge dirigible, which now shook under the concussion.

"Increase range to 15,800," Keen yelled into the microphone.

BR-R-ROOM BR-R-RONG! Two more flashes near the nose of the ship. And then there came a gargantuan roar!

A direct hit!

Searing flame blotted out everything. Keen was blinded for minutes, and he only recovered from the shock when he felt Barney leaning over him and holding the stick.

"Cease fire," Keen radioed. "Your required evidence of this plot will be somewhere near your field in a few minutes. Here she comes now. And goodnight, gentlemen."

The great airship hung in mid-air for a second or two, rolled like a monster animal in its death throes, then broke in the middle. With a creaking groan, the torn colossus began her final flight—to earth!

EXACTLY TEN minutes later, Keen raced up the stairs from the secret Graylands hangar and phoned Drury Lang. The Secret Service man was on the Talbot field, just as he had promised.

"That you, Lang?" Keen asked with a faked tired air. "What the devil is going on down that way? I thought I saw flames in the sky."

"Keen? Why—a—where are you—home?" came back Lang.

"Of course I'm home. But what's up over there? A Fourth of July celebration?"

"Boy, it's a good thing you're where you are tonight, Keen. I was just going to call you—to satisfy myself. I think I will anyhow to make sure where you are. So hang up."

"Thanks, I will, anyhow, I've got a grand glass of beer here that I want to get back to—and a cheese sandwich."

"Cheese, did you say?" asked Lang. *"What sort of cheese?"*

Keen hung up, laughed, then reached for the wet towel Barney was holding out for him and wiped off his perspiration-streaked face.

In a moment the phone rang again, and after kicking off the rest of his flying kit, Keen answered: "Here I am, Mister Lang. Now what is it?"

"Say, Keen! You never heard anything like this in your life! We got the remains of an airship as big as a mountain here. It came down in flames—not three hundred yards from the Talbot field. They shot it down—"

"Who shot it down? And with what?" broke in Keen.

"Talbot's new gun—with the aid of the Griffon. That guy was up there directing the fire, and they got it down. And now I know you can't be the Griffon. You wouldn't take a chance like that, would you?"

"The thoughts of such a thing make me want to reach for Barney's bottle," replied Keen.

"Well, the Griffon actually had them range that A-A gun on him. He flew up close to the airship that was trying to swipe Talbot's gun, and they got it down. Why, everybody's going crazy around here!"

"Look here, Lang. Don't you think you are getting a little too old to believe stuff like that?" asked Keen innocently.

"But I tell you..." blubbered Lang. *"Storrow is the Griffon!"*

"That will be all for this evening, Mister Lang. I can't waste beauty sleep on such rot as that. Good night, Mister Lang."

"Why you... you... you...."

"Cheese-hound," offered Keen And he hung up.

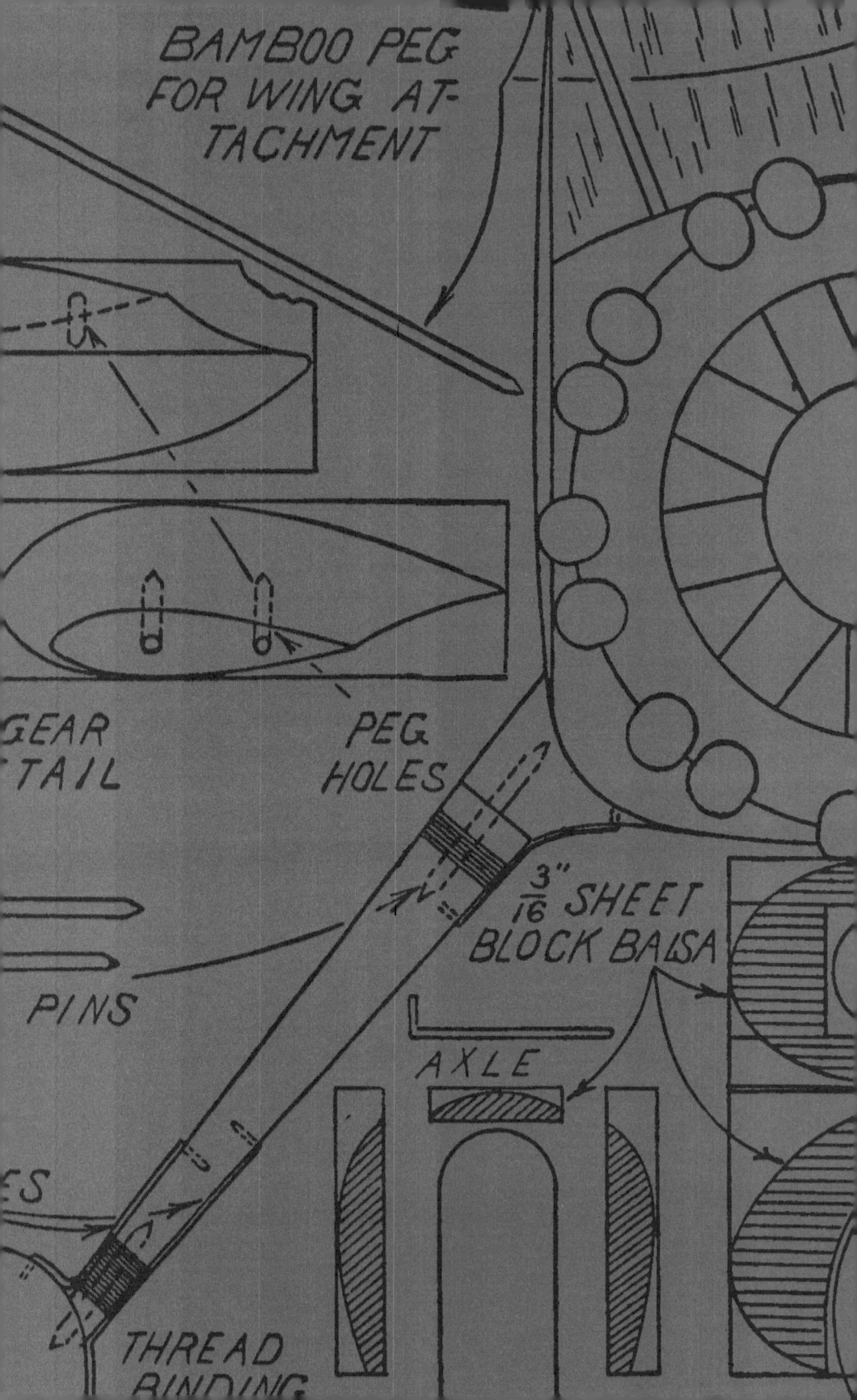

BAMBOO PEG FOR WING AT-
TACHMENT

GEAR
TAIL

PEG
HOLES

PINS

3"/16 SHEET
BLOCK BALSA

AXLE

THREAD
BINDING

ES

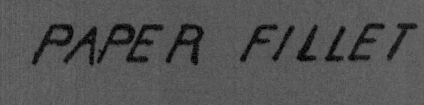

Black-Out Vultures

CHAPTER I
Bomber Bane

ACROSS THE sky, a parachute flare threw a blinding glare of frosted silver. And on the ground below, haggard-faced men on metal saddle seats manipulated knurled knobs and set delicate mechanisms that could hurl high-altitude death through long steel gun barrels.

It was the first in the series of black-out nights that were to throw blankets of inky darkness over Long Island, that protruding finger of land destined to take the brunt of a raiding thrust should some enemy strike at New York City from the east. This was to be a preview of war—a grim game which would offer training for fighting specialists and also give the civilian population some idea of what modern air warfare can be like.

But had Brigadier General Harold W. Thornton known that the ghastly hand of Death had tampered with his well-laid plans, he would have torn every sheet of Army Form No. X177 into shreds long before the ships of Bombardment Squadron 184 had been fueled.

From Governors Island to Montauk Point, anti-aircraft batteries, searchlight crews, and range-finder troops had been detailed to put up the first lines of home defense against the sky "raiders" from the sea.

upright beams of searchlights. A few fighters were speeding by in a safe, wide formation, a handful of Douglas observation planes swept over with slit-eyed observers peering out of their covered cockpits, and here and there kite-balloons swayed, their anxious spotters hugging portable telephone sets to their chests.

This was war as the generals had prescribed it—a scheme to test men, munitions, and equipment. It was war without the actual thud and blood—and yet....

THE MAN in the back seat of the sleek amphibian was a study in Gaelic anxiety. He had been sitting there for more than an hour, staring at the trim head and shoulders of the man in the pit just ahead.

To the right, across the curved top of the engine cowling, both flyers could see the illuminated panorama of "war" that was being waged along the full length of the Island.

"I still don't get why we had to pick this week to pull this one," the man in the back seat of the Black Bullet growled.

"And for the fifty-sixth—no, the fifty-seventh time—I tell you that we had no other choice," replied the man ahead.

Into that withering hail of lead plunged the leading
Hawk. Then with a wrenching screech, its riddled left
wing buckled, fire burst from its cowl, and it plummeted
earthward in the turbulent wake of the falling Fortresses.

"The war games will be on for another six days, and we
certainly couldn't ask old Cap'n Boompjees to sit out there
waiting for us much longer."

"Bah!" spat the man behind. "That old Dutchman wasn't
going anywhere. All he's got to do is kill a few days' time."

"That's where you're wrong. He's headed for Venezuela.
And he put himself out plenty making that contact out there
for us."

"Yeah, and we made it okay. But how we gonner get into
Graylands with all that display going on ahead? Why in the
name of all that's holy did they have to pick Long Island to
play soldiers? I knew we'd come a cropper one of these days."

"You watch me. They'll never figure us, even though
they spot us with a beam. All the raider planes have been
painted black on the bottom, and they'll accept our ship
along with the rest. Very likely the referees will mark us down
as 'destroyed in action' and the gunners will go back home
perfectly satisfied."

"How nice you tell it."

But the pilot had no time to answer, for a sudden shaft of light spanged out from a searchlight mounted somewhere off Westhampton Beach. It spattered its silver blade against the trim wings and retracted pontoons of the Black Bullet.

For what seemed seconds, the pilot sat blinded by the light as the ship was held fast in that betraying searchlight. Then with a quick snap of his wrist and a steady pressure on the rudder pedal, he zoomed the black plane out of the glare and darted back and forth a few minutes. Then, satisfied that he had outwitted the pesterers below, he swung wide.

"Yeah! You'll get in—on the end of a 3-inch gun," growled the bird in the back seat of that funereal amphib.

The Griffon—for it was he who was at the controls—ignored the complaining mutterings of his gunner and worked his way well east of Montauk Light. Then he turned west and zipped toward Long Island Sound. As he swung into a black area over Gardiner's Island, he sighted quadruple pennons of exhaust flame.

"Here's one of those Flying Fortresses," he said calmly over his shoulder. "Watch me join in with him."

"There's three of 'em—in formation," the man behind added with the same complaining tone.

"Right," agreed the Griffon, peering through the slits in his scarlet mask.

With a deft movement, the Griffon eased the Black Bullet into a position behind and slightly above the three-ship group. He nudged the throttle slightly to maintain speed with them, and together the strange formation hurtled on toward Riverhead.

"Now you've done it," growled the man in the back seat. "Listen!"

He snapped on a switch, then from a small speaker set in one side of the front cockpit came an authoritative voice:

"Captain Rollinson speaking:

"Ships of No. 4 Flight watch out for unmarked plane aft of

formation. Am reporting to ground base that it is in restricted area. Keep close watch on it, Plane 98."

"You see," moaned the man in the back seat. "They're wise to us."

"You're goofy! They've only *seen* us; they're not wise to us."

"No? Well, if you stop a burst of .50 caliber stuff in a minute, don't say I didn't warn you."

The Black Bullet hung to its original position, and the Boeing "raiders" thundered on over Manorville. Then from below came the thud of anti-aircraft guns bellowing blanks. More searchlights snapped out and swung their sword-blades of light back and forth across the sky.

"So long, Boeings," grinned the Griffon. "You keep those fellows down there occupied with their big flashlights—and meanwhile we'll duck down to our own little bug-walk."

"You hope!"

As the Black Bullet turned away, the activity from below increased. More searchlights spanged out, and now two parachute flares burst out. Both the Griffon and his gunner realized there were more planes above; but they were so high, they couldn't tell just what they were, or what part they were playing in the game.

Then, as the Griffon completed his full turn, the man behind let out a low cry.

"Look—Look in that glare!"

The Griffon did look—and he was amazed to see the three Boeing Flying Fortresses falter in their flight and break formation. He allowed the Black Bullet to come around again in order to watch the unbelievable antics of the huge bombers. The leading Boeing had nosed up into a sickening zoom, while the ship on the port wing had swung around sharply and let a wingtip drop dangerously. The third had plunged down in a cruel dive.

Then there suddenly came a sharp report and the lead bomber burst into flame.

"What the deuce!" yelled the gunner of the black plane.

"Some fool must have slipped a live round into one of those A-A guns down below."

"What, and hit all three? Don't be silly!"

The burning ship now broke up in mid-air, and the other two plummeted down in its smoky wake, at times narrowly missing one another as they gyrated in gigantic falling-leaf tumbles.

"This is awful!" the Griffon cried.

"And you'll be blamed for it!" came the answer. "Look! Here come some fighters now. Beat it!"

From above, three Curtiss Hawk 75s splashed down upon them. Frantically, the Black Bullet gunner swung out his twin Brownings, poured a series of warning bursts across the blunt nose of the leading fighter. But the Hawk did not halt its dive. Before the Griffon's gunner could release his triggers, it swept full into his withering hail of lead. A wrenching screech followed as its riddled left wing buckled. Then fire burst from its cowl and it plummeted downward.

"Now you've done it," the Griffon barked over his shoulder. "Why didn't you hold your fire? I could have flown rings around them."

"Yeah, but I wasn't firing to hit that guy. I just wanted to hold him off. But gosh, you don't think—?"

The air was now a mad criss-cross design of tracer bullets, searchlight beams, and the flaming curves of engine exhausts thrown like streaked brush marks through the sable sky. There was the thud of anti-aircraft guns along with the harsh scream of motors. There was the wail of slipstream and the scrawnch of wrenched metal.

Black-out night over Long Island!

FOR SEVERAL minutes, the Griffon slammed the Black Bullet through a wild program of maneuvers that completely baffled the pilots in the 75s. The rear gunner refrained from attempting any more shots; in fact, he had all he could do hanging on with his eye-teeth. Back and forth across the sky the amphibian thundered, missing another flight of Flying

Fortresses by inches and cutting across the noses of six Douglas observation ships. Then it abruptly nosed up, stood on its tail a breathless second, and shot out toward the sea.

That was all those in the Boeing and Douglas planes observed of the Black Bullet. They did not see it suddenly twirl, rip over in a sharp flick-roll, and then hurtle down just clear of a sheltering searchlight beam that lanced up from somewhere near Amagansett.

The silver streak of the searchlight offered a suitable guide line for the Griffon and at the same time provided a curtain behind which to escape, Thus in ten minutes the Black Bullet was rolling quietly up the Grayland's lawn toward the Griffon's secret hangar that lay behind what appeared to be an innocent rock garden. A touch of a hidden switch and two great doors opened outward, revealing a wide cavern dug out beneath the rambling home of the man in the scarlet mask.

In a few more minutes, the ship, her wings suitably folded, was eased inside. Then the doors were lowered and the Griffon and his gunner became their normal selves again.

"Well, ye got away with that one!" Barney O'Dare, the muggy Mick, mooned as they ambled through a steel door into the cellar. "But that was only because you were lucky."

" 'Pitch a lucky man into the Nile'," laughed Kerry Keen, removing his mask, " 'and he will come up with a fish in his teeth.' I think a guy named Willis wrote that."

"Yeah?" growled Barney. "Well, James A. Garfield had that one beat a mile. Know what he said?"

"Quote Brother Garfield as you take down a bottle of Bollinger dated 1928," smiled Keen. Then he added: "And you may also bring forth some O'Doul's Dew dated 1938."

"Garfield said: 'A pound of pluck is worth a ton of luck!' What's more, I'll have ye know that O'Doul's is dated 1928 also. It isn't one o' them washes labeled, 'Every drop of this drink is guaranteed to be at least 48 hours old.'"

"Well spoken, my tippling friend. You have the pluck and I'll contribute the luck. Now let's go upstairs and drink a gentleman's toast to Captain Hans Boompjees who has so kindly provided us again with the necessary parts to keep the dear old Black Bullet in service."

"That thick-headed Dutchman—coming here the week the Army decides to fight the battle o' Long Island. Why don't that guy read the papers?"

"Considering what happened tonight," Keen said reflectively as he sipped his champagne, "it may turn out that we're lucky, at that. We certainly needed those gun parts, and I was getting a little worried about our distributor units."

Barney reflected. Then his face went long. "Say, that was queer, though, wasn't it? I mean that business of those bombers going down like that."

"There certainly was something sticky there, Barney. We shall hear more about it later, too. And I'm really worried about that poor devil in that Curtiss you plugged."

"I didn't have time to see if he chuted or not," Barney replied with a shiver. "The-they'll have me for murder, man! What'll I do?"

"Let's see what's being said over the radio," said Keen, twisting around and snapping the switch of his very elaborate set.

The dial clicked into life, and Keen set the vernier for his favorite station while Barney shakily replenished the glasses. There was a crackle of static and finally words began to filter through the speaker, increasing in tone as the tubes warmed up:

"... *Army officials are issuing orders to all airport managers to report any sighting of this mysterious black plane. Later reports coming in state that the third Boeing bomber has been found near Nesconset and that every member of the crew is dead, although the plane is not badly damaged. Army officials are unable to explain what happened. They state, however, that the war games program will be continued as per schedule.*"

AT THAT point, an orchestra broke in, and both Barney and Keen sat staring at the dials.

"You're right! There is something screwy about that," Barney finally said.

"Any minute, now," predicted Keen, glancing about the room.

"What do you mean? Lang?"

As though in answer, a telephone bell jangled. Keen grinned and picked up the instrument while Barney moved across to the radio.

Keen chimed, "Let the radio run a minute. Got to give the old boy some atmosphere." Then he said: "That you, Lang?"

"Sure. But turn that radio down. I can tell you more than any announcer guy."

"What the deuce is it all about?"

"Your pal the Griffon again. You wouldn't know anything about him, would you?"

"Don't be silly. What's up?" replied Keen, nodding as Barney snapped off the radio switch.

"Three of the Army's Flying Fortresses were shot down—somehow—during the maneuvers. If you know anything about solving mysteries, come down here and see what you can make of this."

"Give me some idea."

"I wish we had one, Keen. Anyhow, this is a real mystery. These bombers were taking part in the mock raid. On the way down toward Farmingdale, they spotted this black plane and reported it. Almost immediately all three of the leading group broke up and went down. One caught fire and hit on the beach near Stony Brook, another nosed into the ground near Selden, and they have just found the third, which somehow landed on its belly at Nesconset without much damage."

"Were the wheels down?"

"No! I said it landed on its belly! When Army men got to it, they found every guy in his seat stone dead, stiff, not a bruise or cut, and sitting there with their eyes wide open."

"No evidence of gunfire?"

"Not a scratch of any kind. The Army guys are going nuts."

"Can't blame them. Anything else?"

"Yeah. This guy—the Griffon, I guess he was—also got into a tangle with some single-seaters. He shot one down and they found the wreckage near the Boeing that hit near Stony Point. There was no one in the plane, and no one has any idea who it belongs to."

"You mean it is not an Army ship?"

"No record of it in any squadron connected with the games. Nothing aboard to identify it. But they are going to try to trace it through the Curtiss company in the morning."

"Whew! Anything else?"

"Only that they've swung the job on us, and old Scott is about nuts, too. Can you come down here to Nesconset in the morning and look over this wreck!"

"I can. But if there are no signs of bullet holes, what can I do? The coroner should be able to figure it out if he makes an autopsy. Guys just don't die like that and go stiff. There must be some reason for it all."

"Sure, but no one knows what it is. You get down here in the morning and look it over. Besides, I want to talk to you on something else."

"What?"

"A little matter of a few screwy radiograms from a Dutch freighter which is supposed to be on its way to South America but instead has been seen not far off Hell Rip Light. You wouldn't know anything about that, of course?"

"Not a thing, except that I did get a couple of messages from an old friend of mine, Captain Hans Boompjees. He's the skipper, and he wanted me to join him in a friendly little chess game by radio." And Keen winked at Barney, who had to clap his hand over his mouth to keep from bursting out with a loud guffaw.

"What the devil are you talking about, Keen!" Lang spluttered from the other end.

"You know—pawns, knights, bishops, and white squares. Chess, my good friend, is the game for great minds. Napoleon, Bismarck, Henry the Eighth—and... er... James A. Garfield."

"Oh, shut up! You just get down here at ten o'clock on the dot tomorrow morning," And Lang hung up with a bang.

CHAPTER II
Cannister Clue

BARNEY PREPARED to turn in early, knowing he would have to work on the Black Bullet early in the morning. He had no idea what would turn up, but he sensed that the adventure of the black-out business was not over. No, there was more to come. And Barney didn't like it.

Keen packed a pipe snuggled back in a big chair. Through the open windows, the cool night breezes brought in the fragrance of the trees tanged with the salt of the sea. It also brought the acrid smell of smoke from the sham battle gunnery posts. He sniffed it, smiled.

"Queer thing," he remarked as Barney prepared to leave. "Those Boeings were not shot down, according to Lang. Just went down, cracked up, and the crew of one that somehow managed a landing on its own was found sitting up at their posts—stone dead with their eyes open!"

"Hey, wait a minute," barked the Mick. "This is no time for tales like that. I'm just going to bed."

"There's no ghost stuff about this. There never is. It has a solution somewhere."

"Well, *you* can sit up and figure it out; I'm going to roost with a lot of covers over my head."

"Look out for that bogey man you shot down in that Curtiss. They haven't found him yet, and there is no record of the ship. It doesn't belong to the Army at all."

"Good night!" Barney snapped, and he made for the door.

Keen put a match to his pipe, stared into the blue plumes of smoke. "Queer," he repeated again. "There were a few shots fired from below, and there were a few parachute flares in the sky which had been dropped from some of the Douglas observation ships."

There was very little to work on there.

"Those three Hawk 75s *might* have had something to do with it, at that. They could have discharged some form of death; they might have fired some kind of gas-containing shell capable of snuffing them all out before they could have done anything about it."

He got up, crossed the room and took down a large scrapbook in which he had carefully pasted detail drawings and photographs of the famed Boeing B-17 Bomber. He studied the pictures carefully, worked from the rotating nose turret back as far as the stern post. He calculated space areas and crew positions, then checked the exhaust system of the four engines.

That offered very little hope, so he took a new angle. "They were flying fairly close and maintaining practically the same altitude. What one thing was taking place on each plane at the same time that might have led to their deaths?"

He pondered on that for some time and came to the conclusion that the only item worth considering was the fact that all three were using their radio sets at the same time.

But there was not much to work on there, either.

Finally, he tapped out the heel of his pipe, drew up to his library table, selected pencil, paper, and one or two more books, and prepared to settle down to the problem if it took all night.

NOT MANY miles distant, in a low hall that reflected a stark, military air, stood a group of straight-backed men, stern and defiant. They faced a speaker's dais.

Otto Shanto, a barrel-chested man, well belted, booted, and be-medalled strode up and down behind the gleaming table on the stand. He wore an armlet bearing a totalitarian emblem, a peaked cap with the same emblem, and military orders of high degree on his left breast.

At the table, several other men pored over reports, newspaper clippings, and varied documents. Some wore foreign uniforms and small dirk cases that hung from shiny, silver chains. At one side, two men were taking shorthand notes of radio announcements. And nearby, another man, pasty-faced, hawk-eyed, and lean, hunched over a short-wave set, listening intently to monotone reports.

"It is well," Otto Shanto said in a gruff tone. "So far, our men have carried out their duties well. Antes and Fiata are to be commended. All three went down, you say, Blaut?"

"Yes, Leader Shanto—all three! Grossburg has reported from Nesconset, where one is down. He hopes to be able to remove the cannister."

"One plane caught fire?"

"Yes, sir. It destroyed all evidence. The second is so badly battered forward, it will take weeks to dismantle it and make any sort of examination."

"But the third, landed itself?"

"With hardly a scratch."

"Ah, but these Americans design with skill! Imagine a ship of that tonnage landing itself!"

"We will find out many secrets, Leader Shanto. And now I wish to report that Mostern was shot down in one of our Hawks. He managed to get down safely with his chute, however."

"A Hawk is a minor loss," spat out Shanto. "Most important is the great success of our secret formula. We have taught the Yankee swine a lesson! And they will get a further shock in the morning, eh, Blaut?"

"And another tomorrow night, if they continue with their plans."

At that moment, a telephone bell rang. Blaut stiffened, looked at the Leader who in turn nodded. Blaut—he was a small rat-faced man—raised the instrument and grunted: "Yes!"

He listened intently a minute, scribbled a few notes on a sheet of paper, then ordered the man at the other end to hold on. Turning, he reported to Shanto: "It is Grossburg again. He has information that may be important."

Shanto snatched the telephone, growled: "What is it?" As he listened, his face took on a deeper mask.

"Good!" he snarled. "Then you have the name and telephone number, Blaut?"

Blaut nodded.

"Return to your post, Grossburg," he barked into the phone. "I will try to trace this man Keen. You say the Secret Service man called him, and that he will attempt to find out what caused it? Umm! Well, get that cannister out of there—somehow. Understand?"

Shanto returned the instrument to its prongs with a crash. "Keen is his name, and his phone number is Montauk 4555," he muttered. "Call information and find the address. Get a car ready, Lanta."

Men moved fast at the Leader's commands. They slipped out of their gaudy jackets, pulled on caps and felt hats, and shoved their arms into black wind-breakers. There was a noticeable bulge under the left armpit of each man.

Blaut, having phoned to get the Keen address, scribbled another line, tore off the page, and held it before the eyes of Shanto. The Leader nodded, then together four of them hurried out of the room.

Outside a car bellowed into life. Tires crunched down a cinder driveway and lynx-eyed men stared down the twin paths of silver thrown out by the headlights.

"Keen, eh? A good name for an investigator. I have a feeling we will complete a very important piece of our work tonight," said Shanto with muffled enthusiasm.

TWENTY MINUTES later, a milk delivery truck drew up alongside a car which stood on the highway at a distorted angle, precariously near a deep ditch. Three men huddled together near a front light inspecting something held by the man in the center.

"In any trouble? Can I give you a hand?" the milkman called cheerfully.

"Probably can give us some information," Blaut said, coming up close to the side step of the milk truck. "We've been trying to locate a place called Graylands."

"Graylands? Why that's Mr. Keen's place—just up the road here. I deliver there. You'll find it easy. Got two large granite gate-posts at the entrance to the drive."

"You deliver there, you say? You're on your way there now?"

"Next stop. Shall I rouse them and tell them you're coming?"

"No, never mind. We'll take care of that," said Blaut. "Did you ever see a carburettor like this before?"

The milkman got down from his seat, moved forward to inspect the object Blaut held in his hand.

But the milkman never reached the headlights of the big car. Something crashed down on the base of his skull. The world splintered into a bombshell of silver lights and the poor devil passed into a better land.

It was but the work of a moment to drag the body of the man to the ditch and hurl it, with a grim swish, into the sodden bottom.

Blaut nodded to the man at the wheel of the other car and accompanied by two others climbed up into the milk truck. He carefully let in the gears and started down the road. The black car carrying Shanto followed carefully.

Blaut and his men studied the road carefully. They passed one driveway and looked about but did not see the two granite gate posts.

"There's the place, just a bit further up the road," whispered Lanta. "Two gate posts."

Blaut stopped the truck, and the black sedan behind drew up close again. A few words were passed, then the lights of the sedan were flicked off.

"There are lights on, downstairs," Blaut said, looking across the lawns to the Grayland's edifice. "He must still be up."

"All the better. Drive the truck in and let's get it over," said his companion. "I don't like this sort of business."

"You must learn to like any business, if you expect to stay in this organization," Blaut growled.

They let in the gear again and turned the milk truck into

the driveway, passing between the two granite gate posts. They rolled along, crunching the stones, and finally drew up before the main doorway.

"All right, Lanta," whispered Blaut. "You take a carrier of bottles and rattle it as you go up the front steps. I can see the man. He's sitting in what looks like a library."

"What are *you* going to do?"

"Finish him off, get back in, and drive down as far as the gate again. There we'll leave this truck and get back in with the Leader."

As he spoke, he was fitting the barrel to a chunky sub-machine gun. Lanta watched him anxiously, then began to rattle the carrier of milk bottles. Blaut stepped outside the driving cab, clambered up on the front bumper of the truck, drew the cocking lever of the gun back, and put the weapon to his shoulder.

He took careful aim as Lanta clattered up the front steps.

There was a rattle of fire—and Blaut fell with a scream to the drive-way!

KERRY KEEN was deep in his problem—a small stack of papers, a few scribbled sheets of scratch paper, and three or four rough sketches of cabin interiors before him—when he was startled into a cold shuddery stiffness by the rattle of gunfire outside.

In his deep concentration, he had not even noticed the approach of the milk truck. He had not sensed any danger. But the instant the clatter died down, he had darted across the room, through the door, and into the hallway.

From above came the voice of Barney:

"Look out! There's still one more guy somewhere out there. Don't go to the door yet."

Keen peered about, then slipped across the hall, tapped a panel, and allowed a narrow door to open. From the aperture, he took a short stubby machine gun. He tapped the curved magazine. Then with a crouching glide he moved toward the heavy door.

Outside, another burst of fire rattled out and two desultory spats of flame indicated that some one was running across the lawn.

"That's the other guy," Barney called. "He's cleared off."

"But what the devil is up?" queried the ballistics expert.

"I don't know. But when a milk truck drives up through the main entrance, I want to know what's going on," Barney continued as he came down the stairs. "Didn't you notice it?"

"No. I guess I was too busy."

"Yeah? Well, you're a lucky guy. I heard the truck drive in and knew there was something wrong, so I jumped up out of bed to see what it was all about."

"I should have noticed that," agreed Keen. "They usually come through the service driveway and around the back, don't they?"

"Yeah. That's what made me suspicious. I looked out and saw a guy putting a gun together, and I was just quick enough to beat him to it. He was taking a beautiful aim at you through the window."

Together they opened the door, peered out and reconnoitered the situation. The milk truck still stood there, its motor chugging wearily. Then from somewhere ahead in the darkness, they heard the low, gulping groan of a man.

"Wait a minute! Listen!" whispered the wary Mick. "There goes another car. Hear it… down the road."

"That other bird got away," cracked Keen. "They must have had an auto waiting."

Together they went to the milk truck and then discovered the body of Blaut huddled up over a sub-machine gun. Barney pulled the man over on his back. They noticed the uniform breeches, the black boots, and the incongruous black wind-breaker.

"Looks like one of those guys from that so-called athletic camp over west of here run by those alien-looking ginks," O'Dare suggested. "Look at his belt—that's a military type buckle."

"Never mind the belt. Go through his pockets," ordered Keen.

They searched the man who was now dead. There was a heavy leather wallet with about forty dollars in bills, a mason's union card, a few tickets for one of the society's dances, and a faded snapshot of a young girl, evidently taken abroad. Then in the left trouser pocket they found a sheet of folded paper on which was written:

Grossburg reports Secret S. called M-4555... man named Keen.

Keen examined the paper for a minute under the dim headlights.

"Take everything else he has, except the money, and stick him back in the wagon," he ordered.

"What are you going to do with him?"

"Get him out of here, first. After that, I'm going to look for this guy Grossburg who gave them my telephone number."

With a last glance around, Barney lifted the body of the man and placed it across a stack of milk boxes in the back of the truck. Meanwhile, Keen wrapped his handkerchief around the gun, picked it up carefully, and placed it on the floor of the truck.

"Take it down the road a couple of hundred yards, then let it roll over into the ditch. And get back here safely. I'll be waiting here for you," Keen said.

"I'll enjoy doing that. I never liked milk wagons," grinned Barney, collecting the metal carrier and the bottles of milk that had rolled in the driveway. He climbed up, took the wheel, and let her in gear. Down the curved driveway she crunched and out through the gate. Keeping a careful eye on the road ahead, he selected the spot for the wreck, slipped out of the seat, jerked the wheel around, and dropped off.

The milk wagon careened off the road, dipped a front wheel into the ditch, and with a rattle of glass bottles, rolled over on her side—not ten feet from where Shanto and Blaut had left the dead driver.

Barney stood with his hands on his hips for several seconds

watching the first fingering flames leap up from somewhere beneath the engine. Then there was a dull thudding belch of smoke and a final gush of enveloping fire.

He continued to stand there for several minutes watching the blaze, fascinated by the fantastic flame forms. Suddenly, however, he realized that he had better clear out before the crash and blaze attracted attention.

"I don't want to cut it too close," he said aloud as he turned to move away.

"No?" a voice immediately behind him replied, "Well, you didn't cut that one close enough. Put your hands up—and keep them up, killer!"

Barney made a full turn, stared amazed into the face of—a girl. As he raised both hands under the compelling authority of a small, but efficient-looking automatic, he realized that she was dressed in the trim blue-and-gold uniform of Central Air Lines.

"What the—?" the Mick gasped.

The girl came closer, rammed the snubbed-snouted weapon deep into his ribs.

"Go on, start walking, killer. My roadster is parked in the bushes down there. You and I are going to have a long talk—before I finish your dirty career."

O'Dare was unable to find words. The girl was so slight, so neat, so beautiful—and, in addition so confident. She hurried him past the blazing milk truck, made him keep his hands high.

"What's the idea, Sister?" Barney finally spoke up in an effort to stall.

"I'm no sister of yours, gunman! And if you really have any sisters, keep thinking about them, because I'm just about ready to add a bereavement to your family. I only want to satisfy myself first on one or two points—on those tubes you… you devils have been disturbing."

"I wish I knew who you think I am," muttered Barney as she steered him with the gun muzzle toward her roadster.

"Don't worry, I'll find out," the girl said bitterly. "Get in. Here, give me your left hand. This hand cuff on that wrist and the other fastened to the door handle should keep you quiet."

IT ALL happened so fast. Poor Barney was shackled with one arm across his body before he could get seated.

The girl knew her job. "That's how we take care of tough guys upstairs," she said, slipping under the wheel, her little black automatic still palmed in her right hand. "Now sit quiet until I tell you to move."

"When will that be?"

"When I get you home and safely tied up in a nice quiet cellar."

There was no arguing with this miss. She knew what she was doing, and she knew how to do it. Inwardly, the Mick had to admit she was complete master of the situation. But he still couldn't figure out what she was getting at.

She started the motor, backed out, and drove south-west toward Amagansett. Overhead, planes still roared and long, fingering shafts of light continued to trace the sky. Soon the girl let the car into high and stepped on the accelerator. The needle of the speedometer slipped across the oblong dial toward the 65 mark.

Barney watched her out of the corner of his eye. She certainly was pretty and she most certainly handled herself with all the ease of an air hostess.

"What's in this thing?" she suddenly said, kicking something across the floor of the car.

"In what?" growled Barney. He did not like the situation at all.

"This tube thing you birds planted on my ship the other night. You put one aboard Flight 9 and she piled up outside Cincinnati. Our planes just don't stop in mid-air like that and then dive into the ground, spy." She emphasized the last word.

Barney was looking down at a slender metal tube to which was fitted a cap containing some intricate mechanism. He had never seen anything quite like it before. He was trying to study it under the dim gleam of the instrument board gleam when he caught the word "spy."

"Spy?... spy?" he stormed. "Who says I—"

"Take it easy! I said 'spy,' and that's what I mean. I trailed your gang from your fake athletic camp headquarters. In fact, I've trailed them every night I've been on the eastern end of my run since they downed Flight 9."

"I'd make a swell arm-saluter," Barney grinned, getting at least a small paring of an idea. "My name happens to be Barney O'Dare—I'm as Irish as Donnybrook bacon. And you don't find any shillelah men over there at that camp."

The girl didn't answer. She hammered the car through the traffic that swept through East Hampton. Once on the open road again, however, she again took up the subject.

"So you didn't drive out of that camp tonight and head out for Montauk? You weren't one of the three who stopped the milkman and ran off with his truck? You didn't return later and dump the truck over so that it caught fire, eh?"

"Is *that* what happened?" said Barney, suddenly interested along a new track. "I mean, the first part of what you just said?"

"All that happened—and you know it!" came the fiery answer.

"Listen, girlie," pleaded O'Dare. "You're on the wrong track. And I'll tell you something confidential—if you'll go back with me with that thing you've got on the floor. Don't you realize you're obstructing justice?"

"All I know, killer," the girl replied without looking at him, "is that you and your sabotage spy mob killed the best pilot on Central Air Lines, not to mention the twelve passengers, a grand kid co-pilot, and the hostess. You killed—murdered— Ralph Blaisdell, the man I was going to marry."

"You're okay, sister—but you're on the wrong track."

"I'll find that out when I get you where I want you."

"Listen. I don't know who those guys were you were

talking about. All I know is that they drove into our place tonight—or rather early this morning—and tried to bump off my boss… Mr. Kerry Keen."

"Kerry Keen?" the girl gasped, taking one hand from the wheel and putting her finger tips to her lips.

"No other. I happened to spot them and start shooting first. Then we didn't want that mess about the place, so I stuffed the one dead guy back in the truck—I guess he was one of your pet spies—ran it down the road again, and let it roll over. It was a nice clean way of getting rid of the filth."

The girl braked the car and drew it up to the side of the road.

"Kerry Keen is that young ballistics chap, isn't he? And the police call on him sometimes, don't they?" she asked, her words coming in a torrent from her pretty lips.

"That's the guy. You see, only a short time before, he had received a call to go over to Nesconset to look over one of the bombers that had crashed there. The call came from a Mr. Drury Lang of the Secret Service. You can call Lang at Nesconset and check me back, if you like. Anyhow, Keen was sitting up working out an idea about the bomber crashes. He always approaches a tough case that way."

"Bombers crashed? Big Boeings?" the girl asked anxiously.

"Three of them—during the blackout maneuvers. Three of the new Flying Fortresses. No one knows how, or why—but everybody in the one that practically landed itself at Nesconset was sitting up stiff and stark, with their eyes wide open."

The girl sat helpless, her hands folded in her lap.

"Why didn't you say so before we got this far?" she demanded, swinging the car around.

"You wouldn't let me," cracked back the Irishman.

CHAPTER III
Secret of the Tube

KEEN SAT up, staring at the clock and awaiting the return of the Mick. Nearly an hour had passed since that tell-tale blaze had blossomed out down the road.

"The crazy fool," he growled. "He must have hung around too long and got himself picked up."

He went back to the table, studied the crumpled sheet of paper for the twentieth time. The more he went over it, the more certain he was of his original interpretation.

He was about to pick up the telephone and attempt to make some furtive inquiries when twin headlights flashed through the gates and came crawling up the driveway. Keen selected an automatic pistol from a drawer, slipped in a twenty-round clip, and went to the shelter of the doorway.

Peering through a small peep-hole cut in the decorated doorway, he flashed on a light just as a gleaming road-ster pulled up to the front steps. He watched a slim girl in blue uniform get out, wag a warning finger at Barney who remained in the car, and start up the steps.

Keen stepped out quickly to meet her, his big gun hidden in the large pocket of his dressing gown.

"Hello," he said. "What's up? And who may you be?"

The girl twirled her small automatic in her hand, and came back with a question of her own: "Are you Mr. Kerry Keen?"

"I am. What's wrong?"

"Nothing much—if you can identify this man. I picked him up down the road; caught him wrecking a milk truck."

"Tell her to come and unlock these bracelets," Barney growlingly called.

Keen laughed; there was little else to do. "Sure," he said. "Bring him in. I've got papers for him: Breed, Irish; sex, male; name, Barney O'Dare—no fixed abode and likely to bite unless doused regularly with generous portions of O'Doul's Dew."

"I guess you have him right. I'll go and take the leash off," the girl replied, smiling for the first time.

She selected a small key from her pocket and snapped the metal handcuff that had held Barney to the door handle.

"I'm quitting this job," the Mick grumbled, thumping out of the car and champing up the steps. "When a skirt can nail me with a toy pistol and then put the bracelets on me—I must be slipping!"

Then with a sudden whirl he went back to the car and picked up the strange aluminum-colored tube.

"I'm so glad it worked out all right. I'll admit I was none too game about killing him," the girl said.

"Killing him? What for?"

"She thinks I caused that Central Air Lines crash outside Cincinnati," bawled Barney. "She thought I was one of them spies who goes around putting things in planes to make them crash."

"Come inside, Miss—er—"

"Miss Halliday—Jane Halliday—is the name, Mr. Keen. Thanks, I will. And I'd like some coffee, too, if you can accommodate me. Golly, I'm tired."

"Coffee for Miss Halliday, Barney. Make it two."

"I'll make it three, if you don't mind," the Mick argued. "And what's more, I'll spike it well with rum."

"For once in my flying career, I'll take it, too," the girl answered dropping into a big club chair.

"Now then," assured Keen, "let's find out what this is all about."

Quietly, but with frank concern Miss Halliday outlined the events of the evening and what had caused her to follow the men from their camp headquarters near Medford.

"I was engaged to Captain Ralph Blaisdell, skipper of that Central Air Lines ship that crashed under mysterious circumstances near Cincinnati."

"I'm very sorry. That was a terrible thing."

"Well, I knew that something had been 'fixed' on that ship, and I decided to do something about it—for Ralph's sake.

"I can understand that, too. But what is this tube thing Barney brought in?"

"I wish I knew. You see, it was planted in my ship a few days after the Cincinnati affair. It was attached somehow to the sliding door of my electric heater box where we keep the prepared food. Look, this small lever had been fixed to the latch of the door-handle so that when I went to open the door to serve supper before they turned in, the latch movement would turn this lever on."

"But it didn't," said Keen, studying the tube and the mechanism.

"No. Somehow, in taking off, or because of vibration while warming up the engines, the lever slipped from the latch."

"I see," nodded Keen, as Barney came in with the coffee and a stack of sandwiches.

The food was placed on a coffee table and all three hunched around it and piled in ravenously.

The Mick was as disconsolate as a big bloodhound.

"Swell! I get pinched, kidnapped, and hijacked in the middle of the night by you," he glared at Miss Halliday. "And now I have to get you a supper and serve it."

"Equality of the sexes, or something," the girl smiled. "But whatever your failings and weaknesses, I'll say you can certainly cook."

"Yes," added Keen to the torment. "To repeat an old saw, he'll make some woman a fine wife one of these days."

"Gr-r-r-r," the Mick grated.

"WELL, LET'S get back to business," said Keen who had been staring at the peculiar tube during the refreshment period. "Here's something I don't quite get, Miss Halliday. When you found this thing, why didn't you report it to some one?"

"I did. I took it around to the Maintenance Superintendent, thinking that it might be something one of the shop crew had left around."

"And he saw nothing in it?"

"He just looked at it, handed it back, and told me to toss it on the junk pile."

"So you simply kept it and proceeded to cover the movements of those 'athletic' society blokes. But what for?"

"That's one I can't answer. Just intuition, or perhaps prejudice, I suppose. Maybe I read too many spy stories."

"Well, in this case you happen to be on the right track. These men who came here tonight are connected with that camp outfit. They learned, in some way, that I was to work on the mystery of the Boeing Bombers. By a stroke of luck—an element we require a great deal of in this business—you come along with something that may solve the whole business."

"Aw, quit gabbing. What is that thing?" broke in Barney.

"That's what I want to know. Maybe it's a bomb—a death instrument of some sort. Luckily for us, the lever has not been moved, has it, Miss Halliday?"

"Moved? No, I wouldn't touch it. I still think it would go off if we did the right—or wrong—thing with it. Can you take it apart, with safety?"

"Nuts! Let's go to bed," grunted the Mick.

"A darned good idea. Can we put you up for the night, Miss Halliday?"

"I guess that would be a good idea. I'm awfully sleepy."

"Want to call up and tell anyone where you are?"

"No, that's not necessary. I was going to stay at a hotel somewhere over here anyhow. I'll be all right if you can provide a room."

"Any color room you prefer?" smiled Keen.

"My word! You must have a big place here. Why such a massive home, just for two men?"

"We need plenty of room, especially when we spend our nights opening lethal instruments, bombs, and such things."

"Are you going to work on that tube?" the girl asked with anxiety.

"I think I might as well. I'm going to inspect that Boeing tomorrow and I might get an idea what it is all about via this tube."

"In that case then, never mind the color of my room—I'll take the one farthest away from the seat of operations," the girl smiled. "I can only hope I haven't brought you any trouble."

"Nothing else but," mooned Barney. "Come on, I'll show you to the haunted room. Are you afraid of ghosts?"

"Tell her the story of your Granny McShane," prodded Keen.

"I'd be asleep before she rattles a chain," the girl laughed. "I'll say goodnight now—and hope that you don't blow yourself to pieces."

"Lend her a suit of my pajamas, Barney. They'll be a trifle large but—"

"Oh, never mind. Naturally, I have a week-end bag with me. In my car, Mr. O'Dare."

"I knew it!" the Mick groaned with an elaborate gesture of hopelessness. "She has brought her trunk. Here goes the freedom of Graylands!"

Both the girl and Keen laughed.

"Well, until the morning then," she said. "Unless you break the silence of the night with a Fourth of July celebration."

"—scattering fingers and thumbs all over the room," added Keen.

"Please!" the girl pleaded, covering her eyes with her hands as she followed Barney upstairs.

KEEN CONTINUED his pondering. Somehow, all desire for sleep and rest had left him. The strange tubular instrument on the floor held him fascinated.

He picked it up, shook it, weighed it in one hand, and studied the mechanism set into the cap.

"It might be a gas, or it might be an explosive," he muttered to himself. "I better play safe, I suppose."

He went to his secret cupboard and selected a gas mask. Then with a last look around the room, he snapped off the lights and carried the gas mask and the tube instrument down the cellar stairs. At the bottom he turned to his left, went around to another section of the cellar, and entered his small but very complete machine shop.

He turned on the lights, set the tubular device on a drill bench, and drew a pail of water which he set nearby. Putting on the gas mask he started the drill motor and began to bore a series of holes at the base of the tube. As soon as this operation was finished, he put the tube into the pail of water and allowed it to soak thoroughly.

Almost instantly the water in the pail took on a decided greenish silver tinge. He peered at it carefully through the goggles of the mask and was glad that he had put the safety device on. He went to the door, made certain that it was closed tight.

"Queer," he muttered to himself. "Some chloride derivative. Wonder what the deuce it can be?"

Once he was certain that the contents had been well soaked, he took the tube out of the water. Then he drilled two holes in the cap mechanism and set it to soak again. The water retained the same tinge; so holding it still under the water with a forked stick, he tied a piece of string to the lever and pulled it around.

He held his breath as a low gurgling sound came. Then the top cap flickered in the water and shot off as though it had been snapped off by a spring.

Nothing else happened.

Somewhat disappointed, he removed the two parts. The main portion of the cylinder was now hollow and empty.

The upper portion was nothing but a quick-release mechanism. No detonator, no spark-producing device, no time fuse.

"What the devil!" he snapped.

But he kept his gas mask on.

"There was *something* in this thing," he argued with himself again. "It was a gas, a vapor of some kind. Look what it did to the water. I couldn't see any vapor, but it must have been there. Strange!"

He sat on a box studying the discoloration of the water. Finally, he decided to let it stand until morning when he would apply a few re-agents to the water in an attempt to discover the identity of the gas or vapor that caused the discoloration.

With that, he threw the cylinder on the bench, snapped off the light, and closed the door tightly as he went out. He did not take off the gas mask until he was back in his den. There, he put it away carefully and with a deep sigh of disappointment went upstairs to bed.

THE YOUNG ballistics expert was aroused a few hours later by the mournful-mugged Barney, who was on hand with the regular tray of breakfast.

"Still in one piece?" the Mick observed.

"Sure. Nothing much to that thing as far as I could find out. Just a hollow tube. No explosive, anyway."

"I knew it. That jane is a Jonah. Just playing the beautiful hostess who solves the mystery of the airliner crashes. I'm glad she is buzzing off this morning."

"Is she?"

"Yeah. Up with the lark and singing like hell, she had a breakfast big enough to choke four horses. How do these dolls keep their figures?"

"Don't ask me. Ballistics is my game. Now a quick shower, a noggin of Java, and two slabs of toast will do me this morning, Barney. My respects to Miss Halliday, and tell her her bomb was a dud."

"Nothing will please me better."

"And ask her to wait. I want to see her before she goes."

"You're going to make a dinner date with her?"

"Don't be silly. You know the long line of the Keens has

never been besmirched with feminine entanglements. But I must say that Miss Halliday is easy on the eyes."

"Yeah, but she'll be tough on the pocketbook if she ever gets a strangle hold."

Keen laughed and darted into his bath. In ten minutes he was back, shaved and gleaming. He gobbled the breakfast and dressed quickly. Downstairs, he came upon the young air hostess who was studying the display of guns in Keen's study.

"Good morning!" Keen greeted. "Have a nice night?"

"Not even the prospect of your going through a wall leaving a well-cut impression of your trim military lines interfered. I slept wonderfully. What happened?"

"Nothing. Just messed up a lovely bucket of water, that was all. I'm afraid your lethal weapon turned out to be a false alarm."

"Can I see it now that you have dismantled it?" the girl asked.

"Certainly! Come on, let's go down to my shop."

Barney gave Keen a warning look, but the ballistics expert allayed the Mick's worries with a nod. He had no intention of letting the girl see any portion of the hangar section of the house.

"Lead the way, Barney, and catch Miss Halliday if she slips." The three went down the stairs. Barney, the first one to enter the shop, abruptly let out a gasp.

"Holy Moses, what did you do here!" he barked.

The girl went in next and stared around, noticed that many of the metal parts about the shop had a strange white crustation, giving them the appearance of being covered with hoar-frost.

Keen barged in behind her. "Look here!" the Mick said to him, touching a metal chair. "It's all—"

Before he could finish the sentence, the metal chair broke up under his light touch like a sugary design on a wedding cake.

"Was that a dural-tube chair?" the girl asked quickly.

"You've got it, Miss Halliday! You've got it!" Keen said quickly. "Shut that door, Barney!"

They went all over the shop. Everything made of aluminum or of dural had been affected by the peculiar crustation. Some chloride derivative had apparently eaten off the protective coating of oxide. The items affected crumbled into powder the instant they were touched.

Keen went over to the tube he had thrown on a bench. He picked it up and sniffed, but there was no odor. He glanced about again, watched Barney poking at whitish items all over the shop. A mechanical pencil, a folding drinking cup, an aluminum fishing tackle box, a metal alarm clock. All aluminum or dural parts on the items were affected in the same way.

"This thing," cracked Keen, "contained some gas or vapor that eats up dural."

"And that's what happened to Flight 9—and Ralph," the girl said in a slow whisper.

"Right! And I'll bet a gentleman by the name of Grossburg knows something about this."

"Grossburg?… Grossburg?" the girl said, as if the name twanged a chord of memory. "Wait a minute! I had a passenger on my manifest by the name of Grossburg—on that run when I found the tube."

"Try to remember. Did he get off at Cleveland?"

"No. Flight 12 goes right through to Chicago. No, he didn't go at all. He came aboard and I checked him in at Newark. He was sitting somewhere aft while the berths were being made up. But then an attendant told him there was a telephone call for him, and he disembarked. He didn't make the trip."

"No, but he had planted this tube which didn't click," Barney chimed in.

"Let's get out of here," said Keen. "I've got to get to Nesconset quickly. You stay here, Barney, and keep tabs on everything."

"Can I go with you, Mr. Keen? I'd like to see this through," the girl said.

"Yes, you can help, perhaps. You follow in your car, then you will be able to go on to Newark. You're going out tonight?"

"Yes. About 11:45."

"All right. Let's get going. I'll see that you get through the police lines, if they have been established."

"Don't worry about her. She'd get through anything," growled Barney.

"We're going to get a certain Mr. Grossburg, eh, Miss Halliday?" said Keen with a quiet determination.

CHAPTER IV
Fortress Menace

THE WRECKED Flying Fortress was down in a field not two hundred yards off the Nesconset-Central Islip road, and once he had made inquiries at the local Police Station, Keen had no trouble in guiding his purring Dusenberg to the crash. Miss Halliday had followed him at a respectful distance.

Keen pulled up behind a patrol car, got out and spoke to the Sergeant who was directing traffic. The girl followed suit and on a nod from Keen followed him across the field where an Army truck, a tent, and a cordon of National Guardsmen had formed a temporary base.

"Now listen to me," Keen said out of the side of his mouth as they approached the tent. "I have formed a plan. You do just as I say, but keep one hand in your jacket pocket—on that little gun of yours. Understand? We may run into this Grossburg lad."

"Anything you say," agreed the girl as they were halted by a soldier.

"I am Mr. Keen, and I want to see Mr. Lang of the F.B.I.," the ballistics man said quietly.

"Oh, yes, Mr. Keen. He's expecting you. And the lady?"

"She's with me. It's okay."

They found Lang, weary-eyed, unshaven, and ratty-whiskered, sitting in the tent talking to an Air Service officer. The Secret Service man leaped up when he saw Keen, then gargled something unintelligible when he saw the girl with him.

"This is that guy, Keen, General," Lang opened. "Meet Brigadier General Thornton, Keen. In charge of air operations."

Keen and the General shook hands. Then Miss Halliday was introduced.

"Miss Halliday, who is with Central Air Lines, has some

interesting angles on this thing," Keen said calmly. "As a matter of fact, she has been working in her own quiet way on the recent Central Air Lines crash."

"Hey, wait a minute, Keen," spluttered Lang. "This lady wouldn't be the Griffon, would she?"

"You can never tell," Keen replied in all seriousness. "She might."

The girl looked puzzled but kept quiet. The General was studying her closely. "You have seen the wreck?" he asked quickly, addressing both Keen and the girl.

"No. Why, have you found anything?"

"A most amazing thing has occurred that we cannot explain."

"Well, wait a minute, General. We have an idea—and we have plenty to base it on. But first we want to try something."

"I'll try anything."

"Do you have a man by the name of Grossburg in your outfit?"

"Grossburg? I don't know. But I'll call some one who can tell us."

An orderly was signalled in, and through his information it appeared that an Ivor Grossburg was an Armament Sergeant with No. 184 Bombardment Squadron. As a matter of fact, he had just come on duty.

"Have him stand by to assist in making a special inspection," whispered Keen. "Miss Halliday and I have a plan."

"Wait until you have seen the wreck," moaned Lang. "It's all changed and—"

"Sure, we know—it's all white and the dural is crumbling."

"How did you know?" both the General and Lang gasped together.

"That's what happened to the Central Air Lines ship, isn't it?" the girl broke in.

"Yes," the General admitted, his face a chalky white. "But we thought all that had been kept quiet. You know what this means if it gets out?"

"I have a slight idea," said Keen with a knowing look.

"It means that our Army men will be leery of dural ships until this mystery is solved. The blow to their morale is extremely serious."

"All right, if we prove that something was planted aboard that ship—something that caused this chemical change—it might help a lot, eh?" said Keen, giving Lang a particularly knowing glance.

"This gal ain't the Griffon, is she?" Lang continued to bark.

"I said she might be," smiled Keen. "But let's get on with the work. Have this fellow Grossburg called. Explain to him that Miss Halliday is a special investigator, and that she is to be shown through the wreck. Grossburg is to take her through, and we will follow behind at a safe distance so as not to let him think we suspect anything."

"Why?" asked General Thornton.

"Because Miss Halliday knows what it was that was planted. What's more, we have an idea where it was planted and by whom."

"This man Grossburg?"

"Maybe. That's what we want to find out."

"It sounds silly, but if you say so, Keen," the General muttered, "we'll try it."

Outside, a man stood at ease, his hands folded behind his back. He was fairly tall, grim visaged, and soldierly. He wore the uniform of a Sergeant and he had all the earmarks of a professional soldier. Keen eyed him a moment or two, then stood aside so that the girl could see him. Without a word, she gave Keen a glance that indicated that this was the man they were looking for—this was the man who had planted the tube in her galley locker.

"Are you all set, Miss Halliday?" Keen asked.

The girl rammed her right hand down into the pocket of her blue uniform jacket. She nodded, but her face was white and her lower lip trembled. Keen sensed the chill of the moment and wondered whether he should take this mad gamble. The palms of his own hands were damp with perspiration.

The Sergeant stiffened to attention, snapped a military salute, then said: "Sergeant Grossburg reporting, sir."

Thornton returned the salute and said: "Oh, yes, Grossburg. You're Armament Sergeant with 184?"

"Yes, sir."

"Fine. We're going across to give the wreck another look-over before it is dismantled. I want you to accompany Miss Halliday through the main framework. She is a special investigator. You know the ship well, and I want you to point out every feature of the plane and allow her to inspect it thoroughly."

"Against Group orders, Sir. But if that is the General's command, I am willing."

"They are my *personal* orders, Grossburg," snapped the General.

Again the Sergeant saluted. And it must be said that if he recognized the girl or suspected he was being singled out, he did not show it. A black Colt hung at his thigh, and Keen wished now he could call it off.

TOGETHER, THEY now approached the wrecked ship. Around it, a high canvas barrier had been erected, but at the General's nod they were allowed to enter through a slit in the near side.

The Boeing bomber was a strange and horrible whitish thing resembling the parched skeleton of some prehistoric monster. Large slabs of the dural sheeting had fallen in, and whitish ribs and formers poked through the gashes. The crash had caused very little structural damage, for the ship had slid forward on her curved belly for a hundred yards or more. All four props were badly damaged and two of the motors hung from their nacelles at pathetic angles.

Still, the most striking aspect of it all was the white crustation that covered everything.

"The white skeleton of aviation!" muttered General Thornton. "We *must* get at the bottom of this terrible thing!"

"Leave it to Miss Halliday," responded Keen.

"I'll bet a buck she's the Griffon," Lang growled under his breath.

But the growl was not low enough. Sergeant Grossburg caught the word Griffon, and Keen caught his change of face. Now he knew they were in for it.

The Sergeant moved forward and reached for the door on the starboard side of the fuselage. As he drew it open, flakes of white crustation fell on his neat sleeve and he shook it off petulently.

"This way, Miss Halliday," he said with a gruff tone.

The girl hesitated a second, looked at Keen. Then, with another glance at the Sergeant, she stepped inside. The Sergeant followed and the encrusted door slammed back with a dull metallic clang and showered more white powder to the ground.

Keen's heart sank. Grossburg undoubtedly was suspicious. He might do anything.

Lang stood staring at the swaying door, and the General rubbed his chin nervously.

"What's it all about?" Lang finally said. "Who *is* this jane?"

"Just an air hostess—with a swell imagination," said Keen watching the door. "Has this bird Grossburg been inside the wreck since it came down?"

"No... I don't think so. He's been posted at the Bennett Field base where 184 has been stationed for the war games," the General explained.

"How did he get here?"

"I think he flew over in No. 97—she's outside, on the other side of this canvas. Young Freer flew a few members of the outfit over to help dismantle the Boeing when we are finished with the investigation."

"You're sure he hasn't been aboard until now?"

"Almost positive. Why?"

"I just wanted to make certain. Now we'll find out where he planted it and whether he *did* plant it."

"You mean Grossburg caused this?" said Lang, squinting his eyes at Keen. "How do you know?"

"I don't know. I only have a hunch—or rather Miss Halliday has a hunch."

"What sort of a hunch?" barked Lang. "All this seems screwy to me, Keen. It sounds like another of your wild ideas."

"Don't worry—it is!"

"But we can't be wasting time on hunches, Mr. Keen. We thought you'd have a sound idea as to what caused it," the General argued.

"Trust me, General. I have very good reasons for all this. I'll explain everything later when Miss Halli—"

Before Keen could finish there was a dull thudding shot and a low scream from somewhere inside the Boeing cabin. It sounded well up forward.

Keen was at the door first. He yanked it open, clambered in. For a second or two, the bad light stopped him. But he finally scrambled on through the row of internal bomb racks. Then, after making his way through the narrow passage between the radio cabin and the navigator's room, he found the girl.

She was slumped back against the narrow stairway that led to the pilot's compartment, one hand still in her jacket pocket where a small blackish hole smoked and smouldered.

"What happened? You hurt?" Keen yelled.

Lang and Thornton clumped up behind him.

"Who did the shooting?" demanded Thornton.

Keen drew the girl to her feet, and she smiled weakly. "I'm… okay. I shot him… in the hand. He was go—going to shoot me when I found it…."

"Found what?" Lang growled, pushing around closer.

In her left hand, Miss Halliday held another of the strange tubes. The cap was off.

"Where was it?" said Keen anxiously.

"Where did you find it?"

"In the front gun turret. Fixed somehow to… to the lever that releases the turret-turning mechanisms."

The girl paused, exhausted by her experience.

"And he tried to take it away from you?"

She nodded weakly and pointed toward a great hole in the side of the fuselage: "Out there, he went—ran across the wing."

The General darted to the aperture, saw a tell-tale trail of blood spots on the white-crusted airfoil.

Lang danced about like a silly doll, then grabbed the tube from the girl and stared at it puzzled.

"It was filled with some gas or acidous vapor," explained Keen, "that eats off the protective oxide coating from dural and aluminum. That man Grossburg has planted them on airliners before—and now he's putting them on Army bombers!"

"Where is he?"

As they started to lead the girl out of the compartment and down the passage toward the door, they heard the concerted roar of four engines. There were more shots, then motors blared out louder and drowned all other sounds. All four stood stock still and listened. They feared the worst.

A gleaming Flying Fortress bounced, swayed, and thundered down the field. By the time they had reached the door and had clambered out, the beautiful silver bird swept up in a skilled climb, turned to the east, and roared away into the distance.

"And there goes our man," growled Keen.

Neither Lang nor the General said anything. They were spellbound by the speed of events.

A young Air Corps officer came charging through the barrier. He was holding one arm, and blood was dripping out of his sleeve. He made a game attempt at a salute and gagged: "Sergeant Grossburg has taken Plane No. 97 without orders,

Sir. He knocked out two sentries and… and wounded… wounded me…"

And with that he fell flat on his face, unconscious, before anyone could put out a hand.

"SO WHAT?" Lang said out of the corner of his mouth when they had brought about some semblance of sanity, and the young officer had been rushed off in a Staff car. "What's this all about, Keen?"

"Simple enough. This man Grossburg has been planting these tubes in planes and they have been crashing as a result. Finally we corner him—so he pinches a bomber and gets away," said Keen staring across at the girl who was sitting on a tool box nearby.

"There's more to it than that, though," Lang taunted. "I calls you up last night. You're supposed to be sitting home quietly listening to the radio. You don't know what's going on. But when I begin to put the screws on, you turn up with a blonde!"

"*Is* she blonde?" queried Keen thoughtfully.

"Never mind that. You turn up with this skirt who has all the answers. So I say—what's it all about? Where did you find her? How did she know one of those tubes would be in that bomber? You see, Keen, none of it adds up right."

"I'd say it adds up splendidly—for you. You can go back and tell the big wigs what happened and who did it. Simple, isn't it?"

"No! How can I pull such a gag as that? Who is this girl? Where did she come from?"

"The blue room—that's the haunted room at Graylands," smiled Keen.

"You mean she's been at *your* place all night?"

"Sure! She was a visitor. She found one of these tubes in her airliner, and knowing that the great Kerry Keen was the man to straighten it all out, she came to me—last night."

"Phew!"

"Unbelievable! But true, Lang, old sweet!"

Lang took his hat off, scratched his thin thatch, then suddenly barked: "Yeah, but where does this guy Grossburg come in? How did you know about him? You even knew his name."

"Process of elimination," said Keen, with a haughty stare. Then he told the story of the man who booked on Flight 12 and then suddenly turned in his ticket.

Lang listened with awe and finally replaced his battered felt hat and wagged his chin. "You've got something there, Keen. I've got to give you credit. But down inside me, you chisler, I know you're putting something over."

"It's my turn to say 'So what?' Right, Lang?"

"Maybe. But what are we going to do about this lug who just swiped the bomber? With that Fortress in his hands, anything might happen."

"That's the Army's job, not mine."

"Yeah? Well, listen, you mug. That bomber's got to be back with the Army within twenty-four hours—or I'll spend the next month figuring out this." And with that, Lang pulled a morning newspaper out of his pocket.

Keen took it, stared at the photograph of a burned truck. A glance over the headlines was sufficient.

"That milk truck left your place—Graylands—only a few minutes before it caught fire," Lang said under his breath as he stared at the girl. "The driver was found lying in the ditch with his skull bashed in and he wasn't burned at all. But there was another guy in the truck, Keen. You wouldn't know who that was, would you?"

"No, I couldn't say—but perhaps Miss Halliday can. She passed the truck when it was blazing. But if you ask her one word about it, you can go find your own Boeing Bomber. I won't."

"Miss Halliday, eh?" sniffed Lang stuffing the paper back into his pocket. "She saw it burning—but didn't say anything?"

"No, but I *believe* she saw a man from that foreign athletic camp near her set fire to the truck," lied Keen. "Still, I say, don't ask her about it. Understand?"

"Do we get the bomber back?" Lang pleaded, now disturbed.

"I won't say that. I will say, however, that I don't think Grossburg will get away with it."

"How you gonner be sure? He's fifty miles away by now. That bus has enough juice in it to fly across an ocean. At least, that's what Thornton says."

"He should know. Still, I'll bet Grossburg's somewhere about, waiting to pick up the guy who set fire to the milk wagon," Keen said with a mysterious air.

"That certainly makes sense—I *don't* think," said Lang, fumbling with his thatch again.

"As soon as things begin to make sense, you won't need me," replied Keen, with a laugh. "But perhaps the bomber *will* get back if Miss Halliday can get in touch with the Griffon," he grinned.

"Yeah? Well, I'll bet a buck she's going to do plenty."

"But Lang—do you realize that Miss Halliday will be tucking pretty movie stars and bulbous business magnates into their aerial beds tonight aboard a Century Air Liner headed for Chi?"

"Hey, beat it before you get me as screwy as you," barked the Secret Service man.

"I'm beating it, Mister Lang—and I'd advise you to look up a certain European who runs things in that so-called Long Island Athletic camp. He's absolutely nuts, of course—insane, the alienists would say. But he might know something about burning milk trucks."

Lang picked his brown tusks with a matchstick and watched Keen go over to Miss Halliday and escort her to her car. He never knew what Keen whispered to her as they went off. But maybe they would do something about the stolen bomber—somehow.

CHAPTER V
Transport Trap

ONCE OUTSIDE the area picketed by the Army men, Keen and Miss Halliday parted, one turning a car south-west, the other due east. Both were worried, and Keen's brain felt like a length of gray worsted that had been tangled around a handful of rusty nails.

It was well after noon now, but he was in no mood for lunch. Still, he headed toward Graylands, mainly interested in what had happened there since his departure.

He pondered on the problem in hand all the way back—the business of the strange chemical that ate up aluminum and dural, the mystery of the milk truck and the men who had tried to assassinate him.

"That's it, the milk truck," he muttered, giving the accelerator an extra ounce of pressure.

The scene a few hundred yards west of the entrance drive to Graylands was much the same as it had been when they had driven past in the morning. There were one or two State Troopers lolling around on gleaming motorcycles, a cop directing traffic, three or four plain-clothesmen, and the usual fringe of morbid onlookers.

A Police Captain with a weary eye nodded to Keen as he approached the traffic lane. Recognizing him, he came to the door of the car when Keen slowed up.

"Anything new?" Keen asked.

"Not much, Mr. Keen. It's a pretty messy business, and the fire cleaned up anything we might be able to work on. They found a light German machinegun in there, though. And they tell me the man they found burned inside had been shot first."

"Pretty foul business," agreed Keen. "Nothing else, eh?"

"Nothing of interest, Mr. Keen," the Police Captain smiled. "This is just some sort of a gang murder, I guess, and we'll probably never find out who the burned fellow was, poor devil."

"Quite a night, all told," observed Keen, letting his low gear in.

"Quite! That's what they get for blacking out everything. And remember, they're going to do it all over again tonight."

Keen smiled and let the Dusenberg roll away. He turned into the driveway, hummed up the circular path, and left the car at the door. He found Barney inside, talking on the telephone.

"Here, you take it," said the Mick. "It's that guy Lang again. What the deuce is this all about?"

"The Yanks are playing a doubleheader, I guess," said Keen, picking up the instrument.

"Hello," he said with a weary voice.

"Listen, I heard what you said. Never mind the Yanks. You stay away from ball games until you nail that guy with the Boeing. Now, this is inside stuff and you're lucky to learn it—but Thornton just told me that the full plans for the Eastern Coast defenses are tucked away in a secret locker in the navigating compartment of that bomber. That bomber has got to come back, Keen!"

"How will you have it—in parts or wrapped for mailing?" clipped Keen.

"Don't get funny, Keen!"

And Lang hung up, obviously disgusted.

In a few words, Keen explained the situation to Barney. The Irishman looked painfully bewildered, but he listened intently.

"When ye get a woman mixed up in something, you can bet fifty grand it'll be a beaut," growled O'Dare. "This is the worst yet!"

"How's the Bullet?"

"Ready to go. I went over her carefully."

"We're lucky. All we need now is a plan of action."

"What about this Grossburg guy? He must be miles away by now."

"Perhaps, but he'll be back. They're on a spot now, and he'll have to get the rest of that gang out. The two Hawks they have can't take care of more than a couple of them. Anyhow, those fanatical fools won't stop at anything. That chap Grossburg is down somewhere, waiting for a chance to pick up the others. You can bet on that."

"That girl had a lot of nerve, at that," reflected O'Dare. "I'll bet they'd like to get their hands on her."

Keen jerked as though he had been shot. "That's right, Barney! That's just the angle I've been looking for. Be ready by 11 o'clock tonight. We're taking off then to pick up a bomber—I hope."

Barney wagged his head and sauntered off. Keen immediately went downstairs shut himself up in his shop, and went to work on the film of scum that now floated on top of the pail of water in which he had immersed the tube.

LONG ISLAND was having another war-game spasm when, at 11 o'clock, the Black Bullet eased its throbbing way down the turf from the secret hangar. Overhead, a star-flecked sky was being slashed by a dozen searchlights. A low-flying formation of Douglas B-18s thundered past blinking their navigation lights. Somewhere to the southwest, anti-aircraft guns were coughing seventeen rounds a minute. Again towns were blacked out as great fleets of sky fighters simulated the attacks and defenses of war.

There was a tang of gunpowder in the air. At times, the breezes also brought the pungent odor of burned oil and hot metal. Mechanized cavalry chugged through darkened streets, and National Guardsmen in open formation charged across fields and took up positions facing "the front."

"What a night for a murder," mooned Barney, as he climbed into the Bullet's back pit.

Soon they were at the beach, and Keen drew back the steel lever that set the pontoons for a water take-off. Then, under muffled power, the Black Bullet streamed away, thudded across the top of two rollers, and with the breaking of suction, lifted herself into the air.

Keen let her climb high as he headed well out to sea. At 4,000 feet, he turned her back toward the string of lights that marked the boundaries of Staten Island and climbed even faster. Off to their right they could see the picturesque war-games display of fanning searchlights.

At 12,000 feet, above St. George, Staten Island, Keen turned again, striking a northward course. He was heading for the great illuminated rectangle that was Newark airport.

Now he snapped in the receiving set, cocked an ear toward the loud speaker set into the cockpit framework on his right side. Almost instantly came the words:

"All clear, Flight 12… All clear… Use No. 3 runway."

"There they go, Barney. That's Miss Halliday's ship. Now keep your eyes open for a Boeing Bomber marked '97'—or any Boeing Bomber that approaches that Central Air Lines ship."

"What's the idea?"

"You'll see. Just watch that airliner." Below, they could see the silver monoplane streaking down a runway under the glare of lights. In a few seconds it blocked out a portion of the scarlet ringlet that circled the boundaries, and for a time it disappeared. Keen shot for the red blinker that flashed from the top of the Watchung mountain range near Summit. Then he circled.

The routine reports continued to come over the loud speaker from the traffic tower at Newark, but Keen took no notice of them. He was watching the progress of the airliner.

"Screwy business," commented Barney. "An' to think we still have to get back to Graylands through that 'war'!"

"Never mind. Now when we see that Bomber, remember one thing: Keep all your shots on one side. Just try to make him come down—that's all. In short, get the props. I grant that trained flyers in that ship could turn us away in a flash—but those birds luckily don't know much about fighting tactics of bombers, if my guess is right."

"Shoot the props off?" grumbled Barney. "Who do you think I am—Annie Oakley?"

Keen dropped to about 6,000 feet and kept the airliner in sight. They heard the pilot pick up Bellefonte and make a routine report. Keen winced.

"There's the tip-off," he growled.

"Yeah. Well, here's your bomber, too," hissed Barney into his ear.

Keen looked down. Yes, there was the Fortress, heading for the airliner!

KERRY KEEN shoved the throttle forward, nosed into a dive. The Bullet picked up the challenge and roared a song of speed. There, over the bend of the Musconetcong, he could see the camouflaged bomber with four pennons of flame streaking from her exhausts. Nearer and nearer she hurtled to the helpless airliner.

Keen sensed at once that the Central Air Lines ship was in grave danger. He knew that Grossburg, in his fanatic madness, was out to get the girl who had played such a big part in the day's history. He set his gun gear, drew a bead, and pressed his trips.

The cannon up front barked three times, spat a streak of splintered flame.

The bomber was momentarily headed off just as it was nosing down on the airliner!

From the loud speaker came the frantic reports of the airline pilot:

"*… am being attacked by a Boeing Bomber… and a black plane of some description. Flight 12 calling Newark. Am being attacked by gunfire over.…*"

But Keen did not listen further. He was high-tailing it for the bomber which had turned slightly. Its riding lights were doused. But the exhaust glare gave its position away, and the Bullet went in head-first, pouring a salvo of high explosive shells.

There was a bitter return of fire from a port gun-blister. Barney frantically ripped back the cockpit hatch and yanked out his guns.

"Gimme a shot at him," he yelled.

"Just the engines—on this side if possible," ordered Keen.

Barney steadied himself, drew a clear bead, and let go with two short bursts. Again the loudspeaker barked:

"... *Bomber being attacked by unknown black plane!*"

"You tell the world," growled Barney, giving the Flying Fortress two more short bursts.

Keen whipped the Black Bullet over hard and Barney, hanging on, was just able to get another long burst into the two port engines.

Keen took one look and flipped the wave-length lever of his set. Then snatching up the hand mike he spoke in a clear distinct voice:

"Take the bomber down, Grossburg! Bring it in on the field directly below you—two miles north-east of the blinker. Take it down while you've got wings to get it down. This is the Griffon, speaking."

BARNEY GAVE them another burst, and the Boeing swung sharply into half a spin. She recovered, then went into a dive with the Black Bullet on her tail. She pulled out of the dive to spiral off flatly as though she'd lost part of her control.

"You've got him!" grinned Keen. "He has lost the use of the two port engines."

"Yeah. Now I suppose the bums will take to the silk and let her pile up."

Realizing the horse-sense the Mick had uttered, Keen grabbed the hand-mike again and barked: "Stay with her, Grossburg! If you as much as break a wheel, I'll blow you all to hell. Land the ship just as I ordered. This is the Griffon again."

They circled as the fortress eased out slightly, splashed the sky with two landing flares, and skimmed over a patch of trees. Then, as they held their breaths, the bomber staggered across an open field, dropped her wheels, and skimmed down to a thumpy landing.

The Black Bullet, wheels down, followed her closely, and landed, and half a ground loop to finish up with her guns dead on the bomber.

"All right, Grossburg," ordered Keen over the hand-mike. "All of you come out with your hands up. Line up outside the door. And leave the engines turning over."

In a moment, the door opened and one by one, four men in breeches, black wind-breakers, and caps, stepped out, hands held high. Barney rattled his gun-mounting pointedly, and Keen, well masked, slipped out of the cockpit, a heavy automatic in his fist. Over his forearm he carried a small coil of quarter-inch hemp.

"I know you, Grossburg," he said, stepping up to the group. Then he threw the hemp to the spy sergeant and said: "Tie their hands securely behind them!"

Watching the man closely, Keen then signalled to Barney. Now also masked, the Mick climbed down and came over.

"Now see that this Grossburg fellow is taken care of with rope, Pulski," he ordered.

Within five minutes the four men, silent and sullen, were back in the bomber, all carefully bound to seats.

"What now?" demanded Sharito, who at last assumed what element of command he could muster under the circumstances.

"That's all," answered Keen from behind his Griffon mask. "I'll just fly you lads back to—well, Newark, will do, I suppose."

"But you can't—you can't do that. Two of the engines are dead!" blarted Grossburg, struggling against his bonds.

"Only two? Well, we still have two left. That's enough, isn't it?" asked the masked Griffon. "Surely, you, a Sergeant in the

Air Corps, are not afraid? You know how these things will fly on two engines, don't you?"

"You're mad!"

Ignoring him, Keen released a spring panel near the avigation officer's table and took out a booklet marked "Confidential."

"All right, Pulski," said Keen. "Take the Bullet. We'll go to Newark and deliver."

"Me, too?" asked Barney.

"Oh, yes. Just to make sure we are not molested on the way. Perhaps our friends, here, have a few more export Hawk 75s flitting about that they'd like shot down."

Keen stuffed the "Confidential" booklet into his breast pocket, slipped under the wheel, looked over the instrument panel, and reached for the bank of throttles. The two starboard engines were still ticking over. He waited until Barney was out and had given him the all-clear signal, then he braked on one side and opened the two throttles. The big bomber lumbered around into position to take off again.

Then, holding the rudder over, levering his flaps for the most efficient takeoff, and adjusting the variable-pitch prop blades, Keen drew a long breath, glanced across at Grossburg who was tightly laced to the co-pilot's seat—and grinned.

"Well, my friend," he muttered, "maybe we will—and maybe we won't—get back whole. But we can make a try. Or have you set one of your cannisters aboard with C.T. gas that eats up dural?"

"Cannister be damned!" came the reply. "You'll crack this ship up!"

"Well," said the masked man, "This isn't a milk truck, anyhow. You can't argue me out of it. Here we go."

He gave the engines the throttle and the Boeing stiffened. She began a crabwalk across the field, kicked her tail up. Keen gave her more rudder and she came around and tried to slither into a flat spin. Keen's teeth clenched. But with a final effort he got her off the ground.

Keen then held on, fighting for a sniff of more altitude. He pressed the button that raised the undercarriage just in time. The big Boeing slithered over the fringed tops of some trees with only inches to spare.

Grossburg was sitting tense. His knees drawn up as far as his bonds would allow, he stared wild-eyed through the wind-shield. His mouth was open, his lips drawn back over his teeth, and it was apparent he was expecting a splintering finish any second.

But Keen had no eyes for the sky. He was too busy trying to get the proper balance between rudder and prop pull. Gradually, however, he managed to get a few hundred feet of altitude. Then he let the huge plane come around until she was headed due east.

The run back toward New York was long and laborious. Above, Barney in the Black Bullet S-turned back and forth and mothered them along. Meanwhile, Keen listened to the mad jangle of radio reports that were being sent out concerning the attack on the Central Air Lines ship. Army ships were ordered off their routine duties to seek the mysterious black amphibian and the Boeing Bomber marked "97."

Somehow, Keen crabbed the Fortress along on its crazy run for Newark. As a matter of fact, both Barney and Keen were flying without navigation lights. Once they almost slithered into two Douglas observation ships cruising about over Morristown. Barney immediately splashed on every light, played a wild game of aerial tag with the Douglas gunners until Keen and his crabbing Boeing were in the clear again. Then the Mick doused lights, nosed down, and raced like mad for Elizabeth, where he waited until the Boeing came into view again.

"Now for the fun," he said as he saw the bedaubed bomber slither out of the midst and head for the meadows.

THE REST happened so fast that no one at Newark had any idea what really did happen. All sorts of lights flashed from the control tower as Barney played hide-and-seek over the hangars. Horns blared, sirens screeched, and men ran in all directions.

So well did the Mick play his part that no one noticed the crabbing bomber fly over the main highway cross-wind to keep her dead wing up. Then Keen was down running the Boeing along a bumpy course toward the row of new and as yet unfinished hangars.

Shutting off his engines he grinned, threw Grossburg a mock salute, and said: "So long, Grossburg. I'll see you under guard at Governors Island."

And with that, Keen stepped out, reached in his pocket for his flashlight, and ran away into the darkness. Flicking the beam on and off, he ran well away from the main runways which were now silvery strips of glare lined with dim, searching figures.

Then out of nowhere came the Bullet. Barney brought her around, and before she had stopped, Keen had vaulted to the pontoon-gear, had climbed up on the wing, and plunged headlong into the cockpit. He steadied himself as he felt the Mick hoist her off again.

Once in the air, Keen grabbed for the hand mike. "Calling Newark... Calling tower at Newark... Come in, Newark."

"WREE Calling... All right... Come in!"

"This is the Griffon, WREE... the Griffon speaking... You will find Army bomber No. 97 near new hangars... Advise Air Corps officials at once... Hold men found bound inside. They are responsible for damage and sabotage to Army equipment... Advise John Scott of Secret Service that 'Confidential' papers aboard will be forwarded to him... Okey doke, WREE... Goodnight!"

They got a stuttering reply from the Newark tower and Keen was satisfied.

"Home, James," he boomed to the Mick.

"I'M TELLING you," Drury Lang expostulated, pounding his fist, "this Griffon person has me nuts!"

They were talking it all over the next afternoon in John

Scott's downtown office where a few minutes before a Western Union messenger had delivered an envelope containing the much prized "Confidential" defense measures. The package had been sent by one "Louis Ginsberg" from somewhere in New York city.

"He actually flew that ship with only two motors," cracked Scott. "The German guy, Grossburg, said so. We found him tied up in the cockpit. He simply couldn't have flown it. I tell you it was the Griffon, all right."

"Very interesting," nodded Kerry Keen. "Then you no longer require my services, eh?"

"No... er... that is," said Lang, peering at Keen sideways. "I'm sure you know something about this, Keen. But you've got me beat."

"Well, maybe the girl is the Griffon, after all."

"You dope. She was aboard the Central Air Lines ship— the one Grossburg was trying to shoot down."

"That's right," said Keen sitting up. "Then who did bring the Boeing Bomber in?"

"The Griffon, of course," mooned Lang. "And what's worse, I'm beginning to like the guy."

"Well, there's one thing I *can* do for you—even though I didn't get the bomber or the defense plans back," smiled Keen. "You see, Lang, I figured out what that stuff was that wrecked the bombers. Here's the formula.

"You see," he went on, "this chemical vapor form not only eats away the protective coating from dural and aluminum but also is a killing gas. What's more, it frequently starts fires when released. All that explains the deaths, fires, and wrecking of the Fortresses. Anyhow, you can give this formula to the Government with my compliments—and meanwhile you can forget all about that Dutch freighter business you were telling me about."

"Sure," said Lang, with a confused look in his eye. Then he brightened. "I mean it's okay, Mr. Keen, if you forget that *you* discovered this formula. I've got to show *something* for my efforts, you know."

"All right, Mr. Chemist," tossed back Keen. "But when you take this formula down to Washington, be sure to explain to the boys all about the tetravalents involved. And show 'em how the halogen group fits in, according to Mendelyeev's law."

"The *what*... the *who*—" spluttered the Secret Service man.

But Kerry Keen was already out of the door.

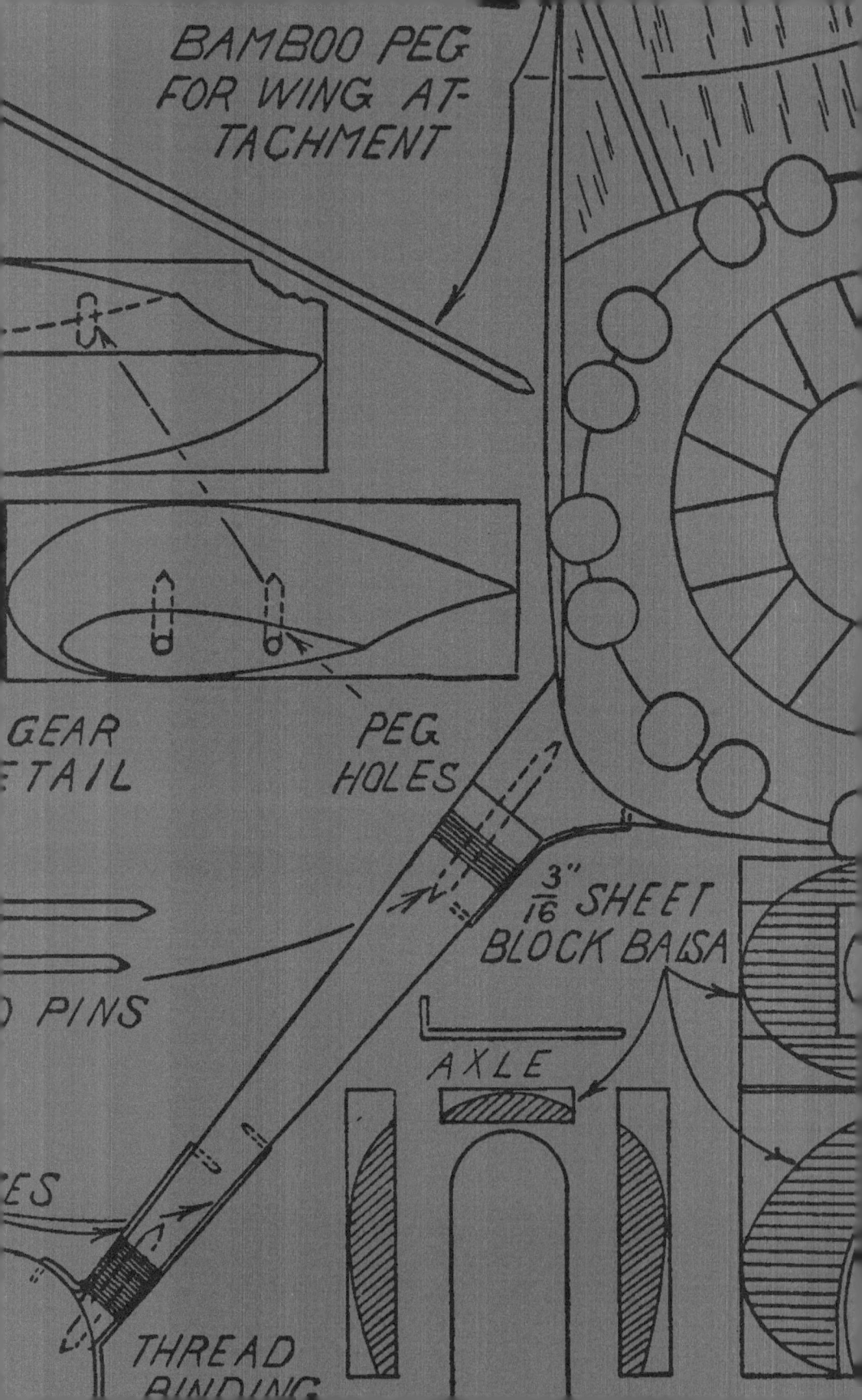

BAMBOO PEG FOR WING ATTACHMENT

GEAR DETAIL

PEG HOLES

PINS

$\frac{3''}{16}$ SHEET BLOCK BALSA

AXLE

THREAD BINDING

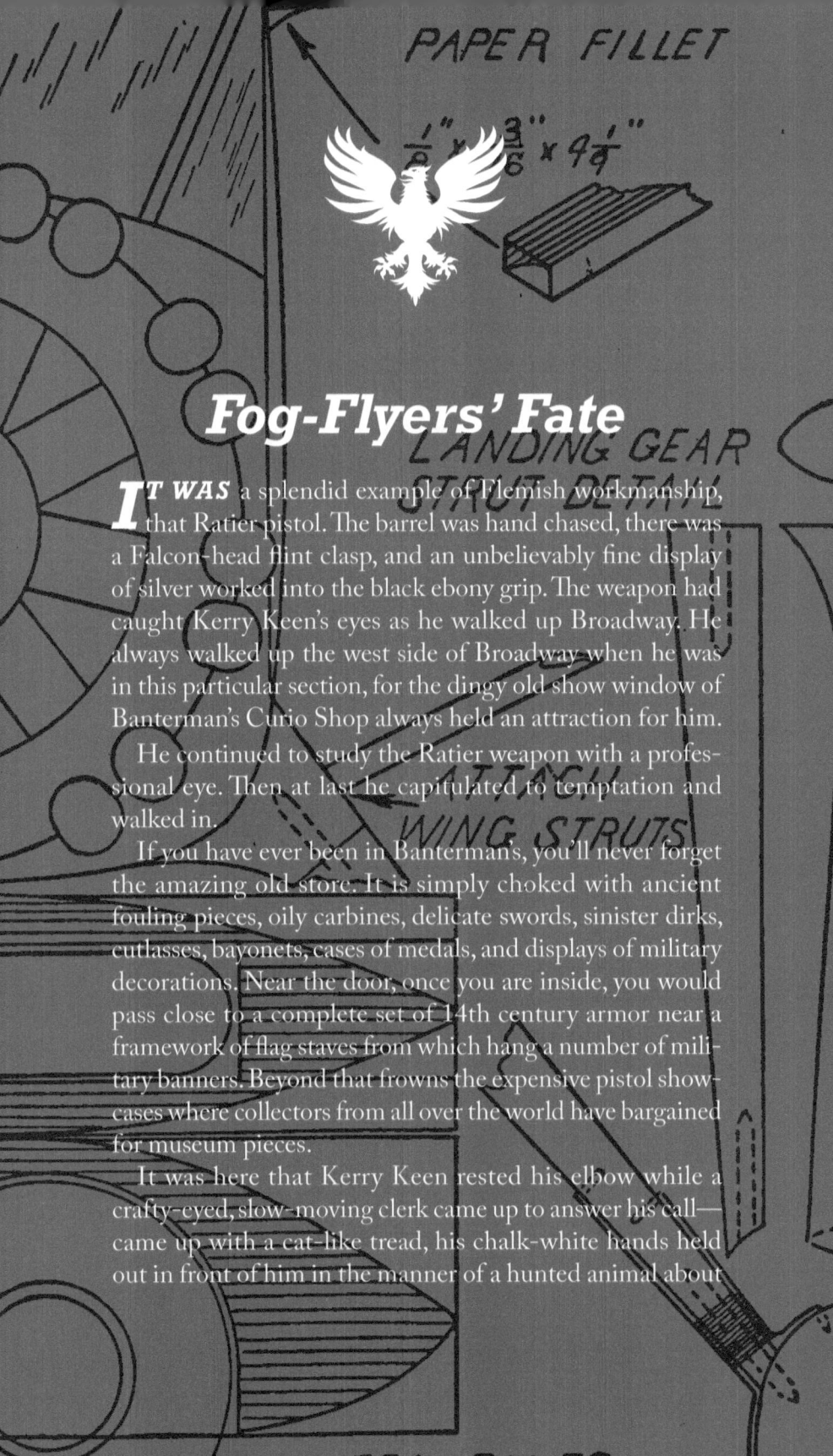

Fog-Flyers' Fate

IT WAS a splendid example of Flemish workmanship, that Ratier pistol. The barrel was hand chased, there was a Falcon-head flint clasp, and an unbelievably fine display of silver worked into the black ebony grip. The weapon had caught Kerry Keen's eyes as he walked up Broadway. He always walked up the west side of Broadway when he was in this particular section, for the dingy old show window of Banterman's Curio Shop always held an attraction for him.

He continued to study the Ratier weapon with a professional eye. Then at last he capitulated to temptation and walked in.

If you have ever been in Banterman's, you'll never forget the amazing old store. It is simply choked with ancient fouling pieces, oily carbines, delicate swords, sinister dirks, cutlasses, bayonets, cases of medals, and displays of military decorations. Near the door, once you are inside, you would pass close to a complete set of 14th century armor near a framework of flag staves from which hang a number of military banners. Beyond that frowns the expensive pistol showcases where collectors from all over the world have bargained for museum pieces.

It was here that Kerry Keen rested his elbow while a crafty-eyed, slow-moving clerk came up to answer his call— came up with a cat-like tread, his chalk-white hands held out in front of him in the manner of a hunted animal about to make a final spring for freedom. He had a sharp face and long straggly hair that hung over his heavy, parrot nose.

"That Ratier pistol in the window," said Keen with a languid air as he hung his heavy bamboo cane on the corner of the case. "I'd like to inspect it."

The sharp-visaged clerk seemed to stiffen as Keen mentioned the weapon. "You are not likely to be interested in that," he said, his face a strange mask of insolence. "That gun is worth a lot of money."

"You have no objection to my inspecting it, have you?" asked Keen, noting suddenly that this man seemed to be new in the shop. "I'd like to see it. I'm a regular customer here. You will find my name in your books."

"And your name is—?"

"Keen—Kerry Keen. I knew the old Mr. Banterman. May I see the Ratier weapon now?"

The clerk seemed uncertain what to do. Then, as if carrying out a duty that was very distasteful, he went slowly toward the window, opened a narrow door, and tip-toed his way through the display exhibits toward where the ancient pistol was resting.

"Nasty devil," reflected Keen, turning back and staring down through the top of the show-case where lay a case of

Suddenly, pistol shots spat from a port immediately aft of the pilot's cab. But Barney was ready. Quickly, he brought his twin guns into play, poured out a terrific double blast of Browning lead.

Venetian dueling pistols. "Acts as though he had another customer for the thing. Wonder where young Banterman is?"

Then he became so interested in the Venetian pistols and their carved case, that for a minute or two he forgot all about the surly clerk. But suddenly as his eye moved along the show-case, he caught sight of a three-cornered piece of mirror back of an adjacent exhibit. That mirror reflected the cascade of flags that hung from the tilted staves behind him. And out from the folds of the banners there protruded a slender, spotlessly clean hand—a hand which gripped a dull blue Hamilton target pistol on which was fitted a silencer!

Keen, restraining his natural impulse to jump, continued to watch, fascinated, in the dusty mirror. The hackles of his neck stood on end as he observed the hand shift farther around and direct the slim pistol barrel at him.

THE HAND was just beginning to show the marked lines of muscular constriction when Keen went into action. His right hand slid under his left elbow and grabbed the crook of his walking stick. Then with a quick twist, he brought the cane around with a slashing swing at the flags—and ducked.

In response there came a series of strange sounds.

First there was a chugging pop and a hiss of a flying missile. A low, choked scream and an oath followed as the misdirected bullet crashed against a display of ancient battle axes. Next there came a jangle as his assailant's weapon fell to the dusty floor.

Keen, now prone, grabbed up the gun. But since it was a single shot weapon, he knew it was useless for further shooting. Quickly, he jumped to his feet and took refuge behind a nearby case.

The stand of flags did not move again, however. And though Keen waited, the clerk did not come out of the window. Finally, he moved forward, poked his stick into the drapery of the flags—and to his amazement discovered that no one was there.

"Where did that devil of a gunman go?" he asked himself. "I could swear that arm came out of those flags. It must have, considering how I was able to hit his hand from where I was standing."

He now inspected the suit of armor, but that likewise disclosed nothing. Whoever had been behind those flags had slipped away by some means not readily apparent.

"And where's that clerk?" Keen asked himself, going toward the narrow entrance to the display window. Here, too, was a mystery. The man was not there, and the Ratier pistol was still on its velvet covered block just in front of a French .75 shell.

"What the deuce?" growled Keen, staring about the shop again. "What's going on here, anyway?"

He stepped up into the window himself, tip-toed through the display, and picked up the Ratier pistol. "I'll have a look at it anyway. That clerk will be back, I suppose."

He returned to the pistol show-case again, keeping an eye on the stand of tattered banners. Here he drew back the Ratier's flint lock, broke the barrel, and inspected the beautiful workmanship. Then, as he tilted the weapon, something slipped out of the bullet chamber. It was a small tube of white paper, carefully rolled, and Keen opened it fully expecting to find it contained some descriptive notes regarding the gun. Instead, he read:

B to leave island at midnight. Musgrove in clear with breech. Must work fast now.

—H. S.

Keen read the message over several times and completely memorized it. But what did it mean? Why was it placed in this weapon? And who was it intended for?

He stared about, waited. But no one came in and there was no one else anywhere about the store. Finally, he slipped the paper back in the muzzle and placed the weapon on top of the show-case.

Then he called aloud. But no one answered. Where the devil had that frowsy clerk disappeared to? Annoyed, puzzled, and not a little upset by his experience, Keen finally flicked his sleeve back, consulted his watch, and remembered he had an important engagement with John Scott and Drury Lang at the Department of Justice headquarters farther uptown.

He left the Ratier pistol on the show-case with full intentions of returning and attempting to complete a deal for its purchase. Then taking up his stick again, he started out of the door—but halted suddenly when he caught sight of a man in a trim gray suit staring through the window at the velvet-covered block which a short time before had held the Ratier.

Keen drew back apace, studied the man. He was tall, slim, and had a queer discoloration over his right temple. He was frowning, and at intervals he glanced anxiously up and down the street. Meanwhile, his long, slim fingers wound and unwound over a folded newspaper, and now and then he fumbled nervously with his cravat.

"Hello. This bird is evidently interested in that Ratier, too," Keen reflected. "Another collector, I suppose, who has been looking at it for days and has finally decided to come into the store and ask about it."

Keen peered again, then sensing that the man was about to enter the store, he quick as a flash stepped back inside, flipped off his hat, laid it on a heavy shell case, and placed his stick near it. Then, assuming the attitude of a clerk, he began setting a few small items in order.

The man came in, stared about in the uncertain light a minute, then saw Keen. He seemed puzzled for a minute. Then Keen spoke up with: "Good morning. What can I do for you?"

The man did not answer at once. But suddenly his eye caught the Ratier pistol on top of the case, and almost instantly his face changed.

"Ah," he said. "Ah, good morning. I see you still have the Ratier pistol. I was afraid you had sold it."

"You are interested, too? I just had another gentleman in here who was also bent on looking over this weapon. Beautiful thing, isn't it?"

"Beautiful!" replied the man. "In fact, I'd like to examine it."

"Help yourself. It's a costly item, though," answered Keen, borrowing the line of talk the frowsy clerk had adopted.

He watched the man palm the gun, saw him deftly slide the rolled note out and conceal it between his thumb and first finger.

Keen made no move to stop him.

"And what are you asking for the weapon?" the man queried.

"Three hundred dollars," replied Keen who believed in making it stiff enough.

The man's eyebrows raised several inches. "That's a lot of money, isn't it?"

"Not for a Ratier in that fine condition. That's a real museum piece. We had a gentleman from the British Museum in London in yesterday. He is quite interested in it and will in all probability be back some time tomorrow to complete the deal. Of course, if you really want it, I would advise that you make a deposit on it. Then we will hold it for you."

The man seemed uncertain as to what to do. But finally he reached inside his hip pocket, drew out a pale yellow pigskin wallet, and extracted a fifty dollar bill.

"Here—will that hold it for me until noon tomorrow? You see, I'd first like to check it with the curator at the Museum of Art. I'll take the markings, if you don't mind."

After pocketing the money with the intention of giving it to young Banterman later, Keen made out a receipt for the fifty dollars, then asked the man his name.

"I'm Dwight Blaine—connected with the Army Intelligence Service. I'll be in town for a few days. By the way, what happened to the other clerk?"

"I wish I knew," smiled Keen, filling in the receipt. "He was here a minute ago. Maybe he stepped out—for lunch." Then signing the receipt, he handed it over and took the pistol.

"I'll see you tomorrow, then?" he said.

"I'm sure you will," replied the man named Blaine.

KEEN GAVE the man plenty of time to move off, then he snatched at his hat and stick and again headed out of the door. And this time, as he passed the entrance, a square of cardboard caught his eye. It lay off in a corner just inside the door and bore the lettering: "Store Closed For the Morning. Will Be Open This Afternoon." The ballistics expert reflected, figured that he now knew why young Banterman hadn't been on hand. For good luck, he re-hung the card, clicked the automatic lock on the door, and pulled it to. Then he hailed a taxi and gave an address in the upper twenties, and in a few minutes he was sauntering into the dingy offices of John Scott, New York District head of the Department of Justice.

Scott glanced up from a sheaf of papers. He was big, sandy-haired, and generous in his proportions. He looked more like a boss longshoreman gone to seed than a Secret Service man.

"About time you came," growled a voice from the interior of the huge office safe which stood open in the far wall. "Where you bin?"

Then an unshaved man with a deep frown and a sodden cigar backed out of the safe. This was Drury Lang, Scott's assistant.

"Is *that* where you keep him now, Scott?" inquired Keen. "You ought to let him get a little air now and again. He'll begin to sprout fungus and mushrooms if you leave him in that safe."

"We got a beaut for you, Keen," said Scott ignoring both the ballistics expert's banter and the belligerent attitude of his assistant.

"You've always got a beaut for me," Keen remarked.

"Either for you or that Griffon pal of yours," Lang broke in.

"Yes," muttered Scott shuffling his papers. "This is where your Griffon guy can help out."

"But I'm supposed to be the Griffon," Keen said making his regular come-on statement. "The Robin Hood of the night skies. The protector of fair damsels and the upholder of the faith in the Secret Service. Last time I saw you, you were both certain the Griffon was a young lady who has a job as a hostess on an airline."

"Yeah, an' I'm not so sure now that she ain't," Lang spluttered.

"Oh, so the Griffon's a girl one time, a man another, and me in odd spots," taunted Keen, taking one of Scott's cigars and inspecting it carefully before he lit it.

"We're looking for the breech mechanism of the new Sprague gun," began Scott again.

"Is that what Lang was doing in that safe?" asked Keen with a grin. Then he went on: "Yes, I know Wayne Sprague, the gun-maker. But I didn't know he had anything worth pinching. Who swiped it—the Griffon?"

"Yes. He did!" said Scott, calmly lighting a cigar. "How did you know?"

Keen gasped, almost allowed his cigar to roll out of his fingers. This was a new one on him.

"Yeah, Mister Keen—this is one for you. Your pal, the Griffon, has stepped out of bounds this time. And we're not playing marbles with him any more. That gun breech has got to be returned."

Lang's speech gave Keen a chance to collect himself.

"Tell me more about it," he said, reflecting that too many strange things were happening to-day.

"Well, in a few simple words, this is the situation," Scott went on. "This Sprague guy has been on the payroll of the Army Air Corps working out a new light cannon-gun for aircraft. Three weeks ago, the first tests were made by three responsible officers of the Air Corps. Yes, and I understand the gun is a pippin, and once the test model has been put through a very stiff series of firing tests, the Air Corps guys will break it up and have it manufactured in great quantities by private firms. Only each firm will be given a special small portion, and they won't know just what it is they are making. All these parts will be delivered to an Ordnance point to be assembled later on."

"Sounds like they have something there," mused Keen. "Taking all those precautions."

"Don't worry. They have. They say it's the most remarkable weapon of its type ever devised. And it is so simple that practically no instruction will be needed by men who have already had elementary machine gun training. Anyhow, they're to be assembled, packed away in grease, and put where they can be quickly distributed in case of a war emergency."

"And some one has swiped the breech mechanism?"

"Exactly," nodded Scott. "And Washington is scared stiff that they will nab the bolt or lock part next—and that'll give 'em the secret."

"What makes them think that's the program?"

"Well, that's what Blaine thinks?"

"*Who?*" said Keen quickly, the name twanging a recent chord of memory in the back of his mind. "Blaine?"

"Yeah. He's the Intelligence Department guy they sent up to work with us. Dwight Blaine. Ever hear of him?"

"Oh, somehow the name is familiar. Go on."

"Well, Blaine is scared they'll lose the lock mechanism next. He thinks the same birds will get that."

"Is this Blaine one of the fellows who was in on the tests?"

"No. He's never even seen the gun."

"But he's afraid some one will swipe the rest of it? Well, where's the lock mechanism now?"

"I don't know. Somewhere in Washington, I suppose. All we have to work on is a pretty rough drawing of the breech mechanism and a general description of it. Blaine knows no more than that, either. We're up against it."

ALL THIS time since the mention of Blaine's name, Keen was mentally sifting a few facts: The name "Blaine"… the note in the Ratier pistol which referred to a man named Musgrove who was "clear with breech"… and the fact that this "Blaine" fellow had walked into Banterman's on the pretense of inspecting a museum piece, knowing full well that there was a message hidden in the barrel—a message that apparently had some bearing on this mysterious case.

"It sounds like a swell spy job," Keen broke in, fencing for time to think. "There's plenty of it going on in this country just now, too. But, I don't see how you can do much here with so little knowledge of the situation. Where was the breech mechanism stolen from? And who could have taken it?"

"All we know is that it was being wrapped in heavy brown paper for shipment to a mid-West firm which had received an order to make three thousand. It was being packed at the office of the Air Corps Ordnance Officer, and it disappeared while one of the officers turned his back to cut off a length of heavy shipping canvas in which it was to be stitched."

"No more than that, eh?"

"Nothing, except that we know that there has been considerable spy activity in Washington, and Blaine believes that the only way we can get a line on the culprits is to try to suck them in to nab the bolt mechanism, because the breech isn't of any use without the bolt."

"Oh! I begin to see now!" nodded Keen, flicking the ash off his cigar. "This Mr. Blaine seems to have some smart ideas."

"Yeah. Quite a change from the average Army guy," growled Lang. "I think he's right, too. I'd put the damn thing right where they could lay their hands on it—and then grab them when they reached."

Keen nodded again, then peered up at the curling plume of smoke above his head.

"What say, Keen?" asked Scott. "You're a gun expert. What would you do?"

"You really mean to ask if anyone has been bothering me—in hopes that I could tell them where or how to get the Sprague lock?" smiled Keen.

"Something like that, Keen. You've always got some ideas—and don't forget, the Griffon left his card, too."

"Oh yes. I was forgetting about that."

"Here it is. Recognize it, Mister Keen?" Lang said flipping a small white card across the table. "Ever see one like that before?"

"Oh, several. You always have one to show me in cases like this," replied the young ballistics expert, fingering the card.

Across the pasteboard in bold, black-ink inscription were the words: *The Griffon.* He was studying it, seeking the curls and twists of the signature he knew so well, when the door suddenly creaked and opened.

Keen started, twisted in his chair—and stared at the same man who only a short time before had given him a fifty dollars deposit on a Ratier pistol!

"HELLO, BLAINE," greeted Scott. "Come in." And he stepped forward to shake hands with the newcomer.

"He *is* in—didn't knock either," Lang snapped. "And here's

this Keen guy we were telling you about, Blaine. Meet Blaine, Keen."

The Intelligence officer was a splendid actor—for he showed no sign of recognizing Keen. They shook hands. Then Blaine sat down, straddling a creaky chair and rested his arms across the top, and directed his gaze on the ballistics man.

"So, this is the great Kerry Keen?" he said in a friendly tone. "I suppose Scott has told you all about the Sprague gun business."

"As much as he knows—for a Secret Service man," laughed Kerry.

"They tell me you're quite a gun man yourself. Got any ideas, Keen?"

"Plenty. None of them worth a dime, though."

"Well, maybe we can get together on it. You've seen the drawings of the breech mechanism?"

"No. Just the Griffon's card—which is quite interesting, Blaine. Quite a smart trick, that!"

"He's quite a smart chap, they say," parried Blaine. "But we'll nab him this time. I'm going to plant the lock mechanism where he can put his paw out for it—then grab him for once and for all."

"He might grab you, Blaine," said Keen with a touch of iced-steel in his voice. "Besides, where would *you* get the lock mechanism?"

"I've put in a bid for it. I think they'll let me have it."

"Why not use a faked lock? It'd be less risky."

"No, I want the real thing. But wait. Perhaps *you* could make us a faked lock, if you looked over the breech drawings, eh?"

"I doubt it, and besides, I wouldn't try. They put guys in the clink for much less than that in these days of spy scares. Not for me!"

"Oh, but under conditions like these *I* would stand up for you."

"Even so, I'd rather not. I have too much respect for the

long arm of Uncle Sam—and the Secret Service," smiled Keen with a bow toward Lang.

He turned and directed his gaze on Blaine again, and his brain worked at trip-hammer speed. Gradually, he was forming a new plan. He was adding up the facts and inserting a few of his own impressions. He sensed that Blaine was a smart Army man who knew how to work to get what he wanted. He had a lot of respect for Blaine.

"But surely you will help Scott here. I understand you have done him several good turns—in your own peculiar way."

"Yes, I have—and suddenly I've got an idea I *can* get that breech mechanism back," said Keen abruptly.

The statement made Blaine jerk back in his chair. He rubbed the strange discoloration at his temple and squinted hard.

"I have an idea I *can* run that guy to earth!" emphasized Keen.

"You mean the Griffon?"

"No—the man who really stole the Sprague gun mechanism. The man who wants to get the lock mechanism."

"Wow!" boomed Blaine. "Here's a man for my money, Scott! But look here, Keen. I'm a sporting guy. I'll bet you fifty dollars—fifty dollars you don't even get your fingers on it within twenty-four hours!"

Keen smiled, stuck one hand in his trousers pocket, and brought out a folded fifty dollar bill—the same bill he had received at Banterman's. He tossed it on Scott's desk, then watched the Army man take out his yellow pigskin wallet, select another, and lay it across the one Keen had put down.

Scott stared at the bills, then at Keen and Blaine.

"Say!" he gasped. "Here's a beaut! These two bills are brothers. Only one numeral difference in their serial numbers. How do you account for that?"

"A twist of fate," smiled Keen. "Both Mr. Blaine and I have much in common. I'll be seeing you, Blaine." And he arose.

"I'll be back for that fifty tomorrow, Keen," said Blaine, getting up as Keen went toward the door.

"I *hope* you will," Keen said.

WHY HE had taken up that bet, Keen had no idea. He only knew he distrusted Blaine—and in the meantime he stood to lose fifty bucks.

He hurried out of the dingy office and called a taxi that would take him to the garage that housed his Dusenberg.

"Kent Garage, Columbus Circle," he snapped at the driver.

He relaxed into the cushions as the car scrawnched into gear again, then poked at his immaculate toe with the ferrule of his walking stick. He was gripping the handle of the heavy bamboo cane fondly, reflecting that it had again come to his assistance as it had done on so many other occasions. That memory brought back the realization that the frowzy "clerk" in Banterman's had completely disappeared, and he wondered what had happened to him.

"He certainly had no idea of letting me see that pistol," Keen said to himself as the taxi lurched up Broadway. "I'll bet he knew a message was in that Ratier. I'll bet he knew that Blaine was coming to 'examine' it, too. Surely, that pistol was selected as a medium of communication between some one—and this guy Blaine. That reminds me. I'd better check Blaine through the Corps Area Headquarters down at Governors Island."

He sat there in a blue study, trying to pierce the dark curtain of mystery that was twisted around the amazing theft of the Sprague gun breech, the chased Ratier pistol, the frowsy "clerk" in Banterman's, the message slipped inside the pistol barrel, the Army intelligence man who *knew* it was there, and—

But Keen abruptly came out of his reverie—to stare at another cab now crawling up alongside as they approached the busy intersection of Herald Square. Something made Keen stiffen as that cab came close. He watched the face of the other driver, then glanced sidewise and checked his position.

Keen now leaned forward to keep his eye on the rear door of the other cab. Then he drew his stick up and held it in a poised lance position.

From the curtained window of the other car a long thin hand now protruded—and it was gripping a blue Hamilton target pistol.

Keen held his position for a few seconds, then suddenly snapped the bamboo stick out of the window as straight as a dart. Flashing across the bar of sunlight that separated the two cars, it struck the inside of the other car's windshield. Instantly, the driver jerked, there was a screech of brakes, then a resounding crash as the cab sideswiped an elevated support.

Keen's driver, who had not seen what had happened, heard the crash, glanced up into his rear-view mirror, saw the other car bouncing toward the curb—and in true cabbie style stepped on the gas to get as far away from the accident as possible.

Keen looked out of the rear window, saw a man in gray slide out of the wrecked cab, thrust a bill toward the driver, and hurry off into the maze of gathering curiosity seekers.

"Why that's that clerk at Banterman's," Keen frowned to himself.

"What hit dat guy?" asked the driver.

"I have no idea," replied Keen dumbly. "He seemed to be overtaking you, then suddenly swerved and sideswiped one of those elevated stanchions."

"Ah, som a dese guys ought to be squattin' on baby carriages, 'steada steerin' taxis," observed the driver.

Keen, examining the inside of the cab, suddenly noticed a small pencil hole of light only a few inches off line from his head.

"Still trying for me, eh?" he went on to himself as the taxi hurried north. "I'd better clean this mess up as soon as possible—if I expect to skip an early hearse ride."

He smiled to himself. The plot was thickening, but like excellent nectar was clarifying itself. Another distorted piece had now been slipped into place in this crazy jig-saw puzzle of intrigue.

BARNEY O'DARE, Keen's combination handy man, chauffeur, butler, and mechanic, was curled up in a great chair avidly devouring a mystery thriller set in the wilds of Outer Mongolia when Keen got back to Graylands, his home out on Long Island.

"Come on, you!" the young ballistics expert chirped. "Get off of it, stick that cork back in that O'Doul's Dew bottle, and leave the flaxen-haired heroine to her fate."

"Wait a minute! Faith an' she's in a terrible mess this time. They got her in a cave with a black leopard and a python."

"Swell! Since when have there been black leopards and pythons in Outer Mongolia—or has the circus gone on tour?"

"Aw, you always spoil everything," the Mick growled, tossing the book down. "What's up now?"

"Well, I've been shot at twice today."

"You went to that F.B.I. office," observed Barney. "You mean that guy Lang pulled a gat on you?"

"No, my friend, this is a new game. My assailant used a Hamilton pistol with silencers. You see, a very spotless hand suddenly pokes out of nowhere and the Hamilton goes 'pop'!"

"And misses?"

"Thanks to my old bamboo shillelah. By the way, order three more next time you are adding to the furnishings. They are grand against silencer pistols."

"Okay. When do we start out?" said Barney with a weary air as he poured Keen a cocktail. "The boiler has been in mothballs for a week. I'll bet there's ivy growing on the pontoons."

"We take off, as usual, just before the witching hour. For where, I have no idea. Sit down and see if this makes any sense to your Celtic noggin." And Keen spent half an hour carefully explaining the events of the morning.

The Mick sat, and sucked on the end of a particularly offensive clay pipe without saying a word.

"Thus," finally concluded Keen, "we have a mysterious Mr. 'B' who will leave an unknown island at midnight, and meanwhile a certain Mr. Musgrove is in the clear with a breech believed to be that of the new Sprague gun. And now we've got to find out what island they refer to, so that we can tell where they are leaving from."

The Mick frowned. "Looks to me like they planted that gun in Banterman's to draw you in, knowing what a sucker you are for useless pistols," he offered.

"They might have. But you forget that the message was slipped in the barrel for Blaine to pick up. I'm sure he came there particularly for that."

"Banterman's!" the Mick gurgled. "O' course that door card you picked up lets them out. That pale-handed, Hamilton-shooting, fake clerk just jimmied the lock, tossed that card into a corner—and waited for business. But that name 'Banterman's'—don't you get the connection?"

"Connection? What connection?"

"Banterman's—and this 'island' business," Barney cracked back in triumph. "And so, it's a good thing you have me around. We leave at midnight, huh? Well, if you want to get there in good time, we'd better leave a little earlier."

"What are you talking about?" asked Keen getting slightly nettled.

"Banterman's Island, up the Hudson river—the old place with the castle where Banterman's store all their stuff!"

Keen slapped his thigh, jumped up.

"After all these years, you big Mick, you get an idea—and it's a beaut! Of course! Banterman's Island! They're holed up there. Perfect!"

Keen went across the room, drew a map out of a file, and studied the situation. Banterman's Island lay just south of Beacon. It had for years been the storehouse for the vast stocks of Banterman military material bought up from various governments, and later resold to other governments, curio collectors, and military organizations.

It was a small, rocky promontory with a garish castlelike building frowning out across the river toward Cornwall-on-the-Hudson.

Keen pored over the map, a Coast and Geodetic Survey chart, and inspected the depth markings off the old island. The eastern side was about a quarter of a mile off the rocky shore of the Hudson. Storm King Mountain lay due south about two miles and the famous Mt. Beacon was some six miles to the northeast.

The ballistics expert marked these points in his mind, for they would come in handy later on.

"Thot's a foine place for to be holing up," reflected Barney, lapsing into his native dialect as the potent O'Doul's Dew began to take effect. "Oi've seen the auld place, and it's a stronghold. Ye can shut yer eyes and see knights in armor, big broad-shouldered men wie' pikes on their shoulders, and… and men in fancy uniforms parading up and down the hall. An' ye can hear chains clankin', if ye listen… and the moan o' men in dungeons…."

"Oh, shut up!" growled Keen. "Let's have less chatter. And now put that bottle away and go get some sleep."

"It's a foine castle, I tell ye. A castle fit for an O'Dare—an' an O'Dare will storm it tonight," quoth Barney standing stiff and proud. Then he clicked his heels in a theatrical gesture, turned sharply, and started for the door.

"An' O'Dare will storm the heights this night, I tell ye," he repeated as Keen hurled a *World Almanac* at him.

KEEN, SETTING to work on the chart, drew up a comprehensive compass course from Graylands to Banterman's Island. He then went through his books and found a fairly recent Banterman's catalog which carried a few interesting details of the old stronghold. It had been built more than a hundred years before as a defense point to protect the cities along the northern Hudson. There was a massive gate on the west side, plus a portcullis bridge which spanned a deep moat. The latter, now dry, was at present used for the outside storage of heavy armament, such as cannon, gun carriages, and pyramids of old cannon shot.

Inside, according to the account, lay long galleries where crates of early-type rifles, hundreds of Civil War muskets, and tons of obsolete World War equipment were stacked. There were bins of swords, lances, cutlasses, and boxes of old uniforms, campaign caps, and the like. In all, enough military equipment of a kind to equip a small uprising.

"Let's see," reflected Keen. "If Barney's crazy hunch is right, Blaine and this gang must have some special reason for being there. Of course, it's a swell spot to work from, well out of the way, and any queer goings on would never be suspected, because of the activity which is always going on there."

He thought again about Blaine, and picking up the phone he called his friend Colonel Mallard at Governors Island.

"You know of a man named Blaine on the Intelligence staff—a fellow who is working on the Sprague gun job?" he asked, after he had properly identified himself.

Colonel Mallard took a minute out, and Keen could hear the flip of pages. "Just a minute, Keen. Have they called you in on that thing, too?"

"They've tried to interest me in it, but I guess this chap Blaine has the case well in hand. Meanwhile, I just wanted to check a bit on him."

"Blaine?... The name is familiar. Of course! That's the famous Dwight Blaine—the fellow who solved the Sperry range-finder case. He's a good man, Keen. Have you met him?"

"Yes. This morning. Have you ever seen him?"

"No, but our dossier on him says he's about six foot tall, and has a wound mark over his right temple as the result of an accident some time ago at the Aberdeen proving ground. Has a fine record, Keen."

"I guess that's the fellow," Keen replied. "I just wanted to make sure so I know where I stand. Thanks for the dope, Colonel."

He hung up, then sat staring into space. There could be no question now about Blaine. But why had he acted so strangely? Had he, Keen, accidentally stumbled on one of the code systems used by the Army Intelligence Service? Had he nearly fallen into a net that was being thrown to catch—to catch the Griffon?

He sat back suddenly, felt all the blood drain out of his face. They were setting the dragnet now. This thing about the Sprague gun might be—just a gag. He really didn't know whether there actually was such a thing as a Sprague gun. But some one had certainly faked a Griffon card and had planted it for action.

"But why," Keen argued with himself, "did they try to shoot me? If Scott and Lang have anything on me, they can pick me up in ten minutes. And surely nobody had to try to blow my brains out like that—twice."

Still, that much did not satisfy him. If this Blaine was the real Blaine—and not a spy as he had first figured—what was he really after? Was it the Sprague gun—or the Griffon?

Yet this same Blaine who had been okayed by Colonel Mallard was somehow connected with the clean hand that pointed Hamilton pistols fitted with silencers. Also he seemed more interested in the Sprague lock mechanism than he did in the missing breech mechanism, and in the interim he used a Ratier pistol in Banterman's window to obtain information.

"There's too damn much Blaine in all this business for me," Keen exploded aloud.

BY 10:30 that night both Keen and Barney were working at feverish speed on their racy Black Bullet amphibian hidden away in the cellar hangar of Graylands. The tanks were drained, checked, and refilled. Ammunition drums and belts were gone over, and six special dartlike bombs were clamped into the narrow racks set under the body.

Barney was as sober as a judge now, and he moved about with that tight-lipped Celtic expression of his that assured Keen that he would be well on his toes when the action started.

The questions now were: what action? And would it take place at Banterman's Island as they had figured?

Two fifty-dollar bills in a small white envelope lay in Scott's safe as mute evidence of two men's belief in their own ability. Who would pick up that envelope tomorrow?

Keen and Barney went upstairs just before eleven and climbed into their black coveralls. They drew on their tight-fitting scarlet masks and stepped into the straps of their black parachutes. They buckled on automatics, then with a last glance around the room, Barney snapped off the lights.

They hurried downstairs into the secret hangar and closed all the steel doors behind them. Barney watched Keen, now in his red-mask role of the Griffon, start the big 1,000-h.p. Avia motor. The Skoda mufflers were jacked in, and the big engine was tuned to a quiet purr.

Keen finally nodded, then the Mick snapped off the lights, pressed another switch, and the big doors opened under the gear-and-lever power of two electric motors.

Outside, the night air was cool, a few stars flickered out over the broad Atlantic, and Montauk's long silver beam swept across the rollers.

Keen ran the Black Bullet out on her land gear. Then after Barney closed the hangar doors to again give the appearance of an inoffensive rock garden, he strode back, climbed up into the rear cockpit, and settled down for the evening's program.

The black amphibian soon was nuzzling her pontoons into the lapping water. Keen let her taxi quietly out past his mooring buoy. Then once in the clear and certain that there was no surface craft in the immediate vicinity, he gave the

Avia the gun and the sleek plane lifted up on her step and took the air.

He let her climb for a bit, then swung her around, crossed the Long Island shore line somewhere near Amityville, and headed a few points west of north. It was about sixty miles by air to Banterman's Island, and Keen knew they could cover that distance at a normal cruising speed in something like twenty minutes.

The air was crisp at 4,000 feet, and now a few fingering clouds, working their way in from the north-east, began to douse the stars. And as the visibility decreased, Keen wondered what their chances would be for getting through.

He managed, however, to make the bend of the river at Peekskill, then he followed the winding waterway as it carved its path past Bear Mountain. Soon West Point slipped by on the left, and they headed over Cold Spring towards the lights of Beacon. Keen then dropped low, cut through the narrow gorge opposite the peak of Storm King Mountain, and circled over the wider stretch opposite Cornwall-on-the-Hudson. Banterman's Island lay below.

AS THEY curled around over the old stronghold at about 3,000 feet, they suddenly lost sight of the lights of Mount Beacon. A filmy something was creeping across the north-east side of the town of Beacon. And it was gradually blotting out the regular lines of illumination which marked the streets.

Barney leaped up, cried one word: "Fog!" Keen turned, glanced at him as though he wondered what the Mick could do about it. Outside, the heavy incoming mist was throwing a muffling shroud over everything.

"We're in-for a swell night now," the Mick observed. "You'd better get this buggy down quick!"

Keen nodded. And as he set the stage for a landing somewhere on the river, the fog got worse, practically blotted out the eastern shore line.

"Got to move fast now," the ballistics expert said as he lowered the pontoons from their retracting slots.

The Bullet screwed down in a series of S-turns, with Keen racing her to beat the fog. Yet it seemed many minutes before they could lose their height and get into position for a set-down.

"We'll be shoved over by an Albany boat," growled Barney.

But Keen was in no mood for such banter now. The fog was racing in with the speed of a forest fire, and he was hunched forward trying to make the Bullet stop ballooning and get down.

At last she settled, scraped her water rudders through the surface water, and with her pontoons gouged out two dirty white streamers which she carried into sodden nothingness beyond.

Now they were bobbing gently on the river. Keen kept the Avia ticking over quietly, headed the plane through the choking mists toward where he figured the island lay.

"Lovely! What a night for an O'Dare," mumbled the Mick, rolling his cockpit hatch back and getting up into the clear.

"The island is about two hundred yards ahead," Keen said. "I'm going to try to ease up to it gently. Keep your eyes open."

The Mick was well out of the cockpit listening and peering ahead intently. The muffled Avia purred low, and the Bullet hardly made a ripple as she edged forward toward where Keen had last seen the jagged outlines of Banterman's Island.

Suddenly, Barney stiffened. "Hold it!"

"What's up?" queried Keen as he cut the Avia engine and let the Bullet drift.

"Get up here and listen."

Keen loosened his belt, raised himself into the clear on his elbows. His ears caught a muffled jangle of metal on metal, voices in earnest conversation, the staccato bark of orders, and the dull flob-flob of some heavy liquid against the retaining walls of some large tank.

"Can you make out what's going on?" Keen whispered,

frowning as he turned to glance at Barney. "And what is that smell?"

"What's the matter with your nose? That's gasoline, ain't it?" the Mick proffered.

Kerry Keen sniffed, then said: "You're crazy. That's not gasoline. That's crude oil—Diesel oil. They're fueling a boat or something."

They could hear the voices more plainly now. Over the heavy atmosphere of the fog came:

"*… but I'm certain I heard something. It must have passed, though. I can't hear it now.*"

A guttural, foreign voice answered:

"*Well, hurry up. We can't hang about here all night. Where's your man, Musgrove? He should be out by now.*"

Both Keen and Barney stiffened at that name.

"*He's finishing up. He had figured to have it open before now, but he found a type of steel there he had never worked on before. He's been at it for hours now, poor devil.*"

"*What about me? If we are caught here, they'll give us plenty of trouble. We're supposed to land at Port Washington tomorrow— that is, early this morning—to cover ourselves up.*"

"*Don't worry, he'll get through—and you'll be away in an hour.*"

"*I'll be away in twenty minutes, gun lock or no gun lock,*" the heavy foreign voice growled. "*And there'll be no money, either, if you haven't got it by then— for the breech mechanism is no good without it.*"

"*I know. We've been through all that before. But you've got to give us a chance. We've been taking plenty. And I tell you that noise I heard has me worried.*"

KEEN WAS trying to identify that last voice. He was certain he had heard it somewhere. Then there came another clatter, the clank of tools, and the rasp of a metal-covered hose over the edge of some sort of a tank opening.

"Listen," said Keen to Barney, "I'm going over there and see what that's all about."

"I get it," snorted the Mick. "That means I gotta stay here and let you have all the fun. I thought the O'Dares did the brave and courageous storming of the ramparts."

"Tough, my lad. But some one's got to stay here and hold the ship."

"Hold the ship? Well, who do you think I am—Commodore Perry or John Paul Jones?"

"No matter, you're staying here while I go over there and do a little investigating."

"But how will you get back? How will you find me in this soup?"

"You'll find *me*. The old signal! Get it? Now, these birds are at the Island to get a gun part that has been hidden there in Banterman's safe, which the Government often uses to put something away for safety. Banterman has worked with Washington on gags like that for years. No telling what else he has in that safe, either."

"Probably the Lost Battalion," mooned Barney. "Okay, go ahead. I'll sit out here and starve."

"I'll use my gun to signal, if I need you. And in the meantime, try to ease the Bullet in close to the Island. Get it?"

"Yeah—in the neck! As usual."

Keen climbed out and stripped off his kit, retaining only his gun, red mask, shirt, shoes, and old flannel slacks. Then he nodded to Barney, slipped into the water, and with easy strokes headed toward where the voices and noise had come from. Soon he came within sight of a large, low-winged monoplane that was bobbing gently on two great twin floats. Four narrow frontage engines were set in the wing and one in the nose, and the large monoplane tail carried two fins and rudders on which were emblazoned the Swastika emblem.

"Wow!" gasped Keen. "It's the very latest Hamburg job being used on the Lufthansa trans-Atlantic flights in connection with a catapult mother ship. They were taking no chances on this one."

But he was uncertain now what to do. The fueling boat, whatever it was, had moved away.

Then he heard the opening thud of an engine, and he sensed that the plane was being run back toward the island. He kept clear, then followed through the water with a noiseless side-stroke. In a few minutes, the engine stopped, and he sensed that the plane had pulled up to some dock or jetty.

He continued his pace for about five or six minutes, then caught the sound of voices again. Now he was in a position where he could clamber up the rocky shore on the far side and approach the gray walls of the old castle unseen.

He waited a minute or two to let most of the water drain out of his clothes, then he worked his way along the old dry moat and edged up toward the dull gleam of light that marked the portcullis entrance. There were voices again, and he could distinguish the dark figures of a few men near the entrance. All wore uniforms of some sort.

Keen watched his chance, cut across the moat in the gloomy yellow pall, and clambered up the side to make his way toward the dim shadows of the gateway. Now he took a small rock and hurled it high over the heads of the men. It fell with a clank among some old cannon about thirty yards away—and that distracted the raiders' attention long enough to allow him to dart inside the gate and make his way toward the doors that led into the old galleries.

Now he carefully examined the wall in search of a window. And finding one a few yards farther along, he peered inside. His eyes finally adjusted themselves to the light, and he could see a number of men grouped about a heavy safe of ancient design. Near one wall, a man was tightly roped to a chair—a man who looked on the proceedings with a calm air of contempt.

Keen gasped. The man in the chair was Blaine—or Blaine's twin brother! He had the same type of face, in general mold, the same cut of hair, and strikingly similar piercing eyes. Then

Keen saw that he likewise had the same mark of discoloration above his right temple.

The young ballistics expert stood there and watched the scene, fascinated. A man was working hard with tools on the safe door. An oxy-acetylene tank and blow-torch set stood nearby, along with a collection of drills, chisels, and wrecking levers.

The men in the background wore uniforms of the Lufthansa line, while those in civilian clothing appeared to be ordinary business men, not far removed from the financial canyons of Wall Street.

"They're trying to get the Sprague gun lock," Keen muttered to himself. "And that must be the real Blaine they have there in the chair. They must have nailed him somewhere, and forced him to come here. Then the other guy—the one I met—impersonated him in order to work through Scott and cover the disappearance of the real Blaine."

The whole story was clarifying itself now!

Keen took another quick look around and saw the fake Blaine he had encountered at Banterman's and Scott's office standing in the group near the safe. The surly "clerk" who had attempted to kill him was there, too.

"I see it all, now," Keen muttered. "I knew he fired at me from the cab—and now I realize that he was the devil who shot at me in Banterman's. He must have slipped through a trap-door in that show-window, come up inside the partition behind the stand of flags, and then taken that shot at me. Right! He's got his right hand bandaged where I cracked him with the cane!"

But then Keen started. The mob was surging forward. And the bound Blaine told the story of defeat in his expression. They had at last forced the safe and were about to rifle the vault!

AS TO what he should do, Keen was uncertain. He saw the first two men enter the vault. They came out with a heavy, greasy package from which dangled a scarlet shipping tag.

Keen could not hear what they were saying, but he could tell by their expressions and gestures that they had been successful in their quest. Now he saw them take the opened package and hold it mockingly before the wrathful face of the bound man. Then they wrapped it up again with a cackle of triumph.

The fake Blaine now handed the new loot over to the heavy German, who also held another package in his left hand. Thereupon, the German took a heavy leather wallet from his inside pocket and handed it over to the fake Blaine. There was a quick inspection of the contents, a cheery exchange of hand-clasps, and another chorus of derision toward the man who, bound with heavy rope, sat glaring at the ruthless despoilers.

Keen's hair-trigger mind completed in full detail every move he intended to make in the next five minutes. His plan was to head the two packages off somewhere between that room and the narrow bridge across the dry moat. A quick rush into the crowd of startled men, perhaps a shot or two— and the rest would be—

But suddenly all this scheming went up in smoke—with one simple move of one man! It was the man with a bandage around his right hand—the man whose hands were strangely clean as compared to the rest of his personal appearance.

"No!" husked Keen under his breath, paling at what he saw. "That's murder!"

The gray visaged clerk from Banterman's store was moving quickly toward the bound man in the chair. His bandaged right hand gripped a massive black weapon—a weapon carrying a cartridge big enough to drop a grizzly bear. And he meant to blast those cartridges into the head of Dwight Blaine, ace operator of the Army Intelligence Corps.

Keen watched helplessly as the gray man moved closer to the trussed Blaine. The others stood off, watched with eyes that were utterly unable to switch their focus from that menacing weapon. The big German seaplane commander cringed, his great shoulders hunching up as if he preferred to draw his head into his body rather than witness this cold-blooded murder.

The man with the bandaged hand now raised the gun slightly, then turned and glared at his audience. Keen could see a snarl form across one side of his face, and he knew that the man was taunting them for being chicken livered.

It was the gray man's moment of triumph—and he was making the most of it.

Then, with a last glance at that helpless mask that was the face of Dwight Blaine, Keen took advantage of that moment. He made two quick moves—and upset the gray man's plans.

Keen's first move was to bash in a window pane with the muzzle of his automatic. His second was when he pulled the trigger.

The crash of glass quickly electrified the raider group. The big German's head came out of his shoulders like a released marker buoy. And the gray man abruptly turned and stiffened at the sight of the red-masked man. That gave Keen the opportunity he wanted—and his well-aimed shot sent the big black Luger crashing across the room to clatter through the jumble of tools at the base of the battered safe door.

For a second, the snarling gray man stood staring at his bullet shattered hand. In that second Keen kicked in the rest of the window.

But before he could clamber over the low sill to cover the rest, some one blasted a shot that put out the light. Immediately, there was a scramble of men rushing out through the firmly lit corridor. But above it all, Keen heard the words:

"The Griffon... The swine!"

"WHO'S THERE?" a voice husked as Keen hurled himself into the room.

"Sit quiet a minute. I'll have you out of there, Blaine," called Keen, and he slammed the door shut, darted over with his pocket knife, and in three quick moves cut the bonds that held the Intelligence man.

"Quick! Somewhere over there. The Luger I shot out of

that chopper-guy's hand. Get it—and get out there after them. And keep shooting!"

"Who are you—the Griffon?" Blaine panted, as he groped over the dark floor in search of the weapon.

"That's what those guys called me," Keen agreed. "Have you got the gun?"

"Yes, here it is. But it's too late now," Blaine said. "They got away with it."

"With both parts, you mean—breech and lock!"

"How did you know?"

"Never mind how. But we'll get them back."

"I wish I knew how. They're getting away in their flying boat."

Without answering, Keen darted down the corridor toward the entrance to the old castle. He had to work fast. The bloodthirsty gray guy had upset all his plans, and now the secret of the Sprague gun was well on its way through the fog to the German plane.

He dropped into the moat, and as he did so he heard Blaine calling him. But there was no time for explanations now. He had to get back to the Black Bullet. Charging up the other side, he clambered over the jagged rocks and plunged into the river again. He could hear the engines of the Nazi flying boat and the ravings of the men aboard.

Keen guessed at the position of the Black Bullet and struck out accordingly. He worked hard for about five minutes, then trod water, got his gun clear, and fired two shots quickly, then followed with a single shot after a short pause. He waited, then after what seemed minutes, he heard a reply:

Crack! Crack!... Crack!

Keen grinned and swam out toward the position indicated by the shots. Then, almost in reply, came a chatter of machine-gun fire from the direction of the big German seaplane. Keen ducked under the water and held his breath. It was eerie, this gloomy, yellow fog punctuated by the m.g. tracers as they spat and hissed into the water.

As he fought on through the water between bursts, he heard Barney break out a gun and answer the Nazi fire. The rattle of the Mick's Brownings aided plenty now in guiding him, and he struck out with more vigor. Across the water came the thud of Diesel engines. Now all four were suddenly opened up and Keen knew the raiders must be moving off.

He finally reached the pontoon of the Black Bullet, where the Mick was on hand to yank him up. Then Keen noticed that Barney was dripping wet, too.

"What happened to you—fall overboard?" Keen queried.

"No, just went for a swim. Got tired of waiting."

"Come clean! What did you do?"

"Forget it! Let's not waste time in talking. Those guys are getting away!" Keen clambered into the front cockpit and waited until Barney drew in a sea-anchor. There was no time for argument with the Irishman now. The starter kicked the Avia over, and she revved up quickly, being still warm. Thereupon, Keen spun the Black Bullet around on her water rudders and roared her down the river after the big Hamburg ship. It was a race now—and a dangerous race, too, in this terrible yellow murk.

The Black Bullet took the air like a charm, and Keen had to throttle her back to play safe. He knew the Hamburg would not attempt to follow the Hudson river any longer than she had to. Soon she would head out to sea, there to sit down and await her time for her scheduled arrival at Port Washington. That much was obvious—but how could he trace her in this choking, blinding fog?

"I'd give a buck to know what that Mick was up to while I was away," Keen growled to himself as he peered ahead. "Something screwy, I'll bet."

"They got away with the gun parts, all right," he bawled over his shoulder. Then he explained to Barney what had happened. "Dirty trick, eh?"

"Dirty trick?" replied Barney. "That's nothing to the one I played on them!"

Keen spun around, tried to fathom the Mick's mind.

Then Barney bellowed: "There they are! Follow that light!"

True enough, a faint beam of light was visible ahead as the fog cleared.

Keen had to throttle back quickly, for the Bullet was now almost on the tail of the Hamburg. He started to fumble for the firing lever to hammer in a long burst, but Barney stopped him.

"Don't worry, they'll come down."

Keen was stunned, but already the big seaplane was in a gliding angle, as indicated by the strange light that lanced back from under the body.

"What is that light? They seem to have all their riding lights off. But that one sticks out like a silver streamer. They're crazy to keep it on."

"I took care of that," the O'Dare grinned again. "Now get ready for an old-fashioned boarding party."

THE HUGE German plane came down almost directly beneath the Bear Mountain Bridge, which was displaying its fog-filmed Mazda necklace of lights across the river. They could see the big transport stagger once, then jerk its nose up and finally swish into a splashy landing. The Mick was up high in the cockpit with two guns trained on the craft's business office. Keen circled tight, then dropped down onto the water and into a broadside position in front of the spy plane.

Now he, too, arose. "We are boarding you at once," he bellowed through cupped hands. "We want two packages you have aboard. And remember, one false move and we will sink your ship and report your illegal landing in United States territory."

At first, there was no answer. Then pistol shots suddenly spat from a port.

But Barney was ready! Quickly, he brought his twin guns into play, poured out a terrific double blast of Browning lead that riddled the window and sent to Eternity the man who had challenged them from behind it.

"We agree!" cried a gruff voice from the control office. "You can have the two packages. In Heaven's name hold your fire!"

"Here!" whispered the Mick to Keen. "Let me do the boarding. I've been done out of the fun so far."

"Go ahead," smiled Keen taking over the two Browning guns. "And there's a matter of a leather wallet in the pocket of the guy with the mark on his right temple. Get that, too."

The Mick went over the side, took cover under the Hamburg's wing, and made his dripping way up the portside pontoon. From there he climbed the inset ladder, crawled over the inboard engine nacelle, and went up the gull-wing portion of the wing-root to the doorway.

"I'm coming in. And I'll shoot the first man who hasn't got his hands above his head!" the Mick boomed. "An' no funny business."

He yanked the door open, rammed the gun inside—and pulled the trigger just in time! The snarling man in gray fell forward. His gun only blasted a hole through the lower portion of the dural cabin wall—for he'd shot too late.

"Anyone else want to argue?" rasped O'Dare. None did. So he called an "Okay" to Keen, then with a quick move slid into the cabin. Inside, he saw the big German commander standing with the two packages. He advanced toward him, then, turning slightly, he flicked one hand like lightning toward the pocket of the man with the discoloration on his temple. Before that individual could lower a hand, the Mick had the wallet.

"Thot will teach ye' not to take money for stealing. An' since ye seem to object to me action, I'll make it certain," the Mick snapped. "I'll put me John Hancock on it."

With that, his short left hook sped with the force of a projectile and landed flush on the man's temple. And the false discoloration mark fell off as the fake Blaine went spinning toward the marine gear locker.

"An' now, Captain," advised the triumphant Mick. "We'll relieve ye of yer bundles. An' if your a wise man, ye'll fill up the radiators I emptied, take off as quickly as possible, and fly outa here."

"I t'ink it's a good idea," agreed the paunchy Captain who spluttered like a fountain pen at 8,000. "I… I vill do dot at vunce. Goot night!"

"Good night, Fritzie. And remember, no tricks!"

Thereupon, the Mick dropped over the wing to the pontoon, then kneeled down and fumbled with a wire binding. His hand came up with a long nickelplated flashlight which still directed a piercing beam. He snubbed it out, tucked it under his arm with the other bundles, dropped into the water, and onehanded his way back to the Bullet.

Keen helped Barney up into the wing. "Open those packages first," he said. "We're taking no chances on those guys."

The Mick first handed over the brown wallet, then cut the cords that bound the packages. The two gun parts were inside, intact and secure.

"Okay. Let's go," the pilot said. "And while we're on our way, you can tell me just what that was all about."

"Easy. While you were having all the fun on Banterman's Island, I swam over to the Nazi boat and opened the release cocks in the radiators, which are built into the legs of the landing gear. I knew they couldn't fly those Diesels far like that."

"But the light?" said Keen as he whipped the Black Bullet around. "That's the one that has me."

"Simple! Your new two-foot flashlight. I wired it on one o' their pontoons just below the water-line, already turned on, ye know. O' course, I put it 'way under. It made a little glow, I'll admit—but with the fog, the dark water, and the fact that it was aimed backwards, I figured they'd never notice it, an' they didn't. So when that boat got into the air, the light showed back underneath. Elementary, huh?"

"O'Dare," Keen said, "there are times when you rise to the occasion. There are times when—"

"—When I'm really worth the O'Doul's Dew you honor me with, eh?"

ALL THE way back, Kerry Keen racked his brain as to how he could collect that fifty-dollar bet money at Scott's office. And meanwhile he schemed how he would have the two packages of gun parts secretly delivered to Colonel Mallard at Governors Island. The Colonel, in turn, would see that they were turned over to the real Dwight Blaine.

As for the wallet that Barney had lifted from the pocket of the fake Blaine, that contained plenty of high denomination bills. They would cover Keen's current expenses and leave a considerable amount over for his favorite charities.

Of course, Dwight Blaine, once he got back from Banterman's Island, would see to it that the Griffon received proper credit for the evening's exploit.

Captain Hans Seefen, chief officer of the Nazi Hamburg plane—and the man whose initials had appeared on the note in the Ratier gun—was the big loser in the sinister game that had been played. He'd have a tough time explaining to his superiors why he failed to get clear with the Sprague gun parts.

But thoughts of the Ratier pistol brought Keen back to normal. What a gun it was! He'd have to drop in at Banterman's in the morning. Why, he'd put a fifty dollar deposit on it—whether he could sneak that fifty-skin note out of Scott's safe or not!